IT'S A CREWEL WORLD

by

Tree Elven

This book is licensed for your personal enjoyment only.

Cover Design: Jenifer Carey

© 2016 by Tree Elven

All rights reserved. No portion of this publication may be reproduced, stored in a retrieval system or transmitted in any form by any means – electronic, mechanical, photocopying, recording, or any other way—except for brief quotations in printed reviews, without the prior written permission of the publisher.

ISBN- 978-1530525744

Table of Contents

CHAPTER ONE - Beige, blue and blackout 5

CHAPTER TWO - Manhattan and Manhattans 23

CHAPTER THREE - Vegas Virgins 41

CHAPTER FOUR - Palo cortado 59

CHAPTER FIVE - A generous husband 77

CHAPTER SIX - Smokescreens 81

CHAPTER SEVEN - The stomach slipped over the edge 93

CHAPTER EIGHT - No more cracks about buttocks 115

CHAPTER NINE - The right sort of beard 121

CHAPTER TEN - The kimono sessions 137

CHAPTER ELEVEN - Red-hot revelations 155

CHAPTER TWELVE - Grab it with both hands 173

CHAPTER THIRTEEN - Set a thief to catch a thief 185

EPILOGUE 200

CHAPTER ONE
Beige, blue and blackout

The story begins here. A station café in Benidorm. Plain – not to say ugly – tiling in the functional everyday style. Not those decorative, colorful depictions of rustic scenes or charming old product advertisements I'd seen in Spain, but just the cheap, dark, ochre-verging-on-red variety, breaking up eternal beige.

It's a beige and blue country.

There used to be trees from coast to coast. Legend has it you could cross the whole of Spain from tree-top to tree-top without touching the ground.

It was a hot day in June.

The fan whirred.

The barman stood.

I sat.

Outside, pale blue letters against a long-suffering white wall announced portions of an old business in Benido-m. The letters, almost intact, were curiously soothing, their pale blue gentle under the scorch of the sun.

Benido-m, they spelt. Benidoom, I mused.

A fly came into the bar. About eight minutes later, it left.

I rearranged my buns on the bar stool and heard the barman shift his weight from one leg to the other behind me. For every second of those eight minutes, we'd both been totally focussed on the fly's activities.

I found it quite healing.

From where I was sitting, and the barman was standing, there was a good view out of the doorway, extending behind the flaked white walls and pale blue letters, out up to the beige hills. A fringe of Benidorm's skyscrapers mussed the left-hand side of the frame, but away from them, my eye roamed free over the hills.

It was quiet.

Presently, out of the silence grew a small roar. The barman and I both stiffened slightly, trying to identify what it was.

The small roar crescendoed into a demanding bellow and then we saw it – a flash of wicked red paintwork up on the windy old hill road tufted with clumps of tenacious almost-greenery and bursts of in-your-face purple blooms. A red glimpse. Now there, now not.

Beautiful.

With satisfaction, I watched its descent towards us. The red flash resolved into a redhot streak of sportscar and the barman murmured his appreciation.

The husky throb of its engines filled our world, its sleek lines filled our sight as it powered past, kicking up a cloud of dust that rose so high it obscured the pale blue letters of Benido-m opposite.

I caught a glimpse of a man's chiseled jaw and short, dark-gold hair, a woman's cheek cut by a slice of black hair, and then it was over.

I half-turned to catch the barman's eye. He raised his eyebrows and nodded in agreement.

"Nice car your friend's got," he commented.

I opened my mouth to protest – where would someone like me get friends like that?! – then shut it. What, after all, did I know about myself right now?

"Sounds like he forgot something," continued the barman, and I realized the roar had stopped. Not left, stopped. Changed. Reversed…

The red beast's rear end showed outside the door. It quieted, a door slammed.

And then a seriously cool dude swung into the bar, lit up by the background of those drab old tiles. Six-two, natural tan, that wavy dark-gold hair…

"Oh thank Christ, you're here!" he cried, spotting me. "Has he been bothering you?" he asked the barman, who chuckled.

The dude slapped my arm and fished out some money.

"Will that cover it?"

"I'll get your change," the barman said.

"No, no, that's good. Adios, adios!"

"Thank you, señor, thank you!" called a grateful barman as my 'friend' ushered me off the stool and out into the sun.

The girl in the car was also gorgeous.

"Oh, thank goodness we found you!" she cried with a dazzling smile.

I grinned at her like the ultimate homecoming. I was so glad. She was so beautiful.

"Will he be okay?" she asked my friend anxiously.

"Sure, sure, but let's put him in the front, just in case…"

In case what?

They organized me in the passenger seat. The engine fired into husky throbs. My world quivered with the vibrations.

I turned to the girl and gazed at her in dazed amazement, smiling non-stop. She was quiet for some moments – a rare thing in a Spanish girl – gazing back at me. Her hand rose gently to my cheek. I stretched back and kissed her full on her willing lips. I caught her hand between both of mine and felt impossibly happy. Cool friend. Gorgeous girlfriend.

Names. Their names would come back to me.

* * *

We skimmed along the winding flanks of the beige coastal hills, through brief mountain tunnels. An azure sky was flung over all, a deeper firmer shade than those gentle letters advertising the Benidorm company up on that peeling white wall.

I relaxed into the back of the seat – the girl had taken away her hand, probably realizing it was dislocating my shoulder to hold onto it – and let the azure breeze patter my cheeks.

We were, it seemed, heading north. I had no idea where or why, yet I felt safe.

To our left, high, pitted beige rocks edged the road. To our right, the road after each mad corner dropped away down to the turquoise and royal blue waters of the Mediterranean.

And set amongst the trees as we wound up into the greener heights, cream and ochre villas proclaimed comfortable wealth, an uncomplicated enjoyment of life.

I was borne along on waves of total tranquility.

The angle of his jaw caught my eye; I smiled involuntarily. The barman had been right – he *was* my friend.

"Jules," I stated loudly, my back and head flush against the seat back.

His head snapped round for a moment, a delighted grin on his face. I knew that the hazel eyes were blazing behind the Ray Bans.

"Old man! You remembered my name!" His hand left the wheel to grip my knee for a second. "Excellent!"

"What's my name?" I asked.

"Can't tell you, old man. Best if you remember for yourself, Dad says."

"What's he got to do with it?"

His glance this time was an assessing one.

"Erm, best for you to remember that too."

"Oh come on!"

"Okay, okay. He's a doctor, knows about these things."

"What things?"

"These, um, episodes of yours."

"Did I black out? Not from booze?" I didn't feel hungover, but I was worried – I wasn't going to hang onto a chica like the one in the back seat by having alcoholic blackouts all over the place.

"No, no," Jules assured me.

"Will he remember my name?" yelled the girl against the wind.

Hello! I'm right here! I thought, but was in fact glad she'd asked Jules because I felt bad that I didn't have an answer for her.

"Don't be offended if he doesn't for a few more hours!" he yelled back, grinning at her in the rearview.

I glanced back. The black hair was whipping around her face. She smiled. At that moment, she didn't need a name.

But I wanted one. I studied Jules' profile, searching for answers.

"You look clever," I said finally.

He laughed out loud, throwing the red beast down a gear to take the next sharp corner.

"This is the best bit!" he called to the girl. "He hasn't got a clue! You can be anybody you want, tell him anything you want!"

I frowned.

"Clever but cruel," I yelled. "You must be Virgo."

The Ray Bans flashed towards me and he laughed even harder.

"Well sorry, but it's true, old man! Nothing to do with that horoscope crap. She could tell you that you two only met yesterday and you'd believe it!"

"We did only meet yesterday," said the girl, sounding a bit cross.

I was shocked, and said so.

"What I feel for you is deep," I told her – Jules sniggered loudly – "I thought we'd known each other for a long time. You're familiar, somehow. Part of my life."

"That is so *sweet*," she said, leaning forward between the seats to kiss my cheek.

"And that's the kind of guy he is," yelled Jules. "He's a good man. Be a good catch if he ever makes any money."

He winked at me and turned off the road up a sandy drive to pull up in front of one of the cream and ochre villas. To its left, a blue blue pool shimmered amid the well-kept greenery. A large arch framed the big wooden front door and provided shelter over a spacious verandah that was scattered with lounger chairs and bright cushions.

People came out of the house and from the pool area as we clambered out. They were pleased to see us. A lovely woman in a bikini top and sarong cried out, "You found him! You found him!" and gave me enthusiastic kisses on each cheek.

"Where was he?" asked one of the men behind her.

"Oh, at the station caff. Just sat there, you know, like Paddington Bear but not cute."

"Has he remembered?" the man asked.

"No, just my name so far."

The man grinned and gripped Jules' arm.

"As usual!" he exclaimed. "Your name always comes back before his own."

We all absorbed that for a moment.

"Bring him down to the pool and let the poor boy relax," said the lovely woman, prodding us towards the house.

"Relax? He's only been sitting on a bar stool all morning!"

"Shush, shush – show him where his things are and come on down."

Nice people. Warm, welcoming, lovely people.

Who the hell were they?

* * *

Jules ushered me up the broad stairs – part wood, part tiled – and into a large bedroom with a spectacular view over beige rocks broken by green out across the bay. White breakers ruched a turquoise curve that shaded to full blue further out.

"Oh man, this is beautiful!" I exclaimed, going straight to the window.

For a moment, Jules paused beside me and stared out.

"It is," he agreed. "We are lucky bastards."

I took a deep breath and said slowly: "Jules, we're not... you know... I mean, you're not my... partner or anything, are you?"

His head snapped round from the sparkling view and he took two involuntary steps away from me.

"Christ no! You couldn't pay me! How could you even *imagine* that? And what about the boner you got just holding that girl's hand?"

"Okay, okay, I'm sorry. It's just that I know we can't be brothers because you have a British accent and mine's American, but I feel that you and I..."

"No! Stop right there!" He flung a hand out in self-defense. "For Christ's sake don't tell me how deep your feelings are for me – I'll throw up. And don't drag the fucking horoscope into it, either."

He turned away abruptly and went to root some swimming trunks out of a white chest of drawers with blue painted flowers on it.

"Okay, you can lighten up! It's not so much fun not knowing who or what you are! Gimme a break!"

"No, I can see that," he admitted, handing me the trunks. "Here, these are yours – honestly, chosen by you, don't try and blame anyone else. Towels over there. See you down by the pool. Chill out, you'll be fine."

"Thanks dude."

"Yeah. I'll see you in a bit. Going to take the girl home."

"No!"

"Oh yes. There are nice people down by the pool and not one of them wants to see your stiffies. What are you looking at me like that for? You only met her yesterday, for Christ's sake!"

He left.

People don't blaspheme back home as much as that, I thought. Home. A question mark. All I knew was what I saw in the full-length mirror as I changed into the trunks.

Early 20s, skinny and sinewy – not like Jules' large hard build – with rather cool blond surfer's hair long enough to run my fingers through, plenty of natural tan, blue-grey eyes, and – I tried it – a great smile!

I looked good, I wasn't an alcoholic or a homosexual, and I knew I felt at home by the sea. Things weren't as bad as they could have been.

I resolved to lie by the pool and be whoever I wanted to be till the real me came home.

Where on earth *was* home?

* * *

For a long, sultry while I lay out by the pool, sometimes swimming, sometimes teaching a random kid to dive or listening to desultory chatter around me, but mainly just lying on my back marveling at how high seagulls can fly.

I found I spoke pretty decent Spanish. Jules was clearly bilingual. At first that made me a bit pissed, but then I figured the real me would have something worthy to bring to the table and set alongside Jules' great looks, rippling muscles, bilingualism, witty conversation, access to an amazing villa and an amazing car in an amazing bit of country, and a group of great friends/relations/whatever they all were.

Yeah, bound to.

Meantime, I built an exciting life for myself – and the girl – in my head, and the afternoon trickled by. Eventually we all sat up and most of them left and the rest of us slumped on the verandah drinking G&Ts and eating huge black and green olives.

"It's been a whole day," said the lovely sarong woman worriedly to Jules when we all went in to get showered and dressed for dinner.

"Yeah, don't worry, he's probably just spinning it out. Giving himself too good an imaginary life to pull back from, eh?" He gave me a wink and a shove and raced me up the stairs.

* * *

"Dr Julius Julius!" I announced suddenly and loudly in the middle of dinner.

There was an outburst of applause and Jules' father grinned back at me across the salads.

"Yes indeed!" he said. "And you are?"

"Jakob Naylor, sir," I replied, pushing back my chair to stand up and bow to the 10 or so people round the table. "Twenty years old, Taurus, from Coney Island outside of New York City. My father's a mechanic there and my mother's a part-time seamstress. One sister. I'm studying Business with Spanish at Emory and this year I'm on an exchange at St Andrews University in Scotland."

They were all clapping and laughing.

"Welcome back, old man!" Jules was on his feet beside me, pressing a wine glass into my hand and raising his own. "Ladies and gentlemen, a toast! To Jake Naylor, old friend and new friend!"

Most of them were Spaniards. It was really noisy. Really good.

"And my girlfriend's name is Carmen," I told Jules triumphantly as we sat down again. "She's Sagittarius – not great for a Taurean, but it can be worked out."

"Girlfriend?! Come on, old man! You only met her yesterday!" he hissed. "Look, what is all this star sign crap? This is a new one."

"Oh yeah, we haven't really gone there, have we?"

"We're not going there now! I just want to know what's wrong with you!" His face was contorted with disgust.

It wasn't the moment to tell him about Nana – the elderly mother of José, who worked in my dad's garage. I liked hanging out at her place. It was full of stuff – old lady stuff I guess, and she was always making tea and Mexican pastries and yarning on about star signs. I guess that's how my Spanish had got good, not just the uni course – Nana had never really learnt much English.

"Okay, okay, stay cool. There's nothing wrong with me. I'll explain sometime."

"Yes, but I can't have you belching on about Capricorn and Cancer in front of people I know!"

"Oh, interesting. You despise 'all that star sign stuff', yet you know the signs all right."

"Oh piss off," he said, passing our plates up for servings of the giant paella that had just been carried out of the kitchen. "I do not!"

"That looks amazing!"

"Yes, my aunt does a mean paella. Here, pass this round. And look, you'd better forget about Carmen."

That stopped me diving into the fragrant mound of saffroned rice and seafood in front of me.

"What? Why? She's gorgeous and she likes me!"

"Yes, but these Spanish chicas are all after one thing. She was asking me in the car this afternoon all about you and your family, how rich you are, what you're studying…"

I nodded and forked some paella into my mouth.

"Oh that is SO good! Deliciosa! Magnífica, la paella!"

Blurry cries of approval, more raised glasses and laughter, music, kids running round the table.

"Jules, those are just the same kind of questions girls in the States ask."

"Really? Blimey. How can you tell if one really likes you? Save it, not my problem. But the Spanish will expect you to follow through in the biggest possible way, Jake. She'll be a prick-tease like the rest. It's not so long since Franco died, so her parents will have lived under the dictatorship and there's no way she'll shag you unless you put the ring on her finger, move to Spain for life and support her, the kids and probably the rest of the family forever."

"Jules!"

"Fact."

"But your mother's Spanish! You're half-Spanish."

"Exactly. That's how I know." The hazel eyes gleamed. He called down the table. "Hey, Mamá! Explain to Jake that all Spanish girls demand a good provider and won't look at a man unless he moves to Spain!"

"Jake, slap him for me!" his mother, the lovely saronged lady, called back. "But you know, he has a point. I don't understand my own son, who lives in the UK. Why? Why would anybody want to live anywhere but Spain?"

She spoke in Spanish and the cheers erupted all around again. We joined in the general toast but Jules slipped me a look of genuine concern when he muttered, "Don't say I didn't warn you."

Everyone was hugging and kissing and shrieking with laughter. I watched Jules' mother clinging to her husband's arm and the way he bent to kiss her and said to Jules, "Dude, I'm warned. But you know, it is good to see couples that age kissing and touching like that..."

* * *

"Jules was just kidding when he said that about Spanish women, right?" I asked his mother next morning.

I'd got up early to go down to the sea – their villa was perched way up above the fishing harbor – and she was already up too; she offered to give me a lift and take me for a coffee at her favorite little place. "Sure, thank you," I'd said, and next thing we were on the winding road again, Sra Julius waving her hands, speaking with her cigarette as she drove.

"Not the sports car, I'm afraid!" she laughed. "That was my husband's 50th birthday present to himself. Well yes, I think Jules *was* serious. His father loves it here, and Jules does too, of course, but ever since he was little he has always been the most English of the children. His father insisted he go to school in England" – she broke off to expertly light another cigarette from the old one – "and he just seems to like it there better. Our girls are both settled in Spain."

Her hands fluttered over the wheel, her bare brown shoulders shrugged.

"And you never wanted to live in Britain?"

She laughed.

"Me? No! What for? Look at this!" Her hand flew out, the burning end of her cigarette sketched an arc across the intensifying sky. Below us, the early sun glittered on a tranquil sea. "I visit. We thought about it, of course; maybe Jules' father would have liked it, but he chose me, and that meant living here."

It was a big thing to have said so simply, with almost arrogance, and I caught a glimpse of what Jules had tried to tell me.

But then her smile flashed again and that expressive cigarette conveyed a confidence.

"To be honest, when we met, Julius had had a huge argument with his family – his father had changed his Will. They were a very wealthy family, but the father got angry at Julius for some stupid thing he did – nothing bad, just stupid boy stuff – and cut him out of his Will."

"What happened?" I asked, fascinated.

"The father was killed in a car accident before things had blown over. Julius was about your age then – all fire and excitement and wanting to set the world alight – yes! like Jules is now! – and he thought his family would make things right despite the Will."

"Ah."

We were drawing into the town now – what used to be a quiet fishing village and now showed a mini-Manhattan skyline bristling with tall apartment blocks and hotels. Yet it had its charm. There was space here still, huge beaches, more curvaceous than the majestic strips of Coney Island, broad promenades fanned by palm trees, and… alegría. An indefinable sense of well-paced enjoyment of life.

"Ah indeed." Sra JJ parked her small car outside a doorway screened by simple hanging beads and mused for a moment. "Families can be very strange. So greedy. Maybe Julius could have obeyed his father, got some inheritance, but he was hurt, you see, angry in that proud way. He was young. He said, 'Fuck them!'" she pronounced it in English, with a laugh, "and came here and just made things happen."

"And he met you here?"

She nodded and opened the car door.

"Come! You need your walk and I need my coffee!"

Already it was hot out. We passed through the strips of beads into a cool, pleasantly dim bar.

"Manolo!" she cried. "Good morning! How are you?"

The leather-faced barman with a cloth over his shoulder continued at the coffee machine while they chatted about their families, the stupid government, the heat. Then he wiped his hands on his apron and leaned across the bar to shake my hand.

"Now, you must be young Jules' friend, the American boy. A pleasure to meet you!"

I was flattered that he knew who I was.

"And what can I serve you?" asked Manolo, placing a small cup of black coffee in front of Sra JJ and adding a spot of milk – the 'cortado'.

"Oh, the same, thank you."

Sra JJ was at the cigarette machine, buying fresh supplies. We perched on stools by the huge old cash register that squatted on the crowded wooden bar and the cigarette in use ordered a couple of magdalenas, small sponge cakes.

"Everyone in the village knows who you are," she said. "I grew up here and spent all my summers here as a student, then we came as a family. So it's still a village to me and friends like Manolo."

"Yes, I can understand that. My parents are both local, they didn't want to move into the big city, just raise their family 'at home'. They said it gives kids a stronger sense of identity."

She smiled through the smoke.

"I am very happy that you are Jules' friend," she told me. "He talks about you a lot – yes, yes, don't look so amazed! Isn't it true, Manolo, Jules talks about his American friend?"

Without pausing for an instant in his ceaseless activities at the increasingly busy bar, Manolo called back,

"As if he were a brother."

"You see?" she said. "I have two sons now – all gain, no pain!"

And I felt, well, really good about that.

* * *

Jules came to find me later down at the harbor, where I'd ended up again after a great swim and beach walk.

"Oh here you are! At last! Are you dry? What are you staring at? Did something happen?"

"No, I'm just, you know, drinking it all in."

"What is *wrong* with you? You are so spaced out. You're too young to be a hippie – snap out of it!"

"I'm in harmony, man," I teased, swinging my legs back over the harbor wall.

"Aargh! Gag me with a spoon! Come on, seriously, it's our last go in the red beast – Dad's only let me use it in exchange for doing his tax returns and time's up at lunchtime today. Carmen's coming for lunch. Wear baggy shorts."

* * *

The overnight 'bus up to Madrid was half-empty. We spread ourselves over four seats. About 20 people had seen us off. I was probably hugged and kissed and passed around more during that farewell than during my entire childhood – and we're not a cold family.

Finally the waves and smiling faces dropped back as the 'bus drew away from the stop.

Jules screwed round in his seat to hiss at me,

"So, do you remember why you blacked out this time?"

"At the Benidorm party? Sure I do."

"You told Dad you didn't! You are such a liar!"

"Didn't want to shock anyone."

Jules' face between the headrests registered interest.

"No! Why? What happened?"

"Do you remember the kitchen catching fire?"

"You bet I do! That broke up the party. That's when we lost you. Why *did* that trollop start frying croquetas? There was plenty of grass and booze. Croquetas! But go on, go on – what happened to you, old man?"

"There was a lot of smoke and confusion in the corner where we were – it was quite scary. I thought I'd grabbed Carmen's hand but it turned out to be that guy dressed – or not – as the Naked Cowboy…"

"Oh Christ!"

"Yes. Must have picked up on my accent. I tried to drop his hand as soon as I realized, but he wouldn't let go. Then the firemen arrived. I couldn't see you or Carmen or any of the others. The Naked Cowboy pulled me off into the garden and tried to kiss me."

"What!" Jules' eyes bulged. "But he had a huge… moustache!"

I nodded.

"Crikey. Yuk. No wonder you blacked out. But that's all he tried, right?"

"Dude! I shoved him away and ran."

"Christ!" Jules stared at me with sympathy for about four seconds then burst into such shrieks of laughter that the driver wanted to know what the joke was so Jules told him – with embellishments – and the whole 'bus had the story within about two minutes. It was like being inside a boom box. They were loving it. I'm surprised the 'bus didn't come off the road, it rocked with such mirth.

Yeah, it was fun. But that night on the journey, I had plenty of time to do some serious thinking, about the other times I'd had blackouts since meeting Jules.

* * *

Further up the east coast, in Valencia, where Dr JJ had his practice and lived with his wife most of the year, a flabby, middle-aged man with a receding hairline and mean, clever little eyes, glared hard at his meeker companion.

He was Juan Antonio Ruiz, the mayor.

"Are you sure this will work?"

His companion, furtive in manner but sharp in expression, eyeballed him with perfect confidence.

"Of course I am. We've been studying it for months. All you have to do is sign off the documents authorizing the buildings. Once they're in the system, central government isn't going to question our accounts showing money going out for maintenance expenses, rates, property taxes and so on."

"But the buildings don't actually exist?"

"Of course not! What a waste to put them up when all we need to do is build them on paper!"

They both chuckled heartily.

"What's it worth?"

"To you? Depends how much building we have to do. But none of the four of us is in this for under six figures."

"Hm. Risk?"

"Minimal, Juan Antonio. There's plenty of EU taxpayers' money to play with, and all the highly publicised cleaning-up of the city you're doing, not to mention your TV show and all the coverage you're getting on the luxury new mansions area... well, there'll be plenty of investors lining up to bring even more money in and show their gratitude to you personally. You have hit the luxury button, you know."

Juan Antonio smirked. They were seated in his study at home, surrounded by dark wood furniture, old portraits, family photos. A reassuring atmosphere for his private, late evening get-togethers, which were soon to include Middle Eastern royalty. The luxury button. Yes. He'd seen what was needed here. The mayor – a lifelong fan of bullfighting – instinctively understood about distracting the public's attention, organising flamboyant clean-ups of drugs and prostitution while quietly paving the way for big outside 'investment'. If a little money got cleaned in those investments, he would turn a blind eye and arrange matters... for a gift.

"Let's try this one." His fat finger stabbed at the most modest of the architectural sketches in front of him. "See how it goes. We can introduce more gradually if all goes smoothly."

His companion smiled thinly and raised his glass in a silent deal.

The two men drank.

"Keep me informed." The mayor lumbered to his feet. "Now, I need to get my beauty sleep – tomorrow's a full day at the office and then I have my programme."

"Of course." His companion picked up his things and left after a hearty embrace.

He went to his car but did not drive straight home. Instead, he went over to the far end of the port area, close to where the first of the new buildings was located on the sketch. It was a rundown area, but he felt no fear. Spain had gone mad since Franco's death, but in a materialistic way, not a violent one. The country had tired of violence, profoundly exhausted by the civil war. He climbed out of his modest car and went to stand by the low sea wall, sniffing the fresh tang of good things to come.

Moonlight gleamed on dark water.

He ran his tongue over his lips, savouring the hint of salt like the first sip of a potent cocktail.

His eyes closed.

The slender stem of the cocktail glass was in his hand, there was music and laughter cradling him among bright lights. And the girls! Shapely, half naked bodies wafted towards him… bare breasts brushed his lips…

It was all to come.

He opened his eyes to glance around quickly. There was no-one. His right hand slid inside his trousers and he rubbed eagerly, with a small groan closed in his throat, his nostrils flared to catch the tang, his lips slightly parted and his tongue moistening them with quick little flicks, tasting the salt.

It was all to come…

* * *

Madrid begins with mad, and takes it from there.

Man, I have never been anywhere so noisy in my life, it's like permanent clubbing. Everybody yells, nobody listens, they all talk at once. A drink in one hand, a smoke in the other. Girls and guys breaking out into spontaneous clapping and singing in the street. Loud music. Old ladies sitting out on their balconies, slapping their bosoms with fans. Old men arguing with each other in doorways.

And it was hot. City hot. Stop hot.

We lay on Spartan beds under a whirling fan during the heat of the afternoon, then went out into the mad throngs crowding the cute narrow streets at night.

Every doorway was a bar. Every bar was heaving.

Jules was in his element – smoke. Every time I glanced his way he was festooned in girls. And I guess I wasn't short of company myself.

I don't really remember how we ended up in the potato field.

"I remember that bar with all the bulls' heads round the walls," I offered as Jules and I sat on a rock under an inadequate moon.

Jules shook his head.

"That doesn't narrow it down much. People here watch bullfighting on the telly like they watch football back home – well, they watch football here too, it's true, but what I'm trying to…"

"Sure, you remember. It was the one with all those pictures of matadors getting gored. That guy right up in the air, looked as though the bull had him perched on his head, then you saw that the bullfighter was kinda attached to the bull 'cos the bull's horn was right through his thigh."

"Oh yes, I remember the bar now. That's a really famous one. Ava Gardner…"

"You know, right up close to his sac, dude, right up here."

"Get off!"

"Sorry. But the horn had pierced him that high up and the bull had tossed him up in the air still attached. Can you imagine the agony of all the nerves and muscles being torn through and ripped around like that? And you could see where the tip of the horn had come right through the other side of his thigh!"

Jules took another drag.

"Oh yes. Brilliant photo."

"Jules!"

"What?"

"Is that all you have to say?"

"You're saying it all."

I shut up. He drew on his smoke.

"I think it's a potato field," he said finally.

I didn't argue. I didn't have a clue. I felt sick.

"Then I remember two or three places with music," I said. "People dancing, you were making out with some girl we lost later."

Jules patted his pockets for his cigarettes.

"Then you took me to some dark quiet place where you said famous writers used to hang out and Ava Gardner picked up bullfighters and you made me drink absinthe 'cos Madrid's the only place in Europe where it's still legal."

"Not that legal," he muttered, lighting up. "Why do you think the place was dark and quiet?"

"There was a party in those girls' friends' apartment, then we got in some dude's car to go to another party and that was insane because the Gran Via was completely jam-packed – at 3am!"

He yawned.

"Yes, stupid way to go."

"Not the only bit of stupid from that guy!"

"No. Piss-poor driver."

I fished around and found some gum. It made me feel sicker to start with but it did freshen my beer-weary mouth.

"Was there a party out here somewhere? I mean, did we actually get to something and I've just blacked out again?"

"Nah." Jules stubbed out his cigarette. "You didn't black out. We got to a place. An angry old man in the kitchen…"

"That's right! Someone's abuelo! I remember now! He was mad at us for disturbing him so late. But dude, he was dressed and drinking, what was he doing up at 4am anyway?"

"Dunno. You ran off…"

"They started frying! I was scared!"

"…and I went after you…"

"And we got lost."

"Yeah. They were only cooking us some food. It would've helped with the hangovers."

"Sorry."

"I'm out of cigarettes. We need to get back to civilization."

"Jules, you don't smoke in your sleep, do you?"

"No."

"So chill! We've been up all night and it's peaceful here. I've often slept on the beach."

"It's not a beach. It's a potato field."

I smiled.

"Close your eyes and listen to the waves."

CHAPTER TWO
Manhattan and Manhattans

I closed my eyes and listened to the waves. It was one year on from the potato field.

I'd graduated and was house-sitting for a friend in Queen's for the summer, visiting my family each week and delivering pizzas while I looked for a 'real' job.

Jules, of course, had got it all lined up much better.

"Got a job yet?" his cheerful voice bellowed down the 'phone.

"Still delivering pizzas." I carried the 'phone out to my parents' small balcony and watched the ocean while we talked.

"You lazy bastard!"

I smiled. His English was impeccable, but at times, something about his choice of language, his intonation, made me think of stuffy old Oxford dons like you see in British movies.

"How's the investment banking going?"

"Great, great, really interesting, I love it. Seriously, aren't you even getting interviews? What's the hold-up?"

"Oh, I was never in such a rush as you, Jules. My buddy needs a house-sitter, and I want to get the right job, not just a job. This isn't Europe. Once you're in, you're locked down on two weeks' vacation a year."

"See what you mean, old man. Hardly long enough for a decent blackout. How are *they* going?"

"None for the past year."

"Good. Thought you might make that an excuse for flunking your degree."

"Wow, I never thought of that!"

"What are you applying for?"

"Oh, this and that. Looking for inspiration. I just don't want to be in something soulless."

"You *are* a hippie! Move to South America!"

I laughed.

"That's an option! But you know, I want to work in something, I dunno... something beautiful."

He made a gagging noise.

"Well, Nana says Mercury is retrograde," I told him. "So communications aren't that great for the next six weeks."

"Oh Christ. I'll call you in six weeks."

He hung up.

* * *

Three days later, I walked into my career.

It wasn't my usual beat, but the other guy who delivered in the area was off sick, so I was covering for him.

I liked delivering pizzas. It was outdoors, I got to whizz around on my bike, people were generally very pleasant and tipped me well, and I enjoyed the precision with which Fat Luke ran his business. It was educational. I got to see how a successful local business cut corners, where it *did* put its money, how personnel influenced the product – it was like seeing my degree course come to life, with visits to Nana keeping my Spanish brushed up. I'd mainly worked in bars before – also an education, but I wasn't competitive or charismatic enough to make it up to the big bucks level in that fierce field. Jules could have done it – with his dynamism, his looks and accent, he'd have been raking in hundreds of bucks a night in tips in no time at all. But I preferred local bars where the regulars hung out. Manhattan and Manhattans were never really for me.

I sometimes wondered if Jules was right. Maybe I was too laidback, not competitive enough. But I did have ambition. I just didn't know where to focus it until I delivered one particular pizza.

It was a Fat Luke Special, which carried a lot of salami, sausage and olives, so I was kinda surprised when I was told it was for an embroidery company.

"You drop that pizza, you make a stain anywhere in that place and I make a stain of you, right here on this floor, capisce?" Fat Luke told me when the order came out. "You're skinny but there'll still be plenty blood, you hear me?"

"Si, ho capito," I said. That was the reason he'd taken me on in the first place – the other guys had given the US slang response 'Capisce'.

He checked the order – a huge spider of a man sitting at the center of a very well-spun web – and waved me out.

"And don't touch nothing there," he called, a fat finger jabbing the air behind me as I headed out to my bike.

No problem, I thought – no way would I want to touch anything in some lacey, precious embroidery place. Probably two weird old sisters trying to make ends meet, doing people's turn-ups and hems and repairs like my mom did, only pretentious about it. But the pizza? Oh well, maybe they had nephews visiting.

In the event, I got buzzed into one of the old warehouses within sight of the Queensboro Bridge and the pizza and I went up in a huge old industrial service elevator clearly built to handle bulk goods.

The doors opened at the sixth floor, and that's when I stepped into a new life.

It was the moment I stopped just gazing around, absorbing, sniffing and pawing what life brought, and instead felt, through every fiber of my being, a bright, determined focus.

From the iron-grey embrace of the service elevator, I stepped into a large, soft, furnished interior. A magical, colorful cocoon of artistic creativity, where harmony flowed through the air punctured by spikes of eye-grabbing design. A 2x3-meter cream fabric stitched with an angular, almost life-size tree pattern, dominated the wall opposite the elevator doors. Below it, a large old wooden chest scattered with beautiful, bulging pillows – one of them leather – stitched in different designs and vibrant colors. To my right, a dummy modeled an intricately embroidered frock coat with broad lapels and skirts – the kind you'd see in a movie like *Liaisons Dangereuses*.

I inched toward it, impelled by natural curiosity; above it hung a photo still from the movie *Liaisons Dangereuses* and a letter of gratitude from the Oscar-winning costume designer to Millards, the company I was delivering the pizza to.

"Hello!" someone called. I started guiltily and turned to the advancing woman.

"Your pizza, ma'am."

While she paid me and took the box out of my hands, I looked past her to shelves laden with heavy gold lace and trims of all shapes and colors, and more stills on the walls showing luscious costumes for films and acclaimed TV series. The big old desks underneath were almost hidden under costume books, cloth samples, bowls of buttons…

"Would you like to place an order?" I suddenly heard the lady say in a sarcastic tone.

"Oh, I'm sorry ma'am! I was just, well, it's my first time here and I wasn't expecting… This is awesome. Thank you, have a nice day!"

I turned back toward the elevator and stopped. Blocking my way was an older man – like the woman, who was calling out 'Lunch is here', in the late 50s. He was of medium height, slender, 'dapper' is the word that sprang to my mind, and his long iron-grey hair was gathered at the nape of his neck with a large blue velvet bow. He was theatrical even though dressed for the factory floor.

China-blue eyes surveyed me.

"Would you like to look around?" His voice was cool and low, his expression calm.

"Oh, thank you sir, I would love to, but…" But Fat Luke will kill me, I was thinking.

"No buts. If you are interested, you will make the time."

He was looking at me with undisguised interest, yet I felt no threat.

"I am. Thank you."

"Follow me, then. I can give you 10 minutes at most. My name is Theodore Danes, the owner. Please call me Theo."

The 10 minutes were a test. I admired his calculation. He invited me back the next day and I stayed for an hour, marveling over the machines in the huge, light, factory-style workshop behind the showroom, at the scale and beauty of the firm.

On the second visit, Theo showed me the "client room", where exquisite stitching samples hung on racks around the walls and row upon row of bright threads to match every possible hue of fabric sat on top of tall, pale blue cabinets. The blue reminded me of the letters on the wall in Benido-m, advertising a forgotten firm. But through the high windows, I saw no beige hills, instead, the Queensboro Bridge and Manhattan's Upper East Side skyline.

"This is the oldest machine we have," said Theo, taking me into a room full of old black hand-sewing machines – a century away from my mom's busy modern machine whose quiet hum had been the sound track of my childhood. This felt like an engine room.

"French, 1876. Now, this one is curious. We use it a lot for monogram work. Would you like to try it?"

I sat at the treadle machine and looked it over. Chunky body built into a wood and iron work table. Solid, solid, solid. I smiled. I trusted it.

"There's a wheel underneath which guides the needle," Theo explained, showing me the lever.

"Oh! Hand-eye-foot coordination!" I was pleased.

There was fabric on the table, thread in the needle.

"Go ahead," Theo encouraged. "Try and write your name."

I put my foot on the treadle, took the fabric in my left hand and the wheel under the table with my right. Table football skills honed in Europe had to help here.

"I have to take this call," Theo was saying behind me. "Carry on, try your name."

Well, I have to tell you it was really, really hard. It went against all my instincts, it was like learning to write all over again but facing the wrong way and with the wrong hand. I hated seeing my letters come out so irregular. But then it got better. I felt fits and starts of joined-up coordination, and the fierce focus people don't often see in me 'cos it's usually only there when I'm riding the waves.

Theo came back after about 10 minutes. He looked at my efforts. His eyebrows rose. I was embarrassed.

"Well, that is actually quite remarkable," he said. He didn't seem to be sarcastic about it.

"Do you think so? The edges are pretty loose, look, and this line here is all wrong. But it was fun! Thank you, sir!"

I stood up. He was still examining the scrap of fabric.

"Jake, I'm busy now, but I'd like us to talk. Are you available for dinner on Thursday?"

My alarm must have showed. It was Queen's, but it was still New York, and well, these creative places…

Theo smiled faintly.

"A strictly business dinner, Jake. I'm busy every other evening this week and my partner has a regular engagement on Thursdays."

* * *

"You're working *where*?!" shrieked Jules. "In a bloody embroidery shop! What is it, two old ladies and some cross-stitch? Jesus fucking Christ!"

"I'm surprised you've even heard of cross-stitch," I put in.

I could hear him breathing heavily in the short silence.

"Jake, seriously old man, I do have some contacts, I could've lent a hand. I didn't realize you were desperate. I swallowed all that crap about you wanting the right job not just a job."

I grinned to myself at his concern and just said, "Come on over and see for yourself. You high-finance guys can always find a reason to take a trip to New York."

"Yes, yes, maybe that's best." His usual bonhomie was in abeyance. "Are you still at your pal's house?"

"Yes, but only till the end of the month. I'm looking for my own place. You can come and look at cockroach-infested dives with me – it'll be fun."

"Fun! Okay, listen, give me your postcode there. The whole address, in fact."

"So that you can find the closest 5-star?" I joshed him.

"So that my assistant can," he said coldly. "I'll call you tomorrow, same time."

By next morning he had it all fixed. There was relief in his voice when he rang me to give me the details. Good old Jules, rushing to my rescue, not in a borrowed red steed this time but by BA and yellow cab. I hung up with a smile and left for work.

* * *

I'd never been inside the St Regis Hotel. It reeked of class. A classic Beaux-Arts 1904 building on the SE corner of Central Park. Wood paneling, yellow lighting. Somber-faced staff managing to be obsequious and snooty at the same time.

"Dude, this place is for stuffy old men!" I reproached Jules, standing up to greet him as he joined me in the bar.

"Exactly!" he said, slapping me briefly against his chest in a hearty hug. "That's where the money is, old man!"

It was the first time we'd met in over a year. He was dressed in a classically tailored dark tan suit with a cream shirt and patterned apricot tie. He looked good. Expansive, confident. Older than 23.

"Looking good, dude!"

He looked pleased, but just said, "Oh, straight from work. Good meetings. Now, howzabout a Manhattan, since that's where we are – me for the first time, and probably you too, you country hick!"

I'd taken to wearing a Texan bootlace tie over a crisp white shirt and narrow jeans. I knew it suited my sinewy frame and just grinned back at him while his British accent and beyond-his-years assurance secured our Manhattans.

As usual, Jules had something lined up for later. Over dinner, we mainly talked about his work.

"What kind of things do we invest in? Oh, everything from water treatment works to hotel development. I love it. Every day is different, I like calculating risk. And I like doing something that's useful, helping people and companies be productive, push ahead. I like being useful. It's like what you said about wanting to work in something beautiful. Don't worry, we'll get you there."

I smiled.

"Shouldn't we make a move? If this gig starts at 10pm, it really will start by 20 after – this isn't Spain."

"Yes, yes, let's go," he said. "Bowery Ballroom – I liked the sound of it and one of the girls in the office said the band's really cool."

"A special girl?" I asked as we hopped into a cab. "I mean, in your life?"

To my surprise, he looked confused. I'd always assumed Jules would wait till he was about 30, then marry a Henrietta type and retire to a mansion in the country. This fluster wasn't part of the image.

"Oh God, it's too early to think of things like that."

"What's her name?" I was amused.

He rounded on me with suppressed fury.

"Nobody! Shhh! Shut up!" He bit his knuckles and turned away to look unseeingly out at the Village streets.

"Jane," he muttered finally. "Her name's Jane."

"Wow," I said, in a non-committal tone.

"She's a bloody pain in the arse," he burst out with a scowl. "She... Oh, never mind, forget it."

"So why are you dating if she's such a pain?"

He glared at me. In the lights from the street flashing across his face at different angles, the scowl mutated into something like... fear? Surely not? Not Jules!

"I've got no choice, old man," he said softly. "I'd stop if I could, but I've just got no choice."

I was silent.

Suddenly the boisterous Jules was back.

"Is this it? Great. Drinks'll be a bomb in here, right? Let's hit up a bar or two before we go in. Still time."

* * *

"I won't intimidate the old ducks, dressed like this, will I?" he asked next morning over coffee. I'd stayed in his room overnight – we'd been out till late.

"You're fine."

"Only I have got another meeting afterwards, and I won't have time to change."

He began to look puzzled when we stopped in the warehouse area, the heart of Queens manufacturing, and definitely suspicious when the huge steel doors of the industrial elevator opened to admit us.

"What are their names?" he asked suddenly, as if realizing his ignorance. I just smiled. He tugged briefly at his tie and scowled at me.

The doors opened and I pushed him out into the gorgeous showroom interior that merged into the machine area and factory floor over on the horizon.

"You little shit!" he hissed over his shoulder, but his eyes didn't leave the explosion of color and craftsmanship that was cushioning his fall from assumption.

"Serves you right, dude!"

"Yes," he admitted, advancing and gazing. "You're right, it does."

To cap his downfall, Theo made a perfectly timed entrance from the adjoining workshop at exactly that moment. Debonair and flamboyant, he flung his arms open and came swiftly forward, giving Jules a perfectly judged hug and a laughing welcome.

"Theo, this is Jules. Jules, this is Theo Danes, the company founder. Aka 'two old ladies'."

"Mr Danes…"

"Theo, please."

"Theo, Jake is a little shit who has completely misled me, but you seem to be in on the joke, and I am very happy to meet you 'both'." Jules was back on the first foot.

Theo threw his head back and laughed.

"Poor Jules! Now, Jake has work to do, but I'd be delighted to show you around…"

They disappeared together and I sat down to the day's assignments.

"That," Jules said emphatically over drinks after work, "is an incredible outfit. Bugger me, the work they do! Every piece a one-off! Those curtains for the rich bloke's Colorado mansion! They had crystals stitched into the design! $100,000 – for a pair of curtains! And as for the film costumes… And you know what? I was really impressed by all that OTT house museum stuff – upholstery for the Rothschild and Vanderbilt mansions and so on. Fucking incredible!"

"Yeah, well, I like it."

"I'm not surprised. My God, that place shifts some money! I know that's not entirely why you like it, but I am gobsmacked. Theo said you're not creative but you are a brilliant copyist, so you can get a sketched design right with the machine, and as for the way you handled that monogram machine on the first day…"

"Second day," I murmured. "First day was pizza delivery day."

" …he said it takes most people, even with talent, about three months to do what you just sat down and did straight off!"

"He said that?"

"Yes! And that you're useful because you speak Spanish and half the team is from South America, and that he has high hopes of you for helping develop the business in the right way – high-end, word-of-mouth luxury market among the younger clients. You could be partner by 25!"

"Wow, that's great. There's so much to learn, but that's exactly the line I want to take. More the business side. I could never learn all they know about different periods and designs, but I do have a good eye for the detail, and it is a… beautiful business. It does no harm, it creates beauty. And it's a good size of team – about 15 of us."

"Theo's gay, right?"

"They all are."

"All of them?! Even Juana and Mamencita? Come off it!"

"Yes, those two were both married and they have kids, but they're both in ongoing gay relationships now. Everyone."

We were in a narrow, candlelit wine bar down in McDougal St. Beautiful girls and good-looking guys were crammed in all around us. Jules was looking at me very intently all of a sudden. Seemed like a waste when there was all of NYC around him, to be looking intently at me, but he was. I was thinking around the team.

"Except Danby, the artist," I corrected myself suddenly. "Did you meet him? About 40, kinda wild eyes…"

"Yep, met him!"

"He's a genius artist, can sketch whatever the ditzy client wants and transform it into a form we can work with on the fabrics, but he's pretty radical in everything else. Says he has a live-in girlfriend and isn't prepared to change. But he's the only one."

A gorgeous blonde in half a dress stumbled against Jules and he barely glanced at her.

"And you, old man. And you."

"Oh yes, of course. And me."

* * *

My life trickled on quietly. Learning the trade from a business perspective, sitting in on meetings, understanding Theo's ambitions for the firm, and contributing to its luscious output stitch by stitch, bright thread by bright thread.

Weaving some kind of pattern for myself, I guess. Like those medieval ladies sitting at their tapestries centuries ago, patient stitches creeping oh so slowly to a complete picture. Hopefully a vibrant one.

Some friends, some dates, family, and always the sea.

Jules and I saw each other every year over the next five years. One of the meetings he'd had on that first visit led to a particularly promising investment for his bank, and they sent him over each spring.

"I'm in favor, old man!" he told me triumphantly. "It wasn't my final decision, but they're trusting me with bigger investments now we're beginning to see the results of the first ones. See you in the Big Apple next month – I know you old ducks don't get enough holiday to come over here at all, let alone have the spare cash. Heard from Carmen at all?"

I thought for a moment, then said, "I'm in touch with Carmen and in love with my work."

He laughed and rang off.

* * *

We went to a speakeasy his first night on that trip. The lights were dim, the liquor arrived in coffee cups. Jules loved it. Until he tried to chat up the girls at the next table and soon found they were gay.

"Christ, it's worse than London!" he moaned.

"Worse?"

"Yes, at least there I don't even have any hope any more. Since Jane and I split... Well, it used to be just pride and parades and all that, didn't it? But now it's just everywhere. Everyone. I called someone a cocksucker the other day and a bloke in my department said he was going to report me and I could lose my job!"

He looked moodily at the guys staring into other guys' eyes, the girls at the next table now tongueing each other, and finished his drink in a gulp.

"C'mon, old man. I can't stand this. It's bad enough at work – but *this*!" He waved an arm round and stomped out of the door.

We did find a more radical bar where the girls eyed us with interest, and he cheered up slightly. But he was more subdued than I had ever seen him. And he kept going on about the smoking ban in Spain.

"In Spain!" he exclaimed, flinging his arms out in one of his infrequent Spanish gestures. "I ask you! The government makes a bloody mint out of tobacco taxes, enough to pay for new roads and railways all over the shop, and they go and ban smoking in all public places! That's the European Union for you! That's Brussels and their straight bananas! No, actually, you know what? It's come from here, from the States. Toxic bloody politically correct crap, and federal blocking of people's right to kill themselves any way they want! But Spain! Going out for a ciggie, old man, I'll be back in a tick."

When he came back, reeling a bit – it was a Friday night and we were out late – I decided to try and head him off at the pass with my good news, but his mouth was open and moving 6ft away.

"…flying bollocks! Half of the small businesses will go bust – remember Manolo's?"

I nodded, gauging my moment.

"How do you think he's going to survive if his customers can't smoke?! Eh?" he dipped his nose into his drink and I nipped in fast.

"Well, I have some amazing news. Theo is taking me to Europe on his buying trip later this year! I can add it to vacation time and pay you all a really good long visit."

He slapped me on the arm in delight and ordered more drinks to celebrate. And it stopped him moaning on about straight bananas, bent colleagues. For that night, anyway.

On Saturday, he wanted to see the new building on Sixth Avenue by Spanish architect Pablo Torres. Recently completed; a soaring, gold-gleaming sheath that reached out and brought you in under its influence with its external elevators and acres of transparent, floating reception.

We stood across the street in silent admiration.

"Amazing. Love it," murmured Jules, gazing upwards. "He's done some absolutely wicked work. One of the top three in the country. That's Spain right now – just blossoming all over the world. Architecture, wine, film, food. And language. More people here speak both languages than either English or Spanish. It is so cool, so avant-garde."

He turned to me with a huge grin.
"But you'll see it for yourself soon!"

* * *

Juan Antonio Ruiz, Mayor of Valencia on Spain's east coast, turned to his sidekick with a huge grin.

"Pablo Torres?" he exclaimed. "Wonderful idea, brilliant! Yes, yes, after all the magnificent work he's done on creating Valencia's trademark new museums and aquarium – of course he is just the architect to go to for this new idea. He does a plan, we pay him a nice fat fee and put it down on the books as a much fatter fee – an obese fee! Excellent! So that the five of us have a lovely little gift out of the obese fee, a reward for our vision and hard work."

His sidekick smiled thinly. Two hundred million euros for a sketch by one of Spain's most acclaimed architects was what it amounted to. He'd thought that they, the group of five, would all make six figures within two years on their various deals, and they had. And now they were up into seven figures. He enjoyed the elegance of it. The mayor was delighted.

One more. One more – a genuinely big operation – and he would retire, thought the sidekick. He would know the opportunity when it came his way. Meanwhile, he guarded his treasure, enjoying it carefully, always on the watch for new schemes where they could cream off big gobs of money undetected. Kickbacks, speculation, greed – these were words beginning to taint Spain's public aura. Ugly words to describe what had always been there and now had free expression. His work was pure art, a process of elegance and innovation based on tradition.

"I am delighted that you like it, Mayor. I'll move it forward this week so that we can finalise the paperwork while Torres is in town."

Juan Antonio, his flab now turned to solid fat, beamed. He'd been a millionaire when he took office on an anti-corruption platform.

"Why should I steal from local businesses or the taxpayers?" he'd bellowed on TV in the campaign. "I'm rich already! I don't need to steal!"

Many people had trusted him and voted him in. After all, it was true – he didn't need to steal.

His companion smiled back at him but his admiration was all for himself. For the creation of the gold-gleaming, elegant structures of deceit he was building day by day, year by year. Unperceived.

One more. The golden cupola to complete the beautiful, beautiful structure of which he was the invisible, genius architect.

* * *

"I'd like you to go to Las Vegas for me next week," Theo said in his quiet way. "We're very close to securing the contract for all the high-roller room and bar interiors at Corey Rosenberg's new casino and I think the personal touch would help clinch it at this point."

I was pretty stunned.

"But won't they want to see you?"

"If they want to see me, they can come to New York," he replied simply, and once again I admired his perfect judgment. The man was a walking lesson in unpretentious distinction. He should have been royalty. I'd have had him as King Theo of the United States in a heartbeat.

" …because you are familiar with the portfolio and have a very persuasive manner," he was saying, "I don't want sales types out there representing this firm, but I do want to close this contract. It is an important one."

"I'll say it's important!" enthused Jules when we spoke at the weekend. "There was a report on the telly the other day over here about the new Corey Casino in Vegas. The man's already got an empire and they more or less say he's just doing this one to out-Trump Trump. The toupé wars! Love the way Theo keeps himself at a snooty distance and sends a presentable underling. Class!"

"Did you seal the deal?" he yelled when I picked up the 'phone the following Sunday. Jules was a demon for the 'phone. I thought it was only teenage girls who were stuck to it like that. Even when he was armed to the teeth with the latest gadgets, he maintained there was something special about a 'phone call. I understood. My mom said the same about letters, mourning the fact nobody wrote them anymore. I agreed with them both and responded to whatever others' preferences were.

"Did you? Did you meet the Big Swinging Dick or were you palmed off onto the General Manager?"

"Meeting with the General Manager, signing and champagne with the BSD," I said.

"No! Really? You did it? Got the signature from Corey himself? Sealed deal?"

"Oh yes."

I didn't tell him I knew the deal was sealed as soon as the General Manager ushered me into an office the size of the entire Millards shop floor and the BSD looked me over.

He was in his late forties; smooth, tight skin and an expression to match. He was dressed with exaggerated style. I guessed that, like me, he had little imagination and, not like me, had someone to dress him for every occasion. I was lucky – his look today was classic suit, white shirt, conservative tie and gleaming, pointed, Italian shoes. My Texan chic image was no threat, just neat and appropriate to the setting – a nod to wealth behind a modestly conservative exterior.

He rose up from a monstrous leather office chair with what looked like the whole of Vegas as a backdrop through the window acreage. It seemed frantic to me – even the fountains were running too fast, it seemed like – and inside I was unsettled by the blare of excitement being pawed around in the giant claws of cold hard calculation.

Corey focused my thoughts with a handshake and a look that undressed me. I thought of Theo, how much this contract meant to the whole hard-working team, and met his enthusiasm with bland politeness.

There was a moment, just before he actually signed the precious document, when he leaned forward and teasingly fiddled with the ends of my bootlace tie. Jules would've decked him for that,

I thought, forcing a playful smile to my lips in response. It was comforting to think of Jules' robust responses to life.

"Well done, old man!" Jules was yelling down the 'phone.

"Thanks, thanks."

I didn't tell Jules either that I'd had another blackout after the trip. It began just after Corey signed and I left his office, his praise of our portfolio ringing in my ears and an urge to take my bootlace tie off right away itching my fingers.

I knew it was happening this time, and I had clues – a trail of breadcrumbs back to myself even as the world began to blank. There was a 'plane ticket showing me where I was headed next, and my 'amnesia card', where I'd put down my name, address, job and other reassuring details. Even so, I rang in sick next day, and sent the documents over by cab, carefully checking the address with a clearly surprised stranger/colleague.

She called me Jakob, which matched my card, and I could see the contract meant lots of work for the firm I appeared to work for – all reason to celebrate. But it was a long night, a long flight, and a long fight to find myself again that time.

"I'll see you in New York soon," Corey had said on parting, hanging onto my shoulder with intimacy. "I'm always in and out of the Big Apple. You can show me some of the cool new places to hang out, young guy!"

What gnawed at me later was why Theo had really sent me.

* * *

Corey Rosenberg put the top back on the Montblanc pen he'd used to sign the Millards contract. Idly, he turned the pages of their portfolio, alive with elegance and colored craftsmanship. The lead interior designer who'd come up with the concepts for the casino's interior had been adamant - Millards was the only firm to be trusted with projects of this calibre.

"In the '50s and '60s, there were literally hundreds of embroidery firms in NYC," she'd told him. "Back when the costume industry was booming and the Garment District was really alive. Now there are maybe three, and only one of them is run by Theo

Danes. The man's an encyclopedia. Any period, any project, any scale, he will do and deliver."

"Is he expensive?"

"Beyond price. Of course he's expensive, he's legend."

"I want leather, not silks."

"I know! And that's another thing – only Theo Danes can handle unusual fabrics. Look, the bottom line is that I won't have any other firm doing the stitching on my designs. The high-roller rooms and the VIP bar are going to be poems of contemporary and classic opulence – I am *not* having some Susie Homemaker wannabe brought in on my designs to wreck my reputation."

They eyeballed each other for about 10 seconds.

"Or yours!" she pointed out, and Corey laughed.

He was irked by her arrogance but also reassured by it, and he had no intention of arguing with Mila, whose edgy take on classical entertainment environments over the past 15 years had brought her single-name status.

She'd looked so earnest, so conservative, with her honey-gold hair loose in a softly-layered shoulder-length cut, and a neat cream skirt suit.

Deceptively respectable, Corey mused, a silent laugh in his throat. He knew that Mila's sketches for the interiors were sublime. Attuned to the fast-pulse, live-hard credo of Vegas, its die-now-if-you-want-to-it'll-be-fun attitude, they yet achieved a scored, tough beauty that Corey knew would cut the high-rollers open and fill them with pride.

Who cared if it was false pride? They'd be deceiving themselves.

Deceit.

Deceit.

The definition of our times.

It was Corey's perception. His job, his satisfaction, lay in designing a laughing, seductive, reaching-out, vibrant embrace for other people's self-deception.

In your face, yet invisible.

* * *

"What's it like?" they all wanted to know, in English and Spanish, asking with different expressions and urgency. But that was what they wanted to know.

"Um, it's very like the renderings," I said. They looked disappointed. I tried again. "The casino is immense. It is vulgar on the outside in a beautiful sort of way – very Las Vegas, I guess. You feel dwarfed at the entrance. Some of them are so vulgar they are welcoming. Corey's is vulgar in a select, British old man's club kind of way."

"Wood paneling? Yellow lighting?" pushed Marianne.

"Yeah… Mila is doing all these odd twists with animals' heads that were never animals to start with, and the wood paneling will be leather, but it's that kind of look at first glance, yes. Clubby. With edge."

We were at the communal lunch table. They were hanging on my every word. I said it in English and Spanish. They were really listening. Theo ate sedately as always.

"Outside, Vegas is very glitzy – we've all seen pictures – it seems mainly orange and blue."

Carmen's blue jeans, her orange ruffled top at that party somewhere outside Madrid…

"Go on!" urged Danby.

"Yes, well, Corey's is downtown on Stewarts Avenue, and you notice it from way off because it's pale grey and green. The two colors are almost indistinguishable, it's so well designed, yet it has definition. Inside, the off-white and the fuchsia flashes come into play, so it's not old-fashioned, but it still seems clubby. You can't see yet what the high-roller rooms and VIP bar will be like, of course, but I should think they'll be dazzling glassy against smoke-green leather. There are mirrors everywhere."

Their heads were all turned toward me. At that moment, I felt more important than food. It was weird.

"It's beautiful," I concluded, suddenly sinking under their intense interest. "It is, it's awesome. Torres is a genius architect. And when we've got the stitching round the bar, all the chairs and the monogram details in place, all in leather, it'll be amazing."

Everyone was silent. Theo said,

"But?"

I'd replied before I was aware he'd asked.

"But it's somehow deceitful," I said.

CHAPTER THREE
Vegas Virgins

Ten months later, Corey gazed out of the window of his limo with satisfaction.

Corey's Casino was complete, a new icon in downtown Las Vegas, the grand opening scheduled for that Friday. Everybody would be there, by invitation only – high-rollers, some minor European royalty, top models, sports personalities, big brand owners, the world's finest fashion designers and artists, the most cutting-edge international chefs, the casino's legendary headline singer…

And the architect.

* * *

"Everybody's going to be there," Theo told Jules. "You'll enjoy it – it'll be a very impressive line-up of top celebrities and powerful people. You'll receive a unique insight into American culture!" His sardonic tone belied his words.

With Theo, you never quite knew.

"Are you sure you don't want to go, Theo?" asked Jules for the third time. "It seems unfair. I'm nothing to do with Millards."

"I have no interest in the PR end of the business," Theo said firmly. "Jake closed the deal and did most of the hand-guided machine stitching on leather for the casino. He's a good ambassador, we need to keep our word-of-mouth reputation alive, therefore I choose to send him on my invitation and it works very well that you're in New York this week and can go as his companion on that invitation."

"Well, I'm not going to argue. I can't wait to see the place. Trump's one is over budget and not done yet – Round One to Rosenberg, looks like!"

I was relieved the dates had worked out. The three of us were sitting in the cocktail bar of the St Regis, which had become Jules' default for invitations to chats over Manhattans. It suited most types of people, he reasoned, and I could see Theo approved.

"You're very quiet this evening, Jake," commented Theo. I wasn't, I just come across as quieter when Jules is around – it's a light and shade thing. It allows me to be more myself. So I just smiled.

"He's a dark horse," put in Jules. "Plotting the next big bit of business – I'm sure he'll rustle up something from all the networking we'll be doing at the inauguration. He's a silent dynamo, aren't you, old man?"

"Well, he certainly sealed the biggest deal we've had in the past five years," acknowledged Theo, raising his glass toward me.

I fiddled with the ends of my bootlace tie and thought, "Yeah."

* * *

"Surely there's some gorgeous girl you could take to this?" Jules challenged on the 'plane trip.

"Not really," I replied.

There was a pause. I ate some nuts and said quietly, "Anyway, Theo doesn't know that… look, I love my work and, well… he doesn't know… know that I'm straight."

I was braced for derision, but Jules just made a strange face and turned to stare out at the glare of Vegas, rising brash out of the dust below.

"I understand, old man," he said quietly. "It's the same back in London. I understand."

* * *

"It is fucking great," enthused Jules on the drive in from Las Vegas airport. He'd insisted on booking us in for an extra two nights and hiring a stretch limo to pick us up. "I am so glad to be here – good old Theo! And you! Look at it! I want to see that casino that has eight miles of neon lights above the entrance. Can't wait to see it all by night. Let's do a proper tour later."

I had us booked for ziplining at dusk. It was good to surprise him. He unbuckled himself after the flight through bursting neon and outsize exuberance with the hugest grin ever on his face and yelled, "Awesome! Let's do it every day!"

"Yeah, it was fun. Bit like surfing, riding lights instead of waves."

We were staying one night before Corey's inauguration – "Need something to compare his place with when we get there" – and one night after – "Recovery time".

I met Jules in the hotel bar after we'd showered and changed on the first evening.

"Feel like I need my shades inside," I said. The monstrous chandelier was repeated in a vast mirrored wall and the dazzle from that and the wall of illuminated bottles behind the bar was pretty blinding.

"I know, it's like that, isn't it?" enthused Jules. "Everything I hoped it would be! Good evening, amigo – what's your recommended cocktail for a couple of gents on their first visit?"

The barman gave us a 1,000-watt smile.

"Two Vegas Virgins coming right up, sir!"

* * *

Without putting her cigarette down, Sra JJ adjusted one of her colourful, elegant little sandals and gave a contented sigh.

"It's a great turnout," she commented, and Dr JJ, a cigarette in one hand and a camera in the other, nodded enthusiastically.

The air around them was thick with smoke. There were hundreds of smokers in and around Manolo's. Smoking. Lighting up. Taking pictures of ciggie stubs. Making noise. Making videos. Passing tapas around. Shouting. Singing. Clapping. Laughing. Dancing.

But mainly, smoking.

Dr JJ got up on the steps of the small square's old bandstand and applied a rudimentary megaphone to his lips. After a time, the crowd quieted.

"Friends! Thank you for coming! This is not just about Manolo's. This is about choices, a way of life, it's about family, friendship, and the small businesses we all love, striving to survive and continue to provide the marvellous community centres we all love and honour. Let's take our cause up to Valencia! What do you say?"

The crowd passed the word and yelled their approval. Sra JJ raised her eyebrows – it was the first she'd heard of this notion.

"Ten am in the square!" her husband of 31 years was shouting. "There will be free buses! To Valencia! We are taking our protest to the mayor of Valencia! Don Juan Antonio Ruiz, you are advised! We will be at the Valencia Town Hall next Saturday, May 4th, to protest the smoking ban! It is a threat to Spain's precious local bars, its wonderful families and communities! The ban would strike at the very core of this economy – we will not permit it! Saturday, 10am! Be here!"

"Be here!" cried a voice at his side, and the crowd roared louder, recognising one of their own, the doctor's wife. He bent to kiss her and the cheers leapt higher above the smoke ring, intoxicating young and old alike.

*　*　*

"Oh, fuck 'em up the arse," bellowed the mayor when he saw it on telly. "Who is this wanker? He's not even Spanish. Got an accent."

His sidekick had done his homework.

"Dr Julius Julius," he began.

"Arse-daft name, for a start."

"British born, more than 30 years in Spain. Has a successful psychiatric practice in Carrer de la Pau." He paused, watching that sink in. Carrer de la Pau was three blocks from the Town Hall. A classy area crammed with established, trusted businesses. The mayor made a sound between a snort and a sigh and re-filled their glasses.

"I shit in the milk. What else?"

"He's been married for 31 years to Rosita-Maria Jimenez Motrillo, born in Calpe, where they have a summer home as well as the Valencia apartment. They have three grown-up children – two girls, who both live in Barcelona, and a son based in London. The family is well-liked."

"I can see that!" snapped the mayor, reaching out a paw for more nuts.

He sat munching and thinking, a man accustomed to turning everything to his own advantage. He was one of the lucky few who can give up smoking without effort. He smoked, he didn't smoke. Depending which way the political winds blew.

"Hm," he uttered, standing up to close the long windows against a cool May night.

His sidekick waited patiently. He never interfered in PR or image. Or decisions at all.

Juan Antonio rooted round in a drawer, found a pack of cigarettes, and offered it before lighting up himself. Re-learning his enemy, remembering his friend, mused the sidekick.

Car horns blared in the street, signalling a football victory.

Juan Antonio pondered.

Damn the central government, he thought. It was okay when they brought in the partial ban, whereby bars under 100m2 could choose whether to allow smoking or not and larger establishments had to provide a non-smoking area. And he, Juan Antonio Ruiz, had continued to enjoy the perks of cosying up to the tobacco companies without any political consequences.

But now… The total ban was different.

The mayor knew charisma when he saw it. His own was of a very different, much more bombastic style than Dr JJ's, but this foreigner had what it took to stir things up to a point where the mayor would have to challenge the state ban and risk falling out with central government, or back the ban and jeopardise his image as a popular champion of local enterprises.

It was a no-brainer, really. He had far too much going on behind the scenes to risk government scrutiny or the wrong kind of press coverage.

The tobacco companies knew the score. They were discreet, and at least he could continue to benefit from corporate events and invites on the sly. It could even be fun.

"How's the Torres project coming along?" he asked suddenly, and the sidekick knew which way the smoking ban decision had gone.

* * *

"Vegas Virgins, brilliant! Listen, old man, talking of that, don't get slaughtered and marry a hooker like in the films. Mind you, I'd love to get married here!"

"You would not!" I protested.

"Yes, seriously. Or come to a wedding here," he amended.

"That's more like it. I cannot see your Henrietta type agreeing to a Vegas wedding."

"No, maybe you're right. But they still do straight weddings, right?"

"Oh yes, they do anything that makes money. They even let you smoke in the casinos and bars."

Jules' face lit up.

"What? Really? Now, that I *hadn't* realized! You mean I can just light up while I savor my Vegas Virgin?"

"Sure can."

The barman set our tall, neon-shaded drinks down.

"Excellent!" Jules whipped out his ciggies. "I'm missing the smoke-in at Manolo's, but this makes it all worthwhile. And I'm doing my bit – you know, stone, ripple effect. Paradise!"

I slipped on my shades and prepared for a colorful night.

* * *

Over in the Sheraton Palace Hotel, Mila hooked up her partner's dress and kissed the back of her neck. For a moment the two looked at each other in the mirror.

"You've done a terrific job for Rosenberg, Mila," said Kathy.

Mila scowled. It didn't sit well with her all-American, conservative blonde image.

"Corey Rosenberg is a misogynistic, greedy prick," she growled. "I hate him. He likes ruining lives."

Kathy put up a caressing hand to her cheek.

"Your work for him is paying off the New York condo," she reminded Mila, reaching for her earrings. "And the new commissions you'll get from this inauguration will put the kids through college!"

Mila slid her arms round Kathy's waist, interrupting her finishing touches.

"Will it keep me you?" she asked intensely.

Kathy swallowed a sigh. Mila's need for constant reassurance could be exhausting, particularly on a night like tonight, when she just wanted to have some fun. Why couldn't Mila reap the rewards with simple enjoyment?

"I'm not about to jump ship when you're hitting the big time, am I?" she teased. "Come on, let's go admire your work. You've earned some fun and I for one am going to have it!"

* * *

Corey popped in his substantial diamond cuff links, glanced once at the smooth, taut face topping the smooth, taut tux and stepped out into the bombardment of popping flashbulbs.

* * *

"There he is!" exclaimed Jules. "That's Rosenberg!"

We were halfway up the mile-wide staircase arising from the Red Square-sized main atrium, so caught the BSD's entrance at just the right moment and from the perfect height. The atrium below us was packed, but the staircase less so, and I could see Corey's cuff links flash as the waiting cameras fired off like 4th of July fireworks.

"Christ, look at those rocks in his cuffs!" Jules muttered in my ear. "Who does he think he is, Liz Taylor?"

The lights went out at that moment. A collective gasp hit the chilled air as the entire atrium, so it seemed, turned to water. The immense green-grey walls melted into sparkling streams illuminated from behind. We were inside a thin, cool, serene and beautiful waterfall. No waves or loud noise, just a cooling stream stroking down the walls, gleaming turquoise and green, mesmerizing in its large, gentle murmur.

It went on for a full minute. Then, just as people began to stir from their silent awe, the lights came up, the wall waters stilled, and the central fountain burst into life, radiating all the colors of the rainbow to a pounding beat, a figure glazed in dazzle arising from the center of the fountain.

"It's Audrey Hepburn!" cried Jules. "Brilliant! A life-size hologram of Audrey Hepburn! Oh no, hold on, it's Justin Bieber. Jesus, what *have* they done to him?!"

I was pissing myself laughing. He did look just like Audrey Hepburn.

"He's going to sing!" Jules said in horror. "What are you laughing about? Sober up, old man, all these people are potential new clients for Millards. Shut *up*! Pay attention – her arm's gone up, she's about to let rip! Sshhhh!"

Justin's rendition was mainly lost on me – I sank down onto the gleaming marbled stair so that my tears of laughter could fall unseen, shielded by Jules' immaculately clad knees.

Up in the coveted VIP rooms later, we found the designer, Mila, surrounded by fans admiring her work, and especially the unusual combination of stitched motifs and patterns on the leather trapunto wall paneling. It was a great cue. She looked kinda relieved to introduce me to the group.

"Network, network, get their cards, give 'em yours," Jules urged, pushing me forward. He himself hit it off straightaway with Mila, and after a while – time spent usefully by me in garnering admiration for Millards' work and several promising leads for new work – she swept us off at Jules' request to meet Corey Rosenberg himself.

"The man knows what to give the punters, he's loaded, he might take a shine to me and throw our bank some business," he explained in my ear as we whizzed earthwards in one of the glass elevators serving the main atrium.

It was pretty obvious from the get-go that Jules wasn't the one Corey had taken a shine to. Mila's reminder of who I was wasn't necessary: No sooner had Corey spotted us approaching than he flung out his dazzling arms and cried,

"Jakob! Our genius leather artist, all the way from the Big Apple! Thank you for coming, young friend!"

The pack around him parted to admit us a clear path right up to and into his welcome. I glimpsed Jules' hazel eyes blazing with excited curiosity as I introduced him, and I have to say, he worked the BSD very cleverly, standing respectfully at my elbow, slightly behind me, and putting in the occasional intelligent and well-timed remark to ease the conversation forward while Corey gazed into my eyes too much but at least didn't try to touch me. By the time I was murmuring that we should leave and Corey was urging us to tour every corner, not to stint on the champers, and not to miss the fireworks at midnight, I'd somehow acquired two definite new contacts Corey promised to follow up on to secure prestigious design contracts – home interiors for his loaded pals.

"Old man, that was brilliant!" exclaimed Jules as we reeled over to a quiet corner for another drink and a quick sit-down. "You've got the BSD of all this eating out of your hand! He's recommending you to his chums! It's incredible! That's going to set Millards up for another five years if all this goes to plan! Oh look, there's Torres! The architect! Come on, I have to meet him." He got up and smoothed his jacket.

"Do you know him?"

"No, no, but can't pass up a chance like this, old man. I love his work, and who knows, it could lead to some investment business for me. This guy is *so* hot internationally, but maybe he's up to something in Spain that I can get in on. He's practically reinvented Valencia's skyline single-handed. You'll see when you're over. And you saw that stack he did on the East River – it's genius! Come on, we should be able to head him off at the bar. No, hold on, he's off for a waz..."

"I am not stalking a world-famous architect in the men's bathroom, no matter how much you want to meet him!" I protested, but Jules, already moving fast, said not to worry, wait here, he'd be fine on his own.

A few minutes later, I saw him come out of the restroom with Torres himself, grinning away and tucking a business card into his breast pocket. They shook hands for about two minutes, exchanging laughs and tactile chitchat in what could only have been Spanish, and finally managed to tear themselves away from each other. I was fascinated once again by Jules' ease at networking.

"That was amazing!" he said, bouncing back to me. "He said the smoke-in at Manolo's was on telly, and my dad was stirring the crowd up to go and protest at the Valencia Town Hall in a couple of weeks – would you Adam and Eve it? He knows the mayor and people. We had a good chat."

"I saw. Any business?"

"Chitchat first, Jake. Trust has to be built before you can do any business. But this is a really good event – thanks old man. Thanks Theo!" He waved his glass toward the striking bar, half a mile long, its leather lower front stitched with a motif based on card suits. Loose knots of people were still stopping to point and admire.

"Those card suits were a pain to do," I mused. "We had to change the leather supplier three times before we could even set a stitch. But they do look awesome."

"Cheers to the two old ladies and their cross-stitch!" cried Jules, and the nearest groups turned and laughed and drank the toast with us, with no idea what it meant.

* * *

Dr JJ was just having a smoke on his balcony when the receptionist buzzed through to say that his new patient had arrived a few minutes early.

The doctor frowned. He worked hard, and valued his decompression time between appointments, usually stepping out through the tall, effectively double-glazed windows that gave out on to the narrow balcony to let the world expand back to a normal size after intense sessions inside other people's often diminished universes.

Today was a nice sunny day and he needed his five minutes out here.

The balcony and the generous dimensions of the rooms were what had drawn him to set up his plaque alongside a mixed bag of established medical specialities occupying an entire three floors of a large block within Valencia's old town centre. Slightly rundown when he'd moved in 11 years ago, it had had a couple of revamps since, and Dr JJ had made the decoration and arrangement of his own suite his first priority.

He'd turned the larger room into his consulting room, laid out as a lounge, with different types of chairs, ottomans and couches close to and away from the central balcony window. Patients could choose where to sit or recline, and Dr JJ could assess quite a lot from that simple choice. A desk backed by loaded bookshelves and with two more formal chairs before it, stood discreetly in an alcove over to the far left of the window – this area seemed to reassure and attract some of his older patients.

The colours were gentle lemons and apricots, with terracotta fabrics; flowering plants stood by and on the balcony; and warm, bright rugs punctuated the old tiled floor which the doctor had liked and left despite – or, as he maintained, because of – its scars and cracks.

He glanced in the modern, gilt-framed mirror which had reflected plenty of moments of struggle, some triumphs, and began to say, 'Ask him to wait just a moment', when Sandra broke in and said in her most confidential voice that this particular patient would prefer not to wait in the public area.

"Of course, send him right through," said Julius at once, hastily stubbing out the cigarette he'd brought in from the balcony when she'd buzzed.

His smaller room had been divided into a tiny bathroom and changing area for himself, leaving another space he'd had converted into what he called the recovery room. Sometimes, patients were too distressed or exhausted to leave immediately after a session, and the two soft chairs, murmur of nondescript music, and flask of tea – from the UK, and quite an innovation in a country that ran on coffee – made a welcome transition zone. It had its own exit, and there was, in fact, somebody in there now, so Dr JJ had no waiting space.

He'd barely had time to wonder why this new patient preferred not to wait outside in the general area – some disfigurement, perhaps, that made being in public difficult for him – when there was a firm knock and the door opened. Dr JJ suspected one hand had knocked while the other was already turning the doorknob, and his first impressions were taking shape as he adapted his neutral position at the desk, away from the door. It gave new patients a few seconds to register the room and come right in before facing another unfamiliar element – the doctor himself. Once the patient saw him, the doctor would take a few steps forward in friendly style, neither forcing nor withholding a possibly unwelcome handshake, so that the patient had time to take things in and perhaps start moving towards a preferred armchair or couch. Or turn and leave, as had occasionally happened.

Today, Julius already knew from the entrance itself that this new patient was not a timid type. He was tentatively relegating most neuroses, depression and suicidal thoughts, and anorexia – which was sadly making a mark now on his client list – was ruled out on the spot as the door closed decisively to reveal the buxom figure of Juan Antonio Ruiz, the mayor of Valencia.

The mayor did a rapid 180-degrees of the room – probably wondering if any of the chairs will stand his weight, thought the doctor, once more grateful that he'd installed a couple of solid, outsize armchairs as well as the daintier options – before advancing and clasping Dr JJ's hand in both of his.

Perhaps he's here to tackle his weight problem, thought Dr JJ, as his voluminous visitor strode over to the window, flung open the balcony doors and stepped out with his arms raised to the sky like a newly elected president. Or a newly married royal. No, they tended to be a lot less bombastic than this character, the doctor reflected, intrigued to know whether the clearly territorial mayor would take his own seat behind the desk when he'd finished inspecting the premises.

Juan Antonio, meanwhile, was using the few seconds on the balcony to process his impressions of Dr Julius Julius. He was accustomed to intimidating people with his height and bulk, and was irked that this rebel-rousing shrink could easily look him straight in the eye. Worse, he was about the mayor's age and was also large-framed, but he was slim. For the first time in a long time, the mayor felt fat.

"Nice place!" he approved heartily, coming back into the room.

"I'm glad you like it. Please, do sit down wherever you feel most comfortable." The doctor indicated the entire room. He was interested in fat. He wondered if the mayor was fat or obese. It was hard to tell behind the well-cut, eye-catching pale blue linen suit he was wearing.

Juan Antonio had taken time picking out the suit, and was glad he'd done so. The doctor wore his Britishness like a second skin. After all these years in Spain, he still clearly bought his casually elegant clothes in London, thought the mayor irritably. But pale blue linen had been a good choice for himself. He cast an experienced eye round the range of seating options, discarding any that could leave him sitting at a lower level than his interlocutor, or unable to heave himself upright without difficulty.

Obese, Dr JJ was concluding. He wanted to see how the fat would distribute itself if the mayor lay down, and silently suggested the sturdier couch with a hand movement, but Juan Antonio went across to the terracotta outsize chair and sank not too far into it.

The doctor pushed a footstool over within his reach and carefully chose a less imposing tub chair of equal height for himself.

He waited for the mayor to begin.

For several moments, the mayor made a play of looking uncomfortable. Suddenly, though, he looked the doctor in the eye and said, "I agree with you!" and burst out laughing. "About the smoking ban!"

Dr JJ nodded slowly.

"Okay, so you agree with me."

"Yes, yes! I will come to Calpe in two weeks' time, on Saturday, May 4th, and meet Manolo and the other good people myself. I have relatives in Calpe!"

The doctor raised an eyebrow.

"Yes, yes, I, the mayor, will come to you. I'll make sure it is on TV. You just set up your protest and I'll come and join you. What do you say?"

"I'm not a negotiator," began Dr JJ.

"Yes you are! You have power!" The mayor paused but Dr JJ wasn't looking too impressed. Juan Antonio heaved himself up out of the chair and put his hand out.

"Do we have a deal?"

"It's not a deal," Dr JJ said carefully, still sitting. "I can't stop you from coming to Calpe next Saturday, it's none of my business."

"Yes it is, it *is* your business! You hire buses and come to me and maybe I'm not there – it's a waste of time for everyone. I will come to you. And I will bring Torres, our most famous architect! And a big smoker! This week he's in the States after the opening of his new building in Las Vegas…"

"The casino? Yes, my son was at the opening."

"Really? Wonderful!" The mayor was not, in reality, at all pleased. No doubt the son was as tall and slim as his father. "Bring him too, for the protest! Is he a smoker too? Fantastic! Calpe on Saturday, at 11am – okay?"

"Okay."

"Good, good!"

Dr JJ was still sitting.

"Are you sure there's nothing else you'd like to talk to me about?"

Juan Antonio looked down at him, suddenly unsmiling.

"To you? No. Thank you for your time."

Dr JJ stood up and held out his hand, which was once again squeezed hard between both the mayor's. Juan Antonio opened the door and swept out, leaving Julius feeling somehow hard done by over the obesity issue.

And a little as though he'd received a threat.

* * *

The fireworks display at midnight was a bit like New Year's Eve. Everyone was happy and blitzed. They had all the performers out for a grand finale – Justin Bieber aka Audrey Hepburn leading the way – and as that finished, they all disappeared behind a curtain of fireworks that then leapt higher and wider, drawing our eyes upwards.

"Brilliant!" Jules said, smoking contentedly at my side. "I cannot imagine a better way to see Vegas for the first time."

He'd made a few thousand at roulette earlier – I couldn't help suspecting that Corey had somehow tipped off the croupier – and he'd been exuberant then. "Call me 007, old man!" he'd cried, bouncing around and making everyone smile with his very British accent. "Come on, let's cash in!"

"Aren't you going to carry on and lose it all back?" I teased.

"No way! Investment banker, remember? Calculating risks. It's all about intuition."

"I thought you lot were all about computer math and scientific elimination of risk."

He looked sober – somber kind of sober, not the unintoxicated sort – for a moment, and said, "Most of them are like that. But I'm a throwback to the old school of gamblers. Intuition, Jake, that's where the thrill is for me. Safer for the companies we back, too. Investment banking used to be full of gamblers and poker players who knew how to really take a risk, go against the crowd – and *that's* how they made the money. Small, dispersed, independent risk-taking. Now it's all about mindless calculators who all come up with the same conclusion and act the same as everyone else."

"So what?"

"So what? So *what?*" We were cashing in. His hazel eyes gleamed with indignation and excitement. "Mass behavior leads to mass damage, that's what."

"Stop pushing your money into my face, dude."

"Just sharing," he laughed, thrusting half his winnings into my top pocket. "Calculate carefully, back your beliefs, pull out when you're ahead, and enjoy what you've got."

"How do they compare with the 4th of July fireworks?" he was asking me now, above the Casino Royale soundtrack and fireworks going off.

"Different." I'd always loved fireworks. Going into Manhattan to get a good view on the 4th of July had been a family tradition when I was a kid. It was a whole day out, a world away from our everyday life. The people on the streets all looked fresh and beautiful and happy in a vibrant way we didn't see so much of at home, even though we lived by the ocean. There, fresh was a bright summer frock, a newly painted rollercoaster; it was innocent, wood and cotton and primary colors. Manhattan was like all that intensified to a degree that separated it off into a whole new bubble. On the 4th of July, Dad scrubbed his hands harder than any other day with the cherry slime of GoJo to scour out the oil black that resided in the creases of his hard-working palms. Looking up at the bright colors exploding across a black sky, my child's mind always imagined my dad's oil-stained workshop, always smelling of grease, suddenly putting out bursts of glorious color like this, a noisy declaration of our status as proud Americans, fine people living in the best place on earth.

Jules' ciggie sketched a small arc as he raised it to his lips, and I thought of his mother, rejecting the UK with a smoke, its glowing end burning home her conviction that Spain was the best place on earth.

"It's different," I repeated. "This is more glitzy. Less patriotic. And not as huge – the 4th of July ones stretch right up the Hudson River, you can see them from just about anywhere on the west side of Manhattan."

"Well, this is good enough for me." Jules raised his glass high to the sky. "Finale! Oh wow! Card suits in fireworks! That is brilliant! I love it! Look at the spades! Oh no – I cannot believe this… Oh my God!"

He fell silent, watching with a kind of disgusted delight as Corey Rosenberg's firework display climaxed, ejecting exploding dollar signs into the sky, blooming huge and high above us, then raining disappearing gold down over our upturned, laughing faces.

Corey looked around at the upturned, laughing faces and smiled with satisfaction.

"Tomorrow at 10am," he said crisply to Torres and Mila, then turned away and slipped into his waiting limo.

* * *

Next morning at the pool bar, he popped a feather-light mini-croissant into his mouth and raised his espresso to his lips.

"What do you think?"

Torres and Mila were both pole-axed, he judged.

They were both in.

He took a large sip of go-get and turned his attention to the exquisitely presented sliced fruit. Relaxed. They were in.

"Well, yes, I think it's an interesting idea," Mila was saying, Kathy's calm good sense tempering her natural dislike of Corey. "I'd be very happy to work on it if you get it off the ground."

Corey gave a snap of laughter.

"Get it off the ground! That's a good pun! What do you say, Pablo? Can we get this Vegas-style project off the ground in your home country of Spain?"

Pablo Torres was smiling easily, his mind turning the idea over in all its ramifications for his prestige and his Cayman Islands bank balance, and its artistic interest.

"We can, Corey, architecturally of course we can. However, land, regulations, legislation – these could be complicated and expensive."

"Expensive because they are complicated," nodded Corey. He sat back, sated. "I'm sure we can take care of that."

Torres hoped so. There was no saying while the damned Socialists were in power. And the Spaniards had a different approach to money from what he'd witnessed in the States. Spain's civil war was still within living memory, people had heard their granddaddies describe hunger and honour, betrayal, fighting and desperation. Torres himself was riding the crest of his career wave now. These thoughts were within him but they were not his own hard-wired memories. He'd been born in 1956, a generation after the civil war ended; he'd come to adulthood as Franco died, leaving him a clear path to success, the world his oyster. And he'd reached out and grabbed it all, wielding his outstanding talent without fear and revelling in material success as well as admiration.

He had three homes now, and the world was more than ever his oyster.

The younger generations though, they were more… what? Hippified? Less materialistic? More in line with looking after everyone else? There was even a movement occupying Madrid's central square, the Puerta del Sol, to protest against corruption in politics, greed in the banking sector. Pablo Torres had a secret admiration for their fervour and conviction. He had it too, but only for his own trade.

He glanced across at Corey's smooth, taut face, laden with confidence, and stretched a hand out for the little pastries that tasted so good. There was an election in a few months' time in Spain, and with the economy tanking, the opposition conservatives were bound to be voted back in and Spain could get back on track.

He nodded, imbibing sun, confidence and coffee. It would be an interesting project, and a lucrative contract. A *very* lucrative contract.

CHAPTER FOUR
Palo cortado

"Eurovegas!" screeched Juan Antonio. "He wants to build *Eurovegas*?!"

"Ssshhh! Shut up!" Torres's face was set hard, almost ferocious. "Keep your voice down! I am only telling you because of this stupid smoking ban protest you've got mixed up in. Corey plays tough – this must *not* leave this room, Juan Antonio."

It was three days later and he was back in Spain, seated in the mayor's embracing den in the heart of their city, Valencia.

"Okay, okay, calm down. You of all people should know that I can keep a secret."

The two men mused their joint secrets – which had delivered six and seven-figure boosts to their bank accounts over the past several years – for a few moments.

"Yeah, I know. But this is huge, much bigger than any other project we've worked on."

"I'll say! A European Las Vegas. A casino resort with three hotels, two casinos, a cinema, all the pools and bars and shops and gambling… " The mayor was rubbing his fleshy hands together in glee. "Why not outside Madrid?"

"I told him Madrid's a big village, too parochial. And it's too close to the central government – there's a danger of instability. The PP's sure to get in with the economy in this state, but if by some freak chance the Socialists were to hang on…"

The mayor shuddered and poured them both another glass of the palo cortado very dry sherry he favoured. On the low, dark wood table between the large leather couches sat dishes of stuffed olives, gleaming salted and fried almonds, rectangular slivers of mojama – the salted dried tuna that infused the sea into your mouth even as the palo cortado wafted earth fragrance way up into your head.

Again the two were silent, drinking, popping delicacies into their mouths. Street sounds reached them – kids laughing, the tearing roar of a scooter.

"Billions," breathed Juan Antonio finally. "That'll be worth billions. And you told him Valencia."

Their eyes met.

"You have always been very supportive of my career," said Torres. "It was an honour to re-shape Valencia, bring it alive in a contemporary sense with my aquarium and university buildings. For this project, we need to find the right site. Then we would require someone with the authority to re-classify rural land, perhaps... Iron out the administrative difficulties."

"I am a master of solutions!" beamed the mayor.

"Of course. But you need to take a stance on the smoking issue. Madrid has banned it nationwide in all public spaces. Corey Rosenberg would need to allow smoking in his casino complex. If there is a ban on smoking, he will not make the investment, he will not bring Eurovegas to this region."

"Ah."

"Exactly. I'll come to the protest in Calpe on Saturday, but only if we have this worked out, Juan Antonio. You must understand that."

"Of course, of course. Leave it with me. We'll talk tomorrow. And now, another glass while you show me again the images of Sr Rosenberg's inauguration of your magnificent casino building in Las Vegas!"

* * *

Dr JJ stayed later in his office the day of the mayor's visit, mulling it over.

"He's a strange old bugger," he told his wife over an outdoor dinner at one of the chic new places down by the sea-front. "I'm not sure what he's after."

Sra JJ took another mouthful of swordfish to give him time, but for once he didn't seem to have any answers.

"Maybe he wants you to take the limelight so that you'll be implicated in the next mess he gets up to," she suggested.

"Maybe," he replied, and she thought he'd taken the idea on board. In fact, Dr JJ was developing pity for the porky politician, whose issues over his weight clearly ran so deep that he couldn't even begin to touch on them but had had to invent another reason for his visit. 'You have power', he'd said just before his abrupt exit. A cry for help. Yes, he had the power to help Ruiz. Could he have done better today? No, not while the mayor was still so buttoned up. Just as well he was, though, literally speaking. Although that made it hard to tell how solid the fat was, whether fabric compression was visually firming it. The doctor poured more of the local rosé wine into their stemmed glasses – *nobody* used to drink wine out of stemmed glasses when I arrived in Spain, except at Christmas or first communion parties, he thought inconsequentially – and began to relax. The important thing was that the mayor trusted him, believed in his power. It was a good foundation for healing.

"Well, it's great that we don't have to lay on all the buses and organise things," Sra JJ continued. "But be careful how much you touch him – he's a nasty piece of work who always has an agenda, and the cameras will be rolling."

The doctor grimaced. No way would he want to touch anyone that fat.

* * *

It was Jules' last night in NYC and we were out on the deck of my dad's workshop. You couldn't hear the sea from here, but you got a view over the Three Diamonds baseball field. It was a favorite place for me to hang out with my dad, having a beer. Tonight we were all there. Jules had insisted on bringing the dinner and the whole family had feasted on smoked salmon and salad, assorted savory pastries, fresh garlic bread baguettes and beer and Bollinger. It all seemed very European. He'd even produced strawberries and the unbeatable clotted cream from Cornwall, which nobody except he and I had ever tasted.

Across the highway that had pumped new life into my dad's business 10 years ago, we could see junior league players duking it out before sunfall, and hear the cheering and clapping, the crack of a decent hit, in short snaps against the steady low drone of traffic along the Ocean Parkway highway.

I sat with my feet up on another chair with nephew Dale, who'd arrived eight months earlier, squirming about on my lap playing with a chunk of clotted cream. His mom, my sister Hannah, worked with Dad in the garage. She ran the admin side, with a little help from me sometimes, and was a pretty good mechanic herself. She came up the rusty old outside staircase now; Dale squealed and bounced and I handed him over.

"Jake, when are you gonna settle down and have some kids of your own?" said my mother, speaking over my dad's opinion of the useless pitcher to Jules.

"Christ, you sound just like my mother, Mrs N!" exclaimed Jules, with a grin that made her smile in spite of herself. He got up and kissed Hannah on each cheek, poured her a glass of champagne – which was not her everyday homecoming, but he made it seem so natural – his ciggie stuck to his lower lip, his profile handsome against the darkening sky. I felt shielded. As usual, I could be my quieter self when Jules was around, dispensing bubbles and bonhomie, making everyone smile. "Pressure doesn't work, take it from me!"

"Well, and what about you?" persisted my mom. "Are you courting?"

"Courting!"

We all laughed.

"Courting!" Pausing in his task of collecting up the empties, Jules stood arrested for a moment, the dark gold hair under a final buffing from the withdrawing sun. He stood with the bottles held by the neck in each hand, the cigarette slack though his lips were turned up in humor. "I don't think I've ever heard anyone say that word aloud, let alone to me. Thank you, Mrs N! Yes, I am and no I'm not, and that is all you'll get from me tonight, but thank you for making me feel… innocent. I feel as though I'm living in the 1950s – the ice-cream parlor, girls and guys and real homes. The American Dream… Look! There's even a couple of finned cars down there in your yard! I'm right here inside an Edward Hopper painting! I love it!"

* * *

It was coming up for 10.30pm when the European Union finance ministers broke the session for sandwiches and coffee. They were all in a bad temper and knew the squabbles would go on all night as the Mediterranean countries resisted their wealthy northern neighbours' economic proposals.

The whole of Brussels looks to be in a bad temper, thought Katy, drawing her coat tight around her and dashing out for a quick drink. It had been a dismal evening ending a drizzly day. A few brave souls sat out on the gorgeous Grand Place, crouched at small tables, poised to spring back indoors if the rain came on again.

You can't say they're nothing to do with the story when in a way they *are* the story.

There were three bright students in their final year who wouldn't be able to find jobs for at least 18 months after graduating; there was a woman in her early 50s, at the height of her competence, who'd just been made redundant from the company where she'd worked for most of her married life and was going to have to work more hours for less pay even if she did get another position; there was a good-looking man of about 30 whose job had just been taken over by a robot and who was seriously considering doing some escort 'work' to be able to hold onto his rented flat; there was a group of having-fun older people who would all have to sell their homes for long-term care in 10 years' time.

They weren't the only ones Katy – an attractive, fully employed 35-year-old financial analyst – saw that night, but they were the ones her experience of the system identified.

It's not about currencies or economic policies, she thought morosely, glaring at her cup. It was plain old fucking greedy human nature that fucked things up. Sure, corruption was endemic in some of the southern European countries and needed to be sorted out. But it was the institutionalized, ruthless greed of the system she had trained up in that was colouring her world now. She gulped a second cup and considered texting her friend Chloe over in London, but decided there was no time. She couldn't be sure her 'phone wasn't bugged anyway, so what was she going to say? That it was raining?

She shivered, pulled her large scarf closer round her suddenly chilled neck, and headed back to the all-night talks.

* * *

Jules had booked me a room at the St Regis and we got up early for a farewell breakfast before he headed off to the airport.

"Dude, this place is so damn' stuffy," I complained as the austere waiter, overdoing his British imitation, cleared the table and put Jules' card through.

"Oh I know, desperate. But it is a good place for me to be on these semi-work trips, you know that."

"Hey, I'm not being ungrateful, I just..."

"I know, I know. Just shut up for a minute, will you? Listen, I know you're coming over to Europe for the big trip with Theo in September, but I would really really really like you to come to London for the long weekend in two weeks' time." He pulled an envelope out of his Loewe briefcase and pushed it across the table to me. "I've got you first-class tickets and I'd have you picked up at the airport, so..."

"I feel like a hooker!"

He gave me a slightly speculative glance and continued, "...so it'd all be straightforward. I've asked Theo about workload over the next month and he didn't seem to think it'd be too hectic; says he can spare you. It's your call. I have a work event I'd like you around for, and, and something else. But think it over and let me know by Friday so I can cancel the tickets if you don't want to do it."

I was still staring. He seemed jumpy, he wasn't explaining stuff. And I did feel a bit like a hooker.

"Where would I stay?"

"At my place, South Bank. Loads of arty-farty stuff going on, you'll love it. It's walking distance from the bloody ugly Tate Modern and all the must-see exhibitions." He looked at his watch and stood up. "Gotta go. Let me know."

A brief hug and he was off. I didn't get a chance to say thanks or for goodness' sake at least let me get the Underground in from the airport. But after speaking to Theo, I did all that by email.

He let me get the Underground in.

Theo and I had knocked out half a dozen monogrammed handkerchiefs for Jules in different colors, and when I saw his place, I was glad we hadn't gone for towels without knowing the décor.

"What do you think?" Jules, a bottle of fizz swinging at his fingertips, watched me drop my bags and automatically cross to the immense expanse of window overlooking the Thames from the South Bank.

"Awesome, dude, it's beautiful! Tower Bridge! Hey, that's St Paul's! Wow!" I turned to admire the huge, loft-like, immaculately furnished space. He was pouring. "A place like this in the FiDi in New York would cost millions and I've heard guys over there complain that London's expensive!"

"Here! Your health! Thanks for coming over. And yeah, it's a fair stash here, too, but I sub-let it out a lot at weekends and holidays and that pretty much covers things. Don't tell the boss that though – he expects me to have this kind of place."

For a moment I thought he looked haggard but the expression cleared in an instant and he bent to pick up some keys and a Google map printout.

"Make yourself at home. This is your set. Here's where to meet me at around 6pm, where the red circle is. Okay?"

I found The Bell with no problem after a great day doing the Tate Modern – no idea why Jules had a downer on it, I had a great time – followed by lunch at a nice big friendly pub on the River Thames. It had a big terrace and I was unfashionably early, so I got a seat and was able to watch the tables filling up with an odd mix of middle-aged women knocking back Chardonnay, and edgy young guys who must've been unemployed or strangely employed to be sitting in pubs at that time of day eyeing women up. There was a table of stunning Russian girls that just got bigger and bigger as more of them arrived until they asked if they could use the spare chairs at my table. It totally took my mind off the William Blake exhibition I'd just seen at Tate Modern, and the low skyline. We chatted for a bit in weird accents. It was all great till one of them sidled very close and put her hand on my thigh.

I remember thinking it was all a bit too much for a homeboy embroiderer like myself, and registering a couple of wholesome English girls perched on the wall of the riverside walk giggling in my direction. They had unaggressive blonde hair and freckles.

The sun came out from behind a cloud. I looked again at the Russian girl who was squeezing my thigh and realized in the enhanced light that she had only recently become a girl. Or even – I couldn't help glancing down – was still a man.

The two girls on the wall were collapsing in giggles.

I wished I had Jules' confidence – anyone's – to be able to carry this off. As it was, I looked at my watch, stood up too fast, knocking over what was left of my drink, and departed to muted peals of laughter all round.

In the afternoon, I did one of those city 'bus tours, which I love 'cos they're so relaxing yet informative, and spent £15 on the London Eye, where I chatted to some nice people as we took in the awesome views, and then I went home for a shower in the ultra-chic bathroom before getting to The Bell slightly ahead of Jules.

I'd loved the pub culture as a student at St Andrews, and still do. I got myself half a pint of Guinness at the ancient-looking bar and settled down to soak up the ambiente. There were a couple of old guys over to my left who looked as though their puffy lined faces had been designed into the wood details and the uneven stone flagging Dr Johnson would have been treading centuries ago. They spoke in slow, gruff murmurs; their conversation seemed grim and desolate, yet they kept bursting into laughter and slapping the table with fists of mirth. Very different from old guys at the bars in Coney Island when I was a kid – they were loud and nosy; asked loud questions, wanted the whole room to get their jokes. Reassuring somehow.

A well-tailored suit cut across my thoughts and Jules said,

"Hello! Great old place, isn't it? Get you another half? Listen, my boss is going to drop by for a swift half. He's 42, likes to think he's the Michael Douglas character in that *Wall Street* film, only better-looking, and he's camp as a row of tents. What was the guy's name? Gordon Gekko. Fuck! My boss is called Gordon too! Back in a mo. He's my boss, Jake, the BSD. My boss. Remember that."

He gave me a doubtful look, took his finger out of my face and went over to the heavy-wood bar.

"Yes thanks, I had a great day," I called after him. "How about you?"

He looked back with a grin that turned to a glazed glare and I glanced over my own shoulder to see an effete Gordon Gekko with ultra-blond hair sashaying over to the tables area.

I stood and intercepted him with hand outstretched.

"Hello Mr Gek… I mean, excuse me, I don't know your name, sir, but I am Jules' friend Jakob Naylor, over from New York."

He took my hand and shook it firmly, eyes rolling in a not unhandsome face that he'd clearly had work on.

"Oh my God!" he exclaimed. His gaze raked me from head to foot. "Oh my God!"

"What are you having, Gordon?" called Jules.

"Well this will do for starters!" he quipped, still holding onto my hand.

"Port and lemon, then, is it?" said Jules, which went right over my head but made Gordon squeak with laughter.

"Wicked!" he admonished, finally releasing my hand to wag a nanny-like finger in Jules' direction and whip his coat expertly off his shoulders. In a couple of seconds, the Burberry was neatly folded over one of the wooden chairs. "G&T, Jules darling – Bathtub Gin, Fevertree tonic and two cardamom seeds. Sebastian knows." He waved at the barman, who had it well underway already and called out, "'Evening, Mr H." with a respectful nod.

I studied Gordon during the exchange. Medium height, blond, as good-looking as these times could make him, Jules' boss was a big swinging dick in the City of London, and none of us was about to forget it.

"So!" he exclaimed, X-raying me with his eyes again. "What have you been up to today, Jakob?"

It wasn't until he stood up to go after 20 minutes of intelligent art review and some more idle chitchat about the best places to eat that it hit me.

At that moment, he was standing and I was sitting. There was a burst of laughter from the desolate old guys across the way, Jules was standing and laughing beside Gordon, and I suddenly said,

"I remember!"

Gordon flicked a suddenly unpleasant glance at me – no sooner seen than gone – and settled the Burberry over his shoulders again.

"What do you remember, Jakob?"

Jules, eyes bulging for an instant, laughed in a higher pitch than usual and cut in.

"The security code for the condo! I bet him earlier that he wouldn't remember, but it looks as though I've lost! Damn, that means tonight's on me!"

I smiled and stood, concealing my shock as best I could and letting Gordon hug me though it made me nauseous and I could feel the blackness of disremembrance at my outer edges, waiting to embrace me when Gordon was done.

He left. I sat. Without a word, Jules fetched me a decent cognac and watched me take two or three gulps before saying,

"Thanks old man. I'm sorry. Don't talk. We're going somewhere quiet. When you're ready."

I was ready.

The cab ride wasn't too long. For me. But then, I am American, distance is different for me than for most Brits.

Neither of us spoke.

As we got out of the cab, I was soothed by the nostalgic fragrance of honeysuckle. Like Nana's embrace. It was going to be okay, I thought, following Jules up the garden path. At the end was a door. In the doorway, a young woman.

We all crowded inside and Jules kissed the girl. I remembered only one kiss of that kind of importance in my life. A girl whose name I couldn't remember, kind to me in a red beast. Kind and confused. The most gorgeous girl in the world.

"Knock it off!" I pushed Jules hard against the wall. It was a narrow hallway.

"What's happened?" cried the girl.

"He's remembered."

She gasped.

"How much?"

"I don't know. Have you got any cognac?"

"Cognac? This isn't Versailles, you know. Come on in, he can have some red wine."

We were in a kitchen – one of those London places that opens out onto a long narrow garden overlooked by about a gazillion neighbors.

I gulped down some wine, thanked the girl, then said to Jules, "Come on. Outside."

He put his glass down and stared at me.

"What? Why?"

"I want to hit you. Shove you over into those things you said sting, since there's a garden."

"Eh?"

"Some leaves. You put other leaves on to stop it hurting. You had them as a kid. Don't play dumb now, you loaded jackass!"

"Nettles," muttered the girl.

"Yes, nettles! Have you got any?" I checked with her.

"Yes, up at the top, under those trees where it's all a bit of a mess. See?"

"Don't *tell* him!" cried Jules.

The girl shrugged. She was an angel. The halo of my revenge shone around her.

"You're cute," I told her. "Would you like to sit on my lap?"

"Before you shove Jules into the nettle patch?"

"Nettle patch, nettle patch. That is so romantic-sounding. Yes, before. Would you?"

"Okay." And she did.

Jules lurched forward then, startled and puce.

"Hey! Why'd you have to tell him about the nettle patch?"

Comfortably connected on the chair, she and I looked at each other.

"He cares more about getting hurt physically than about you being hurt emotionally," I observed.

"You are so sensitive," she marveled. "I think you're right."

"No!" yelled Jules. "No, no, NO! He couldn't shove me in a nettle patch if he tried! I'm bigger than him."

"Not where it matters," I said, and the girl on my lap flung her coppery curls back in laughter.

The 'phone rang and she wriggled off me fast.

"I'll put the kettle on for when you're done. Hello? Katy, hi! How was Brussels?"

With her out of the way, Jules lunged at me and we got up to the top of the garden punching and shoving and shouting all the way. Two or three neighbors stuck their heads over the fences to see what was going on.

"Which one's the nettle patch?" I yelled at one of them. "The nettles! Where are they?"

"Don't tell him!" Jules yelled, then hissed in my ear as he tried to bite it, "Shut up! This isn't Spain, they'll just call the cops on us!"

I shoved him over into a pile of leaves, which got some interest and a bit of muted applause from the onlookers, but one of them called,

"Those aren't nettles, mate. Those are dock leaves."

"Oh, the ones you put on to stop the nettle sting, right? Then the nettles must be near here!"

I looked round at all of them, but that was as helpful as they got – all problem, no solution. Jules was struggling upright. The girl was suddenly there.

"How's Katy?" I asked.

"Fine, thanks! Those are dock leaves."

"Yeah, they said."

"Mad cocksucker!" Jules threw himself at my knees from his half-up position but the girl intervened.

"How much has he remembered?"

"How do I know? He just keeps pushing me around like the typical aggressive Yank – drop a few bombs first, ask questions later."

Murmurs of approval came floating over the fences.

"I remember that you kissed me!" I shouted at Jules.

There was silence. I breathed in the soothing fragrance of the English garden, not just gulps of air from struggling with Jules. Honeysuckle. Nana's embrace. I had never breathed anything so gentle, so fragrant. So forgiving.

The girl was staring at me intently.

"He *kissed* you?" She rounded on Jules. "You didn't tell me *that!*"

"Well, I didn't know how much he'd remember," said Jules, wiping leaves off himself. "There was no tongue."

"Eeeew!" the girl and I cried together.

"Hey, you can kiss me any day! With tongue! Let's start now!" One of the neighbors was climbing over the fence.

"Sod off!" yelled Jules and the three of us ran back down the garden and into the kitchen. The girl sloshed more wine into the glasses and said, "Right! What exactly do you remember, Jake? No interruptions. Jules, you are not to say one word."

I took a sip of wine.

"It was soon after Jules and I had met at a party in St Andrews. He gave me a call after it and the next weekend I went over to Edinburgh with a couple of his friends who had a car to see a production of Romeo and Juliet where everyone was left-handed."

"That's right!"

"Jules! Shh!"

"It was good, wasn't it?" he said anyway.

"It was," I admitted. "I didn't expect that to make such a difference, but there was something about the sword-play and the..."

"Yes! It was interesting how different it was just 'cos of the left-handed thing."

"Jake!"

"Okay, sorry. Anyway, we all went off to hit up a pizzeria after the show with some of the actors, 'cos they were friends of yours, right? and Mercurio was one of them. And it was all great. We had fun. But then Mercurio was going on about being gay and he kept using the word 'poof' and some other dude got angry about that and said *he* was gay and he found it offensive..."

"The stage manager."

"Was it?"

"Yes. Auditioned for the part of Nurse and said he'd take the company to court on grounds of discrimination when they told him he was crap and no way. So they offered him stage manager to shut him up."

"Wow!"

"*Jake!*"

"Yes. So, Nurse was being a bit of an asshole too, picking a fight; we'd all had tons of Chianti out of those wicker baskets, and Mercurio started shouting 'I'll say poof as often as I want! Poof, poof, poof!' Then it became a kind of chant and Jules, you stood up next to him and you were both banging on the table with your fists and shouting 'Poof, poof, POOF!' at the top of your voices, and poor old Nurse went off in a huff, and today there was just something about the way you and Mercurio were standing above me at the table at The Bell that brought it all back."

I had another glug or two of wine and poured us all some more.

"Mercurio?" said the girl, inquiringly.

Jules looked resigned.

"Mercurio was played by Gordon. My boss, Gordon Hecklow. He came and had a drink after work with me and Jake today. At The Bell."

She made a big soundless 'Oh' of understanding with her mouth. After a few seconds, she said,

"But that doesn't explain the kiss. Or anything, really. Go on, Jake."

"Mm. Well, next day I woke up late with a hangover and we were in this amazing apartment with a view over Edinburgh Castle, and nice stuff everywhere. And Mercurio was cooking us breakfast. Brunch."

"In my kitchen," muttered Jules.

"You had an apartment of your own?" she cried.

"Hey! I'd been at Edinburgh Uni for four years and I made enough off the lodgers to pay the mortgage each month! The loan was a good investment for my dad! And I'd got a decent job straight after uni, so I kicked out the lodgers and had the place to myself. What's the problem?"

"The kiss?" she insisted.

"It had happened the night before," I told her. "When Jules and Mercurio were doing their 'Poof, poof, POOF!' chant, Jules bent down and kissed me right on the lips before I could react and they all cheered like crazy. I sort of blacked out that night..."

"That was the Chianti!" yelled Jules. "You drank about two bloody baskets on your own!"

" ...and I've been blacking out ever since, whenever a man makes a pass at me or anything like that. And I've only just worked it out. Remembered."

We were all silent.

"Why didn't you tell me, Jules? That time in Spain, your dad trying to help me work it all out, the Naked Cowboy in Benidorm, Corey Rosenberg… You could've told me!"

"I was sort of hoping you wouldn't remember," Jules admitted.

"What!" the girl and I shrieked.

"I'll show you exactly where the nettle patch is," she promised me, and we both stood up.

"No!" cried Jules. "Stop, both of you! I'm sorry, Jake, but I didn't know what it would all lead to! It was a stupid, stupid thing, but I was pissed and having fun, and…"

We were both staring reproachfully at him.

"For Christ's sake!" he implored. "All I did was shout 'poof' in a pizzeria! How was I to know it was an oath of allegiance? I was 23, I just liked shouting in bars! How was I to know the whole bloody world was going gay? All I wanted was a good job, meet the right girl, enjoy life, but Gordon's had me by the short and curlies ever since and now I'm nothing unless I'm a poof!"

* * *

Corey Rosenberg picked up the lavender-colored 'phone in his private suite at the casino and made a few calls. The press frenzy over the opening had died down and it was time to set the wheels in motion for the next project.

Within a few hours, a name had surfaced: Gordon Hecklow. Corey smiled – it reminded him of Gordon Gekko, Michael Douglas's character in the movie *Wall Street*. But Hecklow was a lot more flamboyant, Corey could see from the press pictures coming up on his screen. He even seemed to welcome interest in his own private investments. Corey raised his eyebrows at a Getty agency photo of Hecklow taking exuberant possession of a Jean Prouvé table at the end of a charity auction earlier that year.

"Let's give the guy a call," Corey said aloud, swiveling round to survey his own Daniel Libeskind chair grouping. It'd be around midnight in London, but there was no saying where in the world the guy was, and he could leave a message if there was no answer.

* * *

Jules was staring at us piteously.

"You have to remember that this was in the pre-poof era!" he said urgently. "Before the Change. You know what I mean. Back when hets were able to live and work, socialize and love where we chose without having to wave our gay credentials just to keep a job or an apartment! Before our sexuality and choices were closed off, restricted to leftovers!"

"Aren't you exaggerating here?" I challenged him.

"No! Look at you! Mr 'Theo doesn't know I'm straight so I'm taking a bloke to the Rosenberg Casino inauguration'!"

I opened my mouth but he stampeded on.

"I can see it's just as bad in the States – we got it from you, we get everything from you except subtlety and great rock – and here it went from old boy network to lavender mafia in a generation."

The girl cut in with, "That is *so* not fair, it was decades and centuries and you know it, but Jake, it is true what he's saying about keeping jobs and you're nobody if you're not gay, and the thing is that he's got a big party Gordon's coming to tomorrow and he wants you to be there. As his partner. Boyfriend. Lover. Jules does."

I stood up, sat down, stood up again and went to open the door for a whiff of that sweet, sensible honeysuckle.

"Why did you have to tell him like that?" Jules was berating her loudly. The girl was filling the electric kettle.

"You'd have taken forever, and that is the situation, isn't it?"

I turned and said, "You must be Jane."

There was a nasty little silence and I said hastily, "Or not," but it was drowned out by her yelling, "Jane! Who the fuck's Jane?" at Jules.

He had his head in his hands.

"Old man," he muttered. "Old man…"

"Stop old-manning him and give me an answer!"

"A straight answer," I put in, and after a tense couple of seconds they both giggled unexpectedly, which helped.

"I lied to you about the name," he told me. "I was stressed out by not being able to go out with her to places where I might get seen and people at work would hear, and it would jeopardize my position with Gordon. You were grilling me about my love life and I sort of wanted you to know but I felt I had to use a different name to protect her and you're all so damn' simplistic over there and I just thought 'Dick and Jane', so I said her name was Jane."

"But it was *you*!" he explained – a bit late, I thought – to the girl. "It was when we were together a few years ago, before we broke up, it wasn't anyone else."

I was still puzzling over the 'simplistic, can't handle subtlety' opinion Jules had revealed. Also the bizarre crack about great rock.

"My name's Chloe," said the girl, holding out her hand as though we'd just met. I took it as it was meant – an honest, fresh start.

She poured tea.

"Dude, you have to stop this habit of lying you've gotten into," I said to Jules.

"You're a fine one to lecture! What about Theo?"

"Don't start that – he's never asked and I've never said anything. I just keep quiet on those things, always talk about weekends with friends or a friend, you know?"

"Yes, well, that's all very well when you spend your entire working life clapped up in an old warehouse doing cross-stitch, but I have to get out there and compete in the City! Impress people! Assess them!"

"Yeah, yeah, whatever. But about this party… I don't see why you need me to be there as something I'm not. Where's that gonna take you?"

This time they were both silent. Chloe poured more boiling water into the teapot – one of those low, black, stone-looking ones that look like dachshunds – and kept her lips pressed firmly together like she was determined to let Jules sort it out now.

"Well, the thing is, old man," he began finally, "the thing is, Gordon believes you *are* my partner. The night I shouted 'Poof!' with him in the pizzeria, he helped me get you home and he stayed over and sort of got the impression you were, you know, with me."

"And you didn't enlighten him?"

"No. To be honest, he'd just offered me a job – it was a really good opportunity, too good to turn down, I knew it'd kick-start my career because he was already doing so well, and I suddenly thought it would be safer to be attached, otherwise I might be open to, er, unwanted attentions from Gordon, or other people. So I let him keep that impression, yes."

"But that was eight years ago! I've been in the States all this time!"

Jules' tone was definitely apologetic now.

"Yes, but the thing is, he didn't know that."

"What!"

"You and I were together here for a couple of years, is what he thinks, then you got a job back in NYC, and a couple of years after that, the strain of a long-distance relationship took its toll, and..."

"You cheated on him," Chloe told me.

"What!"

"I took it very badly and was on my own for about three years – just putting it about a bit and joking in the office about great nights out, having my freedom back, you know… "

"No, I don't!"

" …and then in February last year, a new bloke called Rick was taken on and he made it all really difficult. He's a hotshot, insurance guy, and Gordon adores him. Rick's the misogynistic sort who would step on my career like a cockroach if he even suspected I was het, and unfortunately he got the hots for me and I couldn't afford to offend anyone, so on my visit to New York last summer, you and I got back together again and right now, you're over to see what we can sort out. You know, see where our relationship's going."

"That's why Mercurio was so keen to meet you today," said Chloe.

The tea was lemon and ginger. It was good. I turned the packet this way and that in my hands and said finally, "Dude, have you spoken to your dad about your compulsive lying?"

CHAPTER FIVE
A generous husband

It had arrived. The bulky parcel had been delivered to the home of an elderly friend who lived fairly close to his consulting rooms.

Even the pavements felt vibrant as Dr JJ slipped over after work to collect it. He felt so alive with effort, investigative exertion, care. He cared for and about many people every day – except Sundays, when he mainly just drank sherry and read the paper and ate – but this was a fresh endeavour, and at this stage in his professional life, he was proud to be facing up to something he had long avoided.

"What is it, what is it?" shrilled Alicia, clutching his lapels and dragging him in.

"I told you, I can't say, it's a surprise for my wife."

Alicia, leading him down the cool dim hallway of her elderly apartment, was instantly conspiratorial.

"Ah, Rosario is a lucky woman to have such a generous husband. Always secret presents arriving here. It is *big*, this one."

Well, that was true enough, thought Dr JJ, wrestling the box out of the cab he'd been obliged to take back to the office. He glanced round, picked it up and entered the building as nonchalantly as he could while entirely obscured behind a large box.

Javi the doorman sprang forward to challenge and then, when he recognized the doctor's brogues, to help.

"No problem, Javi! Thank you! It doesn't weigh much."

The lift had arrived. The doctor swaggered in and staggered out four floors later, sweat beading his neck and temples.

At last he was alone in his rooms with his box. Private. Nobody could see. Snatching scissors from the desk, he cut away the tape and opened the box. Lifted out his new treasure. He checked that the shutters of the balcony window were fully closed, and drew the light linen curtains across too.

He slipped a seductive B-Tribe CD into the player, slipped off his clothes and spent the next half hour decking himself in his new garment. Then he swayed over to the full-length mirror and purred to his reflection, a reflection softened by the gentle lighting and those seductive strains of music.

"You're beautiful," he whispered. "Beautiful. Oh yes you are. It's you. Beautiful, beautiful. No-one has seen you like this, but this is the real you. Me. Me, this is the real me." Closing his eyes, he rocked and swayed to the understanding music until suddenly he tired. As he came out of the garment, unaccustomed tears pricked his eyes.

* * *

"Please, Jake." The voice was pleading and gentle.

Jules had gone up the garden for a smoke. I looked at Chloe properly for the first time. She was about 30, with fluffy reddish hair, more red-brown than red-blonde, with a cute little spray of freckles across her nose. Medium height, a little on the plump side. She had wide-set brown eyes which were fixed on me now, and wore flowers but not frills. Although she was feisty I found her restful. Cuddly. Receptive. I wanted to please her but Jules had seriously freaked me out and I still didn't know what a nettle patch looked like.

"It's only one party. We really need to keep Jules' image right for Gordon."

"His image?"

"Yeah, of course, Gordon and the Power Poofs rule, and apart from his own position, Jules' bank gave me the loan to get my workshop up and running."

"Oh right! What kind of work do you do?"

"I'm a milliner. I'm good, I've done my apprenticeship with the best, and now I know I can make a go of the business, but it has to be in the right area – which I've got, in Kensington – so as to attract and keep the right kind of clientele. I'm in for the long haul, I'm not expecting it to take off for another five or six years, but I need to hold onto the location and establish my reputation there, and Gordon and the Power Poofs can get me good clients by word of mouth if they like me. It's because of Jules I got the loan. They think I'm his gay cousin. So, the party's important for me too."

"No way could you say 'Power Poofs' in the States."

"Well, you can't here, either," she said at once. "Of course not. But it's just between us. We have gay friends and some of them are Power Poofs, it's what they call themselves, but not in public. Please, Jake, if they know Jules is a het and he's with me, they will pull the rug out from under both of us so fast… All we need is a couple more years to consolidate."

I looked into her pleading eyes.

"You know, what I really don't like is that it's all so unromantic," I said.

She laughed.

"Men are so romantic! But women have had to be pragmatic. Come on, all you have to do is play up to Gorgeous Gordon a bit, hold onto Jules' arm, look into his eyes now and then, hover round, make sure he doesn't talk to anyone for too long, you know, act a bit proprietorial. It's not hard. Women played this game for centuries!"

"Well, that doesn't make me happier, in fact, quite the opposite."

"He gave me £1,000 so that we can go shopping and get you something nice to wear…"

"Now I really do feel like a hooker."

"You do? Well, that makes it all a lot simpler! You are performing a valuable service, he's paying you for it. Step away from the friendship and be a hooker for a few hours!"

I closed my eyes and listened to the waves. Felt them beneath me, moving me in unexpected directions. Ride the waves, dude…

"Okay then, okay I guess. Let's do it."

She shrieked with delight and I said, now show me the nettles.

"Fortnum & Mason, breakfast at 10am," she told me. "You'll love it. Then we can go shopping. Thank you, thank you!"

"Yeah, yeah," I said, figuring that I could always cheat on the guy again as soon as I wanted out.

* * *

Kathy looked up from her book as Mila came back into the main room. It was 6pm in New York, and they were looking forward to a quiet evening at their Upper East Side home.

"How are they all over there?" she asked, taking off her glasses. "Honestly, the way the Times has been reporting it, I'm surprised you got through to Greece at all – it seems like a total country non grata."

Mila sighed and sank down onto the same couch.

"It is terrible," she said slowly. "Just awful. My uncle told me the old lady two doors down hanged herself last week because she didn't want to be a burden on her family – they're all struggling. And she's not the only one – he says every day they hear of people killing themselves, people dying of heart attacks from financial anxiety. Stress. Anxiety. Stress over money. I help my family, my friends, but I can't save the whole country, Kathy. There has been so much corruption in government for so long – they should punish them, not crush the people with 'austerity'. Someone's grandmother killed herself because of no money. How can such things be?"

"I don't know, Mila," whispered Kathy, taking her hand. "I don't know."

CHAPTER SIX
Smokescreens

Jules' joint was heaving. In a very elegant way. I had never seen such a gathering of posers. Yet there was substance too.

The lighter elements had arrived around 9pm for an 8pm invite; the heavyweights swung by round 11pm.

The catering was superb: Jules had hired a specialized firm, plus a troupe of gorgeous waiting staff who wheeled among the guests on roller skates. The guys were topless with tiny mauve sequined aprons and matching G-strings; the girls wore the same but with thumbnail bikini tops. The aprons were a joke all round, the service was a sensation.

I was 29 and I felt old.

Until the heavyweights arrived. Gordon and the Power Poofs. And the lady players. High rollers, I thought, welcoming newcomers at Jules' side. A lot of them seemed fun, a few made my flesh creep.

I knew what nettles looked like now, and Chloe and I had had a phenomenal day's shopping. I didn't need clothes for the party, so just told Chloe to spend Jules' cash on herself. She took some persuading and I understood why, but we did it, and I was blown away when she and Brussels Katy arrived on the doorstep. Chloe shimmered in a mid-calf, taupe cocktail dress with matt gold sequins that had been sewn on well enough to last the night. The shoe stacks were clearly where a chunk of the cash had gone. And the sleek up-do of the red-brown hair. I could feel myself smiling in delighted welcome, and minced forward to envelop her in a very enjoyable hug.

"Beautiful, beautiful," I breathed in her ear, and she hugged me and blushed and turned to greet Jules just as Gordon and a couple of the PPs arrived behind her.

Jules almost lost it when he touched her.

"Oh my God!" he cried, his light tone belied by the stunned look in his eyes. "Well, hi! Chloe and, Katy, isn't it? Welcome!"

He was still holding 'Cousin' Chloe by both hands and would be showing an erection any second now.

"Oh look, here's Gordon!" I cut in laughingly, as camply as I could, ushering the girls into the room and attaching myself to Jules' arm. "How delicious to see you! Welcome to our humble abode!"

"Well thank you, Jake," said Gordon, stepping across the threshold. "*Our* humble abode, eh?"

"Oh stop!" I squealed, slapping his arm limply. "All right, then, *Jules'* humble abode. But you do see why I just adore his humility, don't you?" I turned and flung my arm out like Corey Rosenberg, only without the blinding cuff links, to indicate the acres of gleaming loft now showing a harvest of laughing, swaying guests, the super-sexy waiters/waitresses weaving among them, trays aloft.

Jules glanced at me sideways as if horrified that I was so convincing. Burnished hair gleaming, he was understated chic in classic charcoal pants under a sleeveless top that breathed ripped edges and a barely discernible pattern – "Subliminal advertising," he'd explained. "It's actually the bank's logo. I had it done by a New Zealand artist who lives in Camden. I'm hoping everyone in the department will want one after tonight, so that I can push some business his way."

I'd packed but never seriously thought I would wear an acid-green loose string singlet stitched with tiny Swarovski crystals that quivered and winked with every movement. Theo, who must have had a much better idea of what I was coming over for than I did, had insisted I take it. He'd worn it to the Broadway opening night of *A Chorus Line* and the Queen of Denmark had admired it. "Always respect what the queens admire," he'd said with a wink. "You wear it over cream or very, very light-grey skin-tight jeans, with this dangly Swarovski crystal in one ear. It's a clip-on."

I'd said thanks, thinking 'No way', but under Queen Gordon's approving eye and a couple of admiring comments from the roller-skating staff, I silently blessed Theo and began to enjoy myself.

Gordon himself, über-camp in a sort of air-force pilot's jumpsuit that was all-the-way lilac, laughed out loud and said, "I do indeed see! Tai and Chi," he added, carelessly introducing a couple of cool-looking young Asian dudes who were wearing about as much as the waiters. "Very nice," he continued, surveying the room. "Rick's on his way."

"Great," Jules managed to say.

Gordon seemed to be waiting for something but Jules still looked to me a bit stunned by Chloe, who'd moved away, so I offered to take Gordon to whatever his heart desired and led him away, telling him sincerely that the stitching on his jumpsuit looked a shade sub-standard and I hoped he hadn't paid for it.

"Paid too much for it, you mean," he corrected me, a little austerely, as I nipped a glass of pink fizz from a passing nudity and handed it to him.

"Too much, of course," I agreed, blandly.

"Oh, here's Rick," he exclaimed.

I turned to see a big guy a few years older than myself – probably mid-thirties – who was crossing the floor to Jules like a heat-seeking missile. He was good-looking in a classic sort of way, with regular features and dark wavy hair rippling back over a well-shaped head. He was tanned and well-presented in what looked like Armani, yet for some reason I shivered slightly as Jules pointed me out and Rick caught my eye.

"He'll toe the line better now he knows you're around," Gordon assured me as I raised a hand and a small smile for Rick. "He's quite keen on Jules, admires his work of course, and everything. You know."

I looked into his eyes, which suddenly registered understanding, and he added,

"Nothing to worry about, Jakob. It's only ever been a professional relationship. And anyway, darling, you're the one who cheated. You're cute, but Jules is doing very well for himself and you might want to tread carefully."

His 'phone rang and he raised his eyebrows as he glanced down.

"Unknown caller. What a treat! Excuse me." He took a few steps away but I could still hear his end of the conversation.

"Well, my goodness me! Of course I'm free to talk, Mr Rosenberg... Corey, then. No problem at all, it's only midnight. Yes, London. Yes... Mm... Mm... Yes, I see. Oh James. Yes, a darling friend, and *so* clever on the golf course! So to speak. I hear he's covered most of Spain in them and is redecorating Croatia now. Beautiful landscapes. Lots of lolly... Yes... Mm... And congratulations to you, Corey! One of my team was at the inauguration, he showed us the pictures – sensational! Hm? Oh, Jules Julius. I understand he was there with his friend Jakob Naylor, who was involved in the… Oh, you *know* him? Well, my goodness, isn't the world a little silk handkerchief?"

It got my attention right off Rick. I stared in horror but Gordon, moving back to me, seemed oblivious.

"You are not going to believe this, Corey, but Jake himself is standing right here beside me in the most darling little outfit. We're at a very pleasant soirée Jules is hosting." He was talking pretty loud to be heard over the party buzz, and Corey would have got quite an earful as Gordon handed the 'phone to me.

"Be quick!" he hissed.

"No problem!" I hissed back. "Hi Corey, how're you doing?"

There was a silence but he was still there, I could sense it. Gordon had his beady eyes fixed on me, reassessing, I imagine. I was glad I'd got in the crack about his crap jumpsuit stitching.

Corey spoke.

"Your voice, young Jake, your voice!" he sighed. "From right across the ocean, it's as though you were right here with me… " He sighed again. "So you know Gordon Hecklow? Well, well, well. Now I remember your friend Jules. Well, listen up, young Jake, I look forward to getting together with you in New York pretty soon and doing more business with you. Major business. Now pass me back to the big guy, and have yourself a ball!"

"Thanks Corey, you too."

This time Gordon stepped well away, and I grabbed a glass of something to calm my jangling nerves. Across the crowded room, I saw Rick. He was on his own for a moment. He raised his full glass with an empty smile and I suddenly realized, even as I saluted in return, why he made my flesh creep. Like Corey, he could be cruel. I had no evidence. It was just a tingling conviction all over my body.

"Well, well, you are *so* well-connected, you sly thing!" Gordon was at my side again. "I'm impressed. Jules! Come here! Corey Rosenberg just rang and said he has a major business proposition for me."

"Christ! Did he?" Jules' stress visibly flowed away at the mention of business. "That's great!"

"It's interesting, yes. He'd heard my name from James Cleaver…"

"Builds mega-posh golf courses," Jules explained to me. "There's one designed by Seve Ballesteros just outside Alicante. My dad's played there a couple of times."

" …and it turns out that he is *very* fond of Jakob here," Gordon concluded, watching Jules closely for a reaction.

"Millards did a good job on Mila's designs for his casino," I said firmly, and Gordon took the hint and backed off, which was just as well 'cos Jules clearly wasn't about to fly into a jealous rage or anything.

"Of course. Anyway, he and I are having a little get-to-know meeting when he's in London next week…"

I shivered with relief. I'd be gone by then.

* * *

"It's a good thing it was televised," said Sra JJ, lighting a ciggie and putting her feet up on the battered leather pouffe they'd wrestled back overland after a trip to Morocco 25 years ago. "Honestly, it looks really exciting, but I don't remember a thing except that some idiot trod on my best sandals and broke the strap. I think it was Manolo's aunt – old ladies are the worst in a scrum like that. *So* rough."

Dr JJ handed her a re-filled glass, his eyes glued to the TV screen. They were recording the news.

"Hm, I know what you mean. Old Fatso did us proud."

His wife watched the footage of the mayor at their smoke-in with a more jaundiced eye.

"Julius, what is he up to?"

"Nothing! What do you mean?"

"Nothing? Wake up! He's bad news!"

"Hm? Maybe. I like the way he comes out strong supporting local business. He made it very clear that he doesn't like the central government's total ban on smoking in public places. Oh look! That's…"

"You!"

"Me!" they cried simultaneously. And yes, there was Don Juan Antonio Ruiz, mayor of Valencia, laying a substantial arm across the doctor's shoulder and smiling broadly into the camera.

"I admire this man!" he was booming. "Dr Julius Julius defends local business and community centres like Manolo's. Manolo himself went to school with the doctor's lovely wife Rosario…"

"Oh, why did you turn away from the camera?" the doctor asked his wife, who just shrugged.

" …they were both born and raised in Calpe. They and others are like them are at the core of this vital community. But my friends, what can I do in the face of Madrid's laws? Socialist Madrid is ruled by Brussels. Our money for good new infrastructure in the Eighties came from Brussels! New roads, high-speed trains – well, okay, only one of those and it just happened to run from Madrid to the Socialist prime minister's hometown, Sevilla, but…"

Laughter from the hordes of protest participants, though many voted Socialist.

"…but it was money well spent, and if our sugar daddy Brussels says no more diamond necklaces this year, well, we have to smile and say, 'yes darling, and of course we'll impose a total smoking ban', don't we? We need a firm hand, the PP conservative party, to defend us in Brussels! And I admire our good friend Dr JJ and his lovely local wife, who support local business, as I, in my humble way, have always done! But I have spoken enough! Let us enjoy another smoke – and don't forget to vote PP in the next election!"

The news moved on. Sra JJ frowned.

"He's setting us up for something."

Her husband laughed indulgently.

"Oh, stop imagining things! It was fun, a good protest and a good turnout. Lots of coverage. A good memory. Did we really expect to stop central government in its tracks? No. but we certainly stirred up a lot more dust than anywhere else in Spain over the smoking ban, and that's an achievement in itself. Should translate into more visitors, too. Here, may as well finish the bottle."

Rosario held her glass out without speaking. Dr JJ was pleased by her silence. As for him, he already had the motivation all worked out. The poor fat mayor was reaching out to him. 'You have power,' he'd said. And today, he'd put his arm across the doctor's shoulders – literally leaned on him for support. It had been horrible, but somehow Dr JJ felt proud. He emptied the bottle into their glasses and wondered when the mayor would contact him again.

It was all about fat. The smoking ban issue was just, well… just a smokescreen. The mayor, this man, was in pain. Crying out for help.

It was nothing to do with smoking. It was all about fat.

* * *

Corey's Cocksucker wiped his mouth surreptitiously and got to his feet feeling pissed. He'd heard the whole of Corey's 'phone conversation with people he didn't know, including someone Rosenberg was clearly coming on to – all while he was busy sucking him off in the immense private suite at the new Vegas casino.

His real name was Earl. He was lithe, beautiful, a dancer and choreographer at the casino, No 1 among the young men referred to as Corey's Cocksuckers. Earl had dreams to fulfil, but for now he laughed at the nickname he himself had adopted and took the money Corey held out in one hand as well as the bulging cock that was proffered in the other.

"That was nice, Earl," approved Corey, stroking the young man's gleaming, naked flanks as Earl stood, breathing a little fast from his exertions.

Corey reclined, at his ease. Satisfied.

"Very nice, you can go now. No, wait." He reached into a nearby drawer and brought out an envelope. "Here. Sleep well."

Earl took the bulging envelope and smiled his thanks. It was only a blow job. It was only a job. Take the money and swallow. Your pride. Another year with Rosenberg and he'd be able to move on – he was a good dancer. He slipped on a silk robe and trod softly over to the elevator, private to Corey's suite. He knew there were cameras inside. He kept smiling.

It was only when he reached his own room that he wiped his lips again and went to the bathroom for a long shower.

It was only a job.

* * *

Toward the end of the party, I heard Jules begging Chloe to stay the night, but she said it was too risky and walked straight out.

Late next morning, we went out to her house for brunch while Jules' cleaning lady came in with a couple of helpers to restore his place to pristine.

"Don't you ever do any cleaning or washing or manual work?" I asked.

"Not if he can avoid it!" said Chloe.

"That's not fair! I do loads of all that stuff when I'm over here."

"That is true," she acknowledged.

"Anyway," he continued, "the two best things you can give in life are love and decent work. I pay Mrs White very well and she'd be gutted if I cleaned up after my own parties. She does the changeovers of the short-term lets as well – she's raking it in."

"The party went really well," said Chloe, taking a second croissant.

"It did. Jake, old man, you were sensational! Everybody was asking where you got that bloody awful top you were wearing!"

"Ah, that was Theo's contribution. I didn't know what he meant at the time, but he said it'd be sure to come in handy at some of the places you'd want to take me to. I'm glad it hit the right spot."

"I'll say. So where'd my grand go, then?"

"I was wearing most of it," confessed Chloe, and Jules beamed.

"What, I hand over a grand and you come out looking like a million? Now that's what I call a good return on investment!"

She giggled and glanced at me.

"Corny but nice, huh?" she said, leaning over to give him a honeyed kiss. "Tai and Chi were overdressed as usual."

Jules looked disgusted.

"God, yes. I never want to see a man's buttocks again. They always do the double act dental floss outfits. But hey, they're our top sellers in the Far East and you can't argue with that. Seriously, Jake, I appreciate you being there – I can feel a lot more relaxed at work again now, even if I do have to sneak around to be with Chloe. The PPs'll be off my back now."

"Rick the Prick looked more than a bit pissed off," said Chloe. "He wouldn't talk to floor scrapings like me, but I did hear Gordon making a comment about you, Jake, being bee's knees with that casino bloke over in Vegas. Didn't catch Rick's reply, but…"

"Oh I did!" cut in Jules. "Gordon told me later. He said Rick was so polite he knows he's up to no good and Gordon told me to watch my back next week when Corey Rosenberg's over in case Rick has me bumped off in a hissy fit so he can step up to the Rosenberg cash cow in my place!" He laughed and stood up to pour more coffee but Chloe looked horrified and I said,

"You know, Jules, I'd take that warning seriously. Rick's one nasty-looking guy."

Jules made a dismissive noise. "Oh, he's just a Power Poof who thinks he can have whatever he wants. It's the City, not Chicago! Oh, text. Hey, my dad says the smoke-in protest is on YouTube – come on, let's watch it! It's the one where the mayor of Valencia turned up."

* * *

"You look very glum, my friend!" cried the mayor, watching the screen. "Ah, that's better, a smile. Sort of. But the main thing is that you were there! The great Torres and the mayor go to a smoke-in – this sends a clear message to Corey Rosenberg without causing any major problems for us with the central government. They just think I'm being simpático, doing a little PR; I uphold my fame for being of the people, with the people. But the total ban stands. I tell people to vote PP, that's expected. But I have challenged nothing, in fact."

He rewound and watched again. He and Torres were in the mayor's den, smoking and drinking, embraced by dark wood, with comfortable street noise as backdrop.

Torres tapped the ash off his cigarette and nodded.

"Yes, it's actually quite good," he admitted. "I didn't want to speak or even be filmed, but you're right, it gives the right impression. But what about the real protesters, and this doctor? He seems popular."

The mayor beamed.

"That is the best part! He has enough charisma to be simpático, to carry our message with his attractive wife, without me having to take any stance! He and his gang will do all the protesting from now; you and I provide a sympathetic backdrop, maintain our popularity. But of course we play by government rules, and when Corey Rosenberg makes his Eurovegas proposal to central government, of course the Valencia region will look better than Madrid, where the Puerta del Sol occupation has led to those troublesome 'Occupy' movements all over the place, or Barcelona, which is alienating everybody with its insistence on only speaking Catalan, putting road signs in Catalan before Spanish, and other moves that will drive away tourists even if the city does have lots of Gaudi buildings!"

Torres stirred and vindictively popped the biggest, finest slice of mojama into his mouth. As an architect, he had his sights on Barcelona, home of Gaudi. As an intelligent man whose father had fought on the Republican side against Franco, he understood Catalunya's desire for retroactive revenge against repression, but he had to admit that he agreed with Ruiz that it was shooting itself in the foot now.

Still savouring the mojama, he glanced at Ruiz and caught the mayor's small clever eyes fixed upon him. He's just needling me, he thought, and smiled without effort. Juan Antonio was pocketing millions, but as Spain approached its economic nemesis, his days were numbered. Whereas I, thought Torres, walk away with my talent. Genius already acknowledged and paid for by New York, Shanghai, London, Qatar. Valencia was the least of it. His springboard. Pocket money. His legacy was already assured. Thousands trod his corridors each day, squinted up at his beauty, blessed him for what he had brought them. Juan Antonio would die unperceived, whether or not he had money. And besides, he was fat. Much too fat.

So Torres smiled easily and the mayor, reassured, said,

"The good doctor wants to keep in contact with me. This is good. I will keep him up my sleeve for now, play him when we need to take the trick."

Both men laughed; raised and drained their glasses. The mayor reached for the bottle of palo cortado.

CHAPTER SEVEN
The stomach slipped over the edge

"Even quicker than I'd hoped!" thought Dr JJ as he glanced at his appointment book for the upcoming week and recognised the mayor's alias. "Excellent! The trick will be to draw him out without scaring him off. Softly softly catchee baboon."

Excited by the figures he was anticipating for the Eurovegas project, the mayor rubbed his fleshy fingers together. "Keep the good doctor and his gang onside," he was muttering to himself. "A good relationship there could help me swing this thing if Madrid cuts up about the smoking ban!"

His sidekick, passing by his door in the Town Hall's older section, heard the muttering and paused. He had suspected for a week or two that Juan Antonio was up to something – something connected to the architect Pablo Torres. He suspected they had a secret they were excluding him from. Well, good luck to them if they thought they could cut *him* out of the action! It's not as though he'd started out with blackmail in mind, but if they pushed him, he could push back a whole lot harder. Prison-sentence hard. Whoever handles the numbers handles the truth, he reflected smugly.

He paused for a second or two longer, but the mayor was simply whistling now. All the sidekick had heard was a gleeful tone and the words 'good doctor'. Perhaps the old baboon has a health problem, in which case I should check all the finances to make they stand up if he drops dead, he thought. But no, he wouldn't sound so cheerful if he was ill. Maybe looking for a good doctor to get a rival out of the way with a temporary health scare, he projected wildly.

Heavy steps approached the mayor's door from the inside and he slipped smartly off down the corridor, a few seconds older but certainly no wiser.

* * *

Corey Rosenberg sat back in the deep mauve, revolving leather chair in his Las Vegas office and touch-started the video link

Torres had sent him. The anti-smoking footage over in Calpe, Spain, flared up smoothly from across the room on a large, wall-mounted screen set in a showy gilded picture frame.

Several minutes later, after watching it three times, Rosenberg touched it off and sat contemplating his impressions of Juan Antonio Ruiz, the mayor Torres said could wangle reclassification of land and smooth out other troublesome little issues to ensure the go-ahead of the Eurovegas project. It was a project that was dear to Rosenberg's heart. The past 15 years had seen him sear through the States and, through a judicious mix of business flair and sheer bloody-mindedness, set up a joint venture with a Chinese firm that would not fulfil its potential for another 10 years. When it did, it would be massive. Torres's contacts and prestige had assisted him in that venture, too. But Europe was yet to be cracked. He thought of the old continent as an unsuspecting young boy asleep in a chair, slack-limbed, beautiful, waiting to be truly awakened, thirsting to be shown...

On the whole, he was pleased with Torres's new recommendation. The mayor of Valencia cut a flamboyant figure, in a way that was unfamiliar to Corey. But he was far from being a buffoon, the casino tycoon was quick to recognise. Those small, clever eyes, in which Rosenberg could read greed as clearly as colour, and those well-calculated gestures bore the right marks for a major project like Eurovegas – the camera was always on him, and even when he looked annoyed, the man carried weight. "Too much damn' weight," Corey muttered to himself. He was awkward with hets, and especially this kind of old-school, fat, confident het who no doubt found women to service him even though he was revolting.

Corey shivered in disgust.

But the mayor was clearly popular, respected in his way, and a little feared – which Corey found essential – and was well able to push through the kind of brazen PR stunts he'd need for Eurovegas as well as take care of the administrative details.

"Good job," he texted to Torres, and turned back to his power shake and the financial news continually pouring across a small screen at his side.

* * *

Mayor Ruiz enjoyed his sessions over the summer with Dr JJ. It was very pleasant to be sitting quietly in a cool room with just a relaxing amount of sunshine oozing goldenly in through the big window shutters. Very peaceful.

He wasn't giving anything away, after all, and these appointments were keeping the doctor onside in case he had to be played, and it was... well, just pleasant. He took to lying on the couch after a while. The doctor gave him a special tea that came from England and sometimes he snoozed. Without reproach.

As soon as he noticed the first time that his patient had nodded off, Dr JJ sat upright in jubilation. Now he could really study this man!

After a few minutes of silence then snoring from Juan Antonio, the doctor stood and approached the couch, contemplating the mayor's buttoned bulk.

It was an opportunity too golden to miss. He slipped a small camera out of his pocket and kept it concealed in his palm. He tweaked gently at one of the two big, strong buttons clasping Ruiz's linen jacket across his vast stomach.

Gentle tweaking was not going to do it. Fascinated, Dr JJ put the camera back in his pocket and went to work with both hands. As the first button eased uneasily through its slit, Juan Antonio continued to snore.

The second button was much more nerve-racking. But it came.

The sudden release of his belly roused the mayor to grunts and snuffles and a shift in position. The doctor made a soft leap backwards and sat in his chair, holding his breath.

But Juan Antonio snoozed on.

Gradually, Dr JJ relaxed, began breathing again, and slid the camera once more out of his pocket. But before risking any more disturbance, he simply sat and studied the mayor's unfettered body.

How had two mere half-inch buttons borne such a load? "Never have so few done so much for so many kilos," he murmured respectfully.

The stomach slipped over the edge of the couch, filling the pockets of shirt that had previously lain, uncalled-for, at Juan Antonio's sides. The doctor studied every pouch, every strained seam. This was loose flesh, it wobbled with every snore and with the slightest movement. This was obese.

For three or four more minutes, there was only intense repose and intense study in that room.

And then, to the doctor's horror, the mayor turned onto his side. His bulk spilled, struggled and heaved. Re-settled to one side... and, with horrifyingly inevitable impetus, dragged Juan Antonio off the couch and onto the floor on his face.

Outwardly calm, inwardly appalled, Dr JJ watched as the mayor shook into startled wakefulness, struggled round and up to a semi-sitting position, and looked around for someone to blame.

"That will have done you so much good," crooned the simpático doctor before the mayor could speak. "You were so relaxed, that's astonishingly rare. Very few people make so much progress this fast."

There was nobody to blame, but there was somebody to praise – himself. A smile broke out over the mayor's face as he did up his buttons and revelled in the fact that, as usual, he was ahead of the pack.

* * *

Carmen let herself into her tiny studio in Madrid's hippy-chic Lavapies area and flumped into the armchair, jacket still on, mail still clutched in her hand. Exhausted. And that, she'd be the first to confess, was to do with her ánimo, her state of mind.

She didn't need to switch on the TV to know that the conservative Partido Popular (PP) party was front-runner to win the elections, and that depressed her. It had been a tough day at work: she headed up social media outreach for the 15M – the anti-greed movement that had inspired similar occupations of central squares in the world's major capitals. Most notably, New York.

Carmen had first camped out at the Puerta del Sol occupation and then, when it dispersed to organised centres that wouldn't disrupt the square's valuable tourism business or local enterprises, she'd offered her marketing expertise free on a part-time basis. She now combined an interesting but not overpaid job at one of the city's alternative art venues with 15M work, which made each working day at least 12 hours long.

She was learning, contributing, proud.

And exhausted.

Faint sounds of bombastic PP campaigning burst in through the small window overlooking rooftops, irritating her.

Carmen sighed and tossed her mail to one side. Except for the postcard.

The postcard showed the New York Occupy encampment right in the Financial District, striking hard at Wall Street's daily activity. It had since been dislodged, but, as in Madrid, the movement was alive and kicking.

She turned the card over and read the words again: 'Hi, I visited this every week to show support. I will be in Europe in September. Would love to see you and visit your movement – you are doing an awesome job. What do you think?'

Until she knew what she thought, she wouldn't reply, she decided.

She got up and went for a quick shower in the minute shower room before slipping thankfully into fresh underwear and a huge T-shirt and sitting down with a beer to call her parents for the almost nightly chat that had all but replaced their physical get-togethers in these pared-down times.

* * *

Juan Antonio didn't like Madrid much. He liked being a big fish in a smaller pond. Here, he just felt big in the wrong way.

Now, where had that thought come from? He patted his paunch discreetly as if to reassure it that it was still wanted, and glanced round to make sure no-one had noticed.

He was in the PP HQ on calle Génova, waiting for the conservative party's regional director to appear. The man's title didn't sound like much, but those in the know knew that it was extremely influential in Brussels.

Brussels the sugar daddy, Ruiz thought irritably. People passing by the waiting area smiled and said hello or called out. They all knew him. He was familiar to the older politicians, a thorn in the side to the younger ones, who were increasingly influenced by the rest of Europe, by appearances.

Appearances! Ruiz snorted quietly. They were marketing people, not politicians. Not one of them could handle the reins of negotiation and maintain popularity while prospering as skilfully as he had all these years. Yet, even as he raised a bulky hand and hollered jovially at a passing acquaintance, he felt a pang of awkwardness. They were all so slim.

Slim! Where had *that* come from?!

"Don Ruiz? This way, please." A slim young man led him forward along the corridor into the arena where the present could be played, the future won. Juan Antonio swelled with confidence.

"He's too fat!" the regional director was muttering to his colleagues as the slim young flunky went to fetch him. "He embodies corruption. Everyone in Spain – everyone in Europe – knows he's making a mint out of dodgy deals all along the east coast, and has been for years. Brussels wants us to crack down on corruption. We need to be seen to be doing something."

"Exactly," piped up a senior aide. "Ruiz is ideal for that. Everyone knows him, as you say; he's a TV personality. We throw him to the wolves on some trumped-up charges, let him 'retire' – Brussels happy, Spain glued to the telly, business and politics as usual."

"Don Ruiz!" announced the slim young flunky, and the mayor of Valencia lumbered in.

"Gentlemen," he nodded as they all rose, with grudging or sincere respect. He knew from fairly recent experience that the chairs on offer were uncomfortably tight around the hips, and he had planned accordingly. He stood and beamed.

"Gentlemen!" his voice boomed over the various cries of welcome. "Let me not waste your time. I thank you all for your presence. Especially our revered Don Gonzalez" – he embraced the regional director and stayed, picture perfect, at his side as he continued. "We all want PP to win in the next general election. Now, rising unemployment is the main concern of our voters. This is a true problem. Do I have the solution? No. No man does. I have *a* solution."

To an awed silence, he flung down a single, gleaming black portfolio.

"Eurovegas."

A ripple of excitement ran round the table, and Ruiz swelled, feeling the attention upon him.

"The French think they have it. The British think they could have it. They are arrogant, unseeing, and *wrong*! Gentlemen – and lady – *we* have it! I have the US tycoon Corey Rosenberg, I have the world-famous architect Pablo Torres, I have Eurovegas – with the tens of thousands of jobs and the billion-dollar investment it will bring – in the palm of my hand!"

He struck one hand against the palm of the other and beamed at the stunned assembly.

"I don't waste your time, gentlemen," he continued with a slight bow – the only sort he could execute. "I am in Madrid until Thursday, entirely at your disposal. The figures and guarantees are all in this confidential portfolio. Adios, dear friends!"

He turned on his heel, leaving men half-rising, half-sitting, seven men and one woman stunned, perplexed, irritated and excited.

The ripples grew as they all spoke at once, then gradually died to silence. They all contemplated the gleaming black portfolio lying on the polished dark wood table. They all looked to the regional director.

"I don't care what's in this," he said peevishly, picking it up and opening it. "The man's still too fat."

* * *

I'd come back from that crazy London weekend a worried man. Sure, it'd been fun – and Theo had loved the photos of me draped around Jules, myself draped in acid green and sparkly crystals. It was, as I'd once said to Chloe, the fact that it was all so unromantic that bothered me. And Jules must have picked up on something because he'd offered to call Carmen and invite her over for my last evening in London.

"We can have an old-fashioned foursome!" he'd said. "No, not that sort! I just mean a nice lunch or something. Chloe and I know a great little het place, tucked away, discreet – you'll love it!"

And he'd looked so crestfallen when I'd said,

"No thanks dude. Until I can do this without creeping around and hiding, I'm not gonna do it."

Chloe had sighed and shrugged in what looked like resignation. Jules, always so 'rubbery', so bounce-back, just said I'd better go and live in Spain then, 'cos things were 10 years behind and hets weren't being hounded yet, although it was seen as trendier to be gay and already the best jobs were being ring-fenced.

"Why don't *you* go and live there?" I'd asked and they looked at each other and I knew I'd said a troublesome thing.

"It's my fault," said Chloe.

"No it's not!" he said.

"Well, mainly mine. I really want my business to work here, you see, and here in the UK, it's a different look, a different color palette, a different style of women even. Shape, size, style, habits – it's all inter-related. And climate. That's a big factor. It'd be too big a risk to change location before I've made enough of a name."

"And I want to be in the UK," Jules said firmly. "No blame anywhere. And come on, old man, the States is huge – you're not telling me you can't find a place where you could be het and not hassled."

"Sure, sure." I thought of my modest home in Queen's. Rented, comfortable, unpretentious. Fairly safe. For now. It was all 'for now'.

"Cheer up, old man," Jules said suddenly. "We can winkle Carmen out of Spain if she's The One."

Chloe looked immensely cheered by his sudden show of romantic sensitivity, and I had to smile.

"Let's see where we are in September," I said.

"Yes, and way before that, let's see where we are after Corey Rosenberg has his little tête-à-tête with Gordon next week," said Jules.

"I'm worried about that," said Chloe. "He sounds awful and I don't like what Gordon said to you about Rick."

Jules waved his hand dismissively.

"Oh, bollocks to Rick. I'll tell you what worries me, and that's Dad. Mum says she thinks that fat old bugger Ruiz..."

"Mayor of Valencia Ruiz?"

"Him. She thinks he's pulling some kind of fast one on Dad. I watched the video again of them at that smoking ban thing, and I have to say I think she's got a point. It's weird, 'cos Dad's always had a thing about fat people – wouldn't go near one unless it was a medical condition not just porking out the whole time like Ruiz does – and now suddenly he's all cosy with the fat boy. I don't know what's going on."

I pondered. Now he mentioned it, it was pretty weird.

It wasn't why I left London worried, but it's true that now, when I closed my eyes and listened, I couldn't make out what the waves were telling me. About anything.

It felt like I'd lost my center. It made me cling more closely to the old sewing machines, the solid feel of their old bodies against my palm, the calming thump-thump of their work, their precision and inevitability.

Theo said I must be in love.

"I hope it's not Corey," he said, and seemed reassured when I said,

"Oh man! No way!"

More than reassured. Glad.

I didn't tell him I'd remembered about Jules kissing me and that that had been giving me blackouts over the years. That would be too much sharing. I was very fond of Theo, but, he was gay, and he was my boss. I loved my job, the incredible new opportunities he'd given me, and there was no way I could contemplate jeopardising it.

It was all so weird. Everything had a 'but' attached these days. Except the stitching under my hands, the uncompromising beauty of my work.

Business as usual. The rest – not.

* * *

In his luxuriant lavender office, Corey Rosenberg looked up from the financial data screens and stretched.

He was happy with the Eurovegas project and looking forward to his flight to London next day to meet Gordon Hecklow. Torres had assured him that the mayor of Valencia, that fat Ruiz fellow, had got things well underway on the Spanish side.

"It'll all be clear and clean," he'd told Rosenberg at a brief meeting in Chicago, where Torres was advising on a new downtown development. "Legal."

"Good. I'm seeing Hecklow in London to firm up the financials," Corey had replied. "I'll give it to the press after that, if it's all going to plan. The right press. Give me time to deal with the eco-crazies. You'll be seeing in the press that we're taking in bids, assessing locations – whip up the expectation. But it's all Spain's."

"Fine." Torres and Rosenberg knew that taking in bids meant substantial sweeteners for both of them as major developers vied for the contracts. They worked together well. Torres looked around the sweeping hotel lounge, deploring the vulgarity of its atrium. "Our friend the mayor needs three or four months to handle the formalities."

"That works." Corey took a gulp of his designer beer and waved a hand round the atrium. "Nice place, classy. Maybe we can do something like this at Eurovegas."

Torres smiled to conceal his contempt and said,

"It'll be everything you ever dreamed of, Corey. Hecklow's got what it takes. You might want to ask him about media management on that side of the pond, too. He's well-connected and we don't need even a whiff of bad press."

"I might," agreed Corey.

"I might," he said aloud now, smoothing his hair in the mirror. "Depends on how solid you really are, Hecklow. The figures check out, but I'll know when we're eyeball to eyeball. Pity Jake won't be in London."

He caught himself up on the thought. Maybe it was for the best. That young man is too much of a distraction, he chided himself. He'd need to be careful around Jake's partner, Jules. But Jules was young.

"Plenty of flash, plenty of promise," he told himself. "But no substance. Young Jake needs stability, no ifs or buts. Substance." He turned his face this way and that. Satisfied. "Hecklow's the big fish, the one who can help me make Eurovegas happen. Forget about Jules and Jakob."

The thought of Jakob stirred him; he picked up an in-house 'phone and said,

"Earl? I need a little company. No worries if you're busy yourself, but send someone up now. Thank you."

He closed the Eurovegas portfolio on his desk and went into the adjoining bathroom suite, pulling off clothes as he went. A long hot shower. He enjoyed getting serviced in the shower.

* * *

Spain's EU regional director opened Mayor Ruiz's gleaming black portfolio one more time and closed it immediately with a frustrated gesture. He knew what was in there. It all made perfect business sense. And on a political level, Spain was itching to pull one over on the increasingly arrogant wealthy countries who'd made Spain their playground for the past 30 years, raped and ruined her coastline, and had now begun their greedy invasion of the poorer nations obliged to flaunt their wares cheaply in exchange for membership of the EU trading bloc.

But Spain! Spain is different! A sardonic smile curved Mariano Gonzalez's lips. We have better gastronomy than the food-whore France, we have more style than Italy, more sun than the Brits, and way more fun than the Germans. Our architecture, our cuisine, our dancers and choreographers, our film directors, are all achieving worldwide recognition...

Gonzalez realised he was mouthing the words and throwing his arms about, as if addressing his counterparts in Brussels, and checked himself. His kids ragged him when he went into what they called promo-rant mode.

Focus, he told himself. Take the next logical step. Get Ruiz back so that he can start the dirty work quietly – all the reclassification of rural land and other little details he knew perfectly how to handle while creating nice juicy distractions for the news reports on telly.

He wrinkled his nose briefly in distaste and picked up the 'phone.

* * *

"You're giving it to *Spain*?" squeaked the French delegate to Brussels.

"They've only just had the Olympics!" objected Britain.

"It's not a question of giving it to Spain," Germany said irritably. "They've taken it."

"But we can't let that happen! France needs it!"

"They've only just had the Olympics! It's not fair!"

Italy wondered quietly why its extremely 'sweet' bid hadn't been picked up by Rosenberg.

"Look," said Germany, as if explaining to a dim child, "Spain has the biggest construction industry in Europe. None of us can compete with their legions of cheap labour, combined with their decades of practice at this kind of thing, thanks to the fact that we've all used the entire country as our holiday home. From Rosenberg's point of view, Spaniards are the biggest gamblers in Europe – look at the amount the average Spaniard spends every week on lottery tickets, not to mention the Christmas 'Fat One' – so he's got a head start with them for a major casino."

"Actually, the lottery is a nice money-spinner," admitted UK. "We've managed to loosen things up a bit at home to get people spending on that. Keeps them happy, too – stops them seeing what's really going on with the economy if there's hope of winning obscene amounts of cash."

France nodded, still glum.

Italy was bending down to tie its ridiculously elegant shoelaces and thinking under the table about all the black market spin-offs it would enjoy from Eurovegas. Italy had the management skills to assist with this kind of thing at the informal level which these stuffy rich nations didn't really get. But Spain did. Getting things done at a local level without tiresome accountability was a forte in both their countries.

"What *are* you doing down there?" scolded Germany. "Sit up!"

Italy reappeared, muttering an apology.

"Well, exactly," Germany resumed. "Then there's…"

"But it's not fair! They've only just had the Olympics!"

"Oh shut up, UK! You can have the Olympics soon!"

UK looked pleased.

"Really? Promise?"

"Go for it," said France. "Expense, public transport mayhem, bunch of useless buildings that get you criticised, and all kinds of opportunities for terrorism. You're welcome to it."

"Getting back to the agenda," Germany said heavily, "Spain also has Torres – the architect. We all know how much weight he swings."

"He's only a bloody architect," said UK.

"He's the bloody architect who's in bed with US tycoon Corey Rosenberg, who rivals Donald Trump in wealth, ambition and ability to swing the financial backers his way. And Spain is fun. None of us can compete with that either."

Silence.

Germany refilled her glass and contemplated the water.

"It's a done deal, my colleagues," she said. "We need to accept that and make the best of it."

France pouted. Italy's smooth olive face was serene.

"Fine!" said UK. "As long as we get the Olympics. Anyone know what's for lunch?"

* * *

"Do you think he's right?" Chloe asked Jules one night in bed.

"Who? What?" He was half asleep, cosy and sated after making love. It was a weekend; he could lie in with Chloe and they could spend the next day together with hardly any fear of being seen by people they knew from work. No holding hands or shows of affection in the street, of course, but hets were used to that now. These Friday evenings were pretty much paradise.

"Jakob."

"Oh him. No, 'course not."

Chloe was silent. Jules sighed and tried to focus.

"About what?" he mumbled.

"About it not being very romantic."

"What? What not being vuh-wuh-man?"

"Our life together, such as it is. All this skulking about, not being able to kiss in the street in case someone sees us – all that."

"Oh right. Well, there's no choice, is there? Been through all this. 'Night, 'night."

Unreassured, Chloe stared at the ceiling, remembering what Jake had said about Carmen: "Until I can do this openly, I'm not going to do it at all", or something like that.

How many stunted lives, she thought. Am I making the right choices?

* * *

Dr and Sra JJ sat looking out over the marina. The sun was setting, sending bright tints of orange and ochre flickering over the gleaming bodies of the gently bobbing boats in the water. Children were running about, older folk gathered in vociferous knots at water's edge.

Neither of them spoke. There was no need. They'd spent so many times in this colourful tranquillity together. Dr JJ quaffed deeply and his wife drew on her ciggie, profoundly contented.

Her mobile rang. She frowned as she glanced down, then her face brightened.

"Oh, it's Jules!" She answered while her husband took another gulp of his cold gold beer. "Jules! Hello darling, how are you? Yes, he's right here. Hold on."

"What's the hurry?" Dr JJ said, not taking the outstretched 'phone. "Hasn't he heard of sundowners?"

"He's gone to the loo," Sra JJ told Jules. "Do you want him to call you? Oh. All right. Yes. Hm. I see."

After a couple of minutes of this, her husband flapped an impatient hand at her.

"Give me that damn' thing!"

She hurried her goodbyes, hung up and said, "He thinks Mayor Ruiz is trying to pull something over on you, too."

"Oh for God's sake! That boy needs a hobby, apart from yakking on the 'phone."

"Well, it's what he said. He's been watching the video of us at that smoking ban thing again, and he said – like I said – that Ruiz is setting you up. You can see it in the body language."

Dr JJ snorted and signalled for refills.

"Where do you want to have dinner?" he asked.

"He's in denial, but I agree with you," Sra JJ texted her son later.

* * *

Corey was impressed. He'd seen plenty of good-looking guys in his time, but even so, the welcome committee sent by Gordon Hecklow to meet him at Heathrow airport was a spectacle in itself. Pared-down and precise, the two young men with Asian features and impeccable English tailoring introduced themselves as Tai and Chi. Their formal welcome held a promise of something more exotic, Corey was, with his experience, quick to sense. Just something about the way they moved, and ushered him expertly into the waiting helicopter, he decided, enjoying every flash of eye contact, every small touch. These boys would look after him in every way.

In his discreetly sumptuous office, Gordon sat alone in the dusk. His face wore no particular expression, and in the fading light, he looked weary, and heavy about the jowls.

After some minutes, he fished out the 'phone that only he and one other person knew he had, and pressed the quick dial. The lines around his eyes softened as the loved voice answered.

"Hello darling," he said caressingly. "How's your day been?"

For a minute or two he listened, murmuring, smiling, his body relaxed, no movement in his office except for the shifts in light across his windows.

"I'll be late tonight," he said finally. "Rosenberg's coming into the office around now. I had Tai and Chi pick him up earlier – what? No! No dental floss thongs! Savile Row suits, actually – and he'll be here any minute. I need to do the wine and dine after our meeting, take him along to a club and get him settled there. But I'll be with you as soon as I can, I promise. Enjoy the film, darling. Bye now."

As he ended the call, a small light on his desk flashed, indicating that the chopper had landed on the building's rooftop helipad in the very heart of the City.

Gordon rubbed his cheeks hard, splashed a little Czech and Speake scent – foreigners could never identify it because it was only sold in a single outlet in London – straightened his jacket and called for Jules and Rick to join him.

"Oh, Jules is not our main man on this, Corey," he was reassuring Rosenberg some hours later over a perfectly judged dinner at a clearly elitist club restaurant. "But, of course, he is bilingual and – more importantly – bicultural, and he's very familiar with the area where you plan to build the Eurovegas site. And, as you're aware, he also knows the architect, Torres."

Corey nodded in satisfaction. Hecklow was everything he'd been cracked up to be. He'd had time to freshen up at his hotel after they'd covered the main financials in record time. There was no sensation of haste – merely knowledge and smooth operations. Jules had swung by to say hi, along with a guy called Rick Hanbury, who struck an immediate chord with Corey. Business in safe hands, he instinctively knew. Gordon himself exuded intelligence and status. He lifted a hand now in a small gesture and the maitre d' appeared instantly, attentive but not obsequious.

"Sir?"

Rosenberg leaned back and breathed a deep sigh of contentment as Gordon took care of the bill and called for the car.

"Now, Corey," smiled Gordon, "not to tire you out on your first evening here, but we do have an entertainment proposal for you." Again, the tiny gesture, and Tai and Chi appeared to escort them to the waiting Silver Phantom Rolls Royce.

That same evening, Juan Antonio Ruiz moved ponderously about his Valencia home. The doorbell rang and he went to let his sidekick in.

The two men went into the den. The long window was open, dusk hung fragrantly outside. It was warm. The final days of pleasant warmth before the heat hit.

The mayor's sidekick eyed the tapas laid out for their delectation. As always, they were appealing, of fine quality, and yet... Ah yes. Boquerones y patatas – anchovies to be eaten balanced on potato crisps. His favourite. They had never been lacking. But this evening, they were. Somehow, it bothered him.

Ruiz was way more forthcoming than usual. He outlined the Eurovegas project. His sidekick struggled to keep the astonishment, indignation, admiration, whatever these mixed emotions were, out of his face. He was being admitted into the secret. Now he knew why Ruiz and Torres had been plotting together! He was not excluded. He had been kept in the dark until now, Ruiz was explaining, only until the financials were solid and their vital work could begin.

Exultation flooded through him. Perhaps Ruiz would now fetch the boquerones, seal the deal with his favourite.

The mayor's mouth kept moving. There was no need to speak of confidentiality – they were brothers in scheming and profit. Adept, discreet.

"So there you have it, my friend," beamed Ruiz. "I know I can rely on you to put all the necessary measures in motion." His clever beady eyes bored into the sidekick.

"Of course," nodded the sidekick impassively. *Has he forgotten?* I have never, ever, ever been here with no boquerones offered.

"Have some of this fuet," suggested Juan Antonio, pushing a platter forward.

His sidekick accepted with a brief smile of appreciation, his mind racing, casting about, diving here and there to identify what was wrong... Maybe he couldn't see it because it simply wasn't in sight yet.

There was a small silence. He was aware of paint peeling away from the bottom of the window shutters. At floor level, it was barely perceptible. He'd never noticed it before.

The warm air, with an oppression full of summer pulling at its heels, crawled in past the peeling bottom of the shutters and smothered his feet.

Ruiz's voice was an extra layer to the warmth. Pleasant still, but now with something of oppression dragging it down, down... The sidekick reached for another morsel, chiding himself for indulging in fancies, forcing his mind back to the facts.

"Warm, isn't it?" Ruiz was saying. "It's getting hot these days."

"Yes, indeed."

Again a small silence.

"Summer approaches," the mayor pronounced in a genial tone. "Yes, yes, the summer heats are almost upon us." His clever beady eyes played over the other man. "And this year, once again, we have to fear the fires. The fires that lay waste so many precious hectares of our beautiful countryside."

Ah.

"Indeed," the sidekick said quietly. Alert.

"But at least there is a positive side to such devastation," said the mayor, heaving himself up to fetch – not boquerones, but a fresh bottle of sherry.

His sidekick looked an inquiry.

"Re-classification."

The sidekick nodded. This was familiar territory.

"Such a shame to waste the land laid waste by Nature," Ruiz rolled on, smoothly pouring sherry. "Fortunately, we can take the ruined rural land, re-classify it and put it to excellent use for building beautiful homes and centres for our local people. And for our valued foreign visitors."

"Of course, Juan Antonio, this is easily and completely understood."

But still, the sidekick burned to know *where* this mighty new project, this Eurovegas comprising three hotels, a casino, sports complex, wellbeing centre, shops and conference spaces, was to be located. It would, there was no doubt about it, be a huge boon to whichever town was closest. Jobs, investment, a brand *name*.

The silence drew longer.

At last the sidekick broke it.

"Juan Antonio, can you tell me exactly where the centre of this amazing new development is to be? I need to know in order to prepare the terrain, you understand."

The mayor broke into fat chuckles. He leaned over and slapped the sidekick on the knee.

"Yes I can! Yes I can, my loyal friend! And I guarantee that you will be blown away by the sheer brilliance of this! Oh but first, some boquerones! What was I thinking of?" He stood and filled their glasses, fetched plump white boquerones with crisps. Looking over the sidekick with the drugged warm air dragging itself inevitably around his bulk, he stood unmoving and said simply,

"The Salinas of Calpe."

The heavy air fell silent for several moments.

The Salinas. Sacred waters. A lagoon forming an oasis of peace and natural beauty behind the tower blocks and apartments that jostled along Calpe's desirable beaches. An oasis of peace and serenity, even if only glimpsed through a car window in passing. Healing, calm, smooth, glistening water reflecting the slender legs of pink flamingos, with hard high hills as a background. No other town on the built-up coast offered such a treasure.

"We will drain the Salinas!" cried Ruiz, the sky dark behind him through the long open windows. "A feat of engineering to be proud of, many construction jobs, the opening-up of fresh opportunities, new horizons for our beloved local people!"

A slow, grim grin pulled at the edges of the sidekick's mouth.

"Of course," he said quietly. "Of course."

* * *

"Are you all right, Gordon?" Jules asked anxiously. "You look a bit knacked."

"Oh lord, do I?"

"No, you're fine, it's just that I thought for a moment... Forget it! I just thought that hooking a big fish like Rosenberg for whatever this big hush-hush deal is would have lit you up more."

They were crouched together at a large, gleaming table in a heaving club called Duro, which, in a discreet area up in the galleries, catered for pretty much every gay and lesbian taste. The music was loud – "has to be, to cover the screams from up in the galleries," Jules had once quipped to Chloe – and every body in sight was a body that wanted to be seen. Except for Gordon and Jules, who both needed, rather than wanted, to be seen.

Gordon smiled.

"You're right," he said. "I should look happier. It is a big deal; basically we're handling all the European side of the financials.

I'm putting Rick in as their point man, and we'll be using you for the PR and cultural side of things."

Jules stared.

"What do you mean, PR and cultural?" he said.

"Tell you tomorrow."

"Okay, whatever you say. No problem. Wow, Tai and Chi doing a great job out there! Love the transformation from sharp suits to burlesque. Anyway, just going for a quick waz. Gordon, then I'm ready to head off with you. Won't be a mo."

Gordon nodded. He sat staring idly down at the floor, which in that section of the club was glass, affording an excellent view of the huge pool underneath, where lithe, naked bodies frolicked and a water sex show took place every hour.

Corey had been so delighted he'd gone down to take a closer look. Gordon smiled thinly to himself and glanced at his watch. Time to make a move. He was dropping Jules off on his way home. Taking his time in the loo, Gordon thought.

In the men's room, Jules stared wanly into the mirror, willing Friday night closer. Dinner at the het place, a bottle of good wine, the sedate walk home followed by squeaks and giggles from Chloe as soon as they got in the door and he could get down to business, pent-up and eager after a week's separation.

"Jules!"

A hearty slap on the back jerked him back to reality. With a gasp, he turned to see Rick grinning at him in the cold blue strobe light.

"Hi," he said, and made a move to the door. But Rick blocked his way and edged him swiftly, firmly up against the wall at a secluded end of the facilities.

Suddenly scared, Jules felt a chrome hose attachment pressing into the small of his back. Christ knows what goes on in this place, he thought.

"Rick, get off me, what are you playing at?" he croaked, trying to push his way out from the large, hard body pressed against his. He could feel Rick's breath on his face.

"Corey likes your whore-boy Jakob," Rick said into his ear. "He can have him, can't he, Jules? Keep our multi-million-dollar deals sweet. Hm? What do you say?"

His hands slid down the front of Jules' body. Jules felt his palms turn wet, heard his own breath short and rasping.

"Don't be daft, Rick. Get off, leave me alone."

Rick's hand moved to his crotch and Jules' eyes opened wide in horror.

Outside, Gordon glanced at his watch again and frowned. Suddenly Tai was at his side, bending over to ask,

"Everything okay, sir?"

"Oh, Tai! Thank you. Listen, I have to leave and I need Rick out here hosting Mr Rosenberg in my place. I'm giving Jules a lift home and he's taking his time in the loo. Go and powder your cheeks, would you? And Tai, keep things dainty."

Tai nodded briefly and was gone, Chi appearing at his side as he moved to the men's room with those spare movements that all at once held a hint of menace.

"Rick, where have you *been*?" shrilled a fluttering voice.

A familiar voice. The weight of Rick was pulled away from him, Jules opened his eyes, shaking and sweating, to find Tai and Chi festooning his assailant and bearing him away in a cloud of flutter that was somehow fast and sinister.

"Mr Rosenberg's been missing you," he heard Chi say.

Tai turned, stepped swiftly back to Jules and said,

"Gordon's ready to leave. You ready?"

"Yes, of course. Be right there."

Tai glanced him over, nodded as if satisfied.

"Go straight out to the car. I'll bring your things out," he said, and left.

Jules straightened his tie, ran cold water over his hands until the shakes abated and closed his fly before heading out to the car.

CHAPTER EIGHT
No more cracks about buttocks

"Jake! It's me, Jules!"

The familiar bellow. I smiled involuntarily. Monday night was movie night and I'd just got home from my cocktail class with *Solaris* under my arm.

"Dude! What's up?"

"I'll tell you what's up – Rick nearly was! He just tried to rape me!"

I dropped *Solaris*.

"What?"

"I'm not joking! It was the most scary thing that's ever happened to me in my life except when I practically cut my toe off with the garden hoe when I was 13 and had to have it sewn back on, but even that was interesting because there wasn't much pain till afterwards and then they gave me some good drugs, but this was just plain bloody terrifying! And I'm calling you, old man, to apologise, because frankly I've thought all these years you were being a bit of a princess, having blackouts all over the place years after, just because I'd given you a smacker when we were both pissed anyway, but my Christ, I totally get it now, and I have to say I am sorry, old man, I really am!"

I was too stunned to speak even when he paused for breath.

"Jake! Are you there?"

"Yeah, yeah, sure I'm here. Jeeze man, that is bad. Are you okay?"

"No! I told you, the bastard tried to rape me! We were in this club called Duro, entertaining Corey bloody Rosenberg, and Rick rammed me up against the wall in a dark corner of the men's room and said Rosenberg's got the hots for you..."

"What!"

"...and I was to let him have you to sweeten this big deal Corey and Gordon are working on..."

"You didn't say yes, did you?"

"Of course I bloody didn't! But that pissed Rick off, and he started trying to get to work on me, and I tell you, old man, if Tai and

Chi hadn't come and got him off me, I'd have been done for. He is *strong*. He'd got his tongue all over my face and his hands inside my trousers and as for him – well, I always thought a boner was a good thing, but the thought of getting his rammed up me... Ugh, God, I'm still shaking."

"Hey, hey, calm down. Seriously, are you okay?"

"I'll be fine. Just shook me up."

"Have you told Chloe?"

"Are you mad? It's 2am here and she was scared of Rick to start with – the last thing she wants to hear is that now I am too!"

"But she should know."

"What for? There's no need. And don't you tell her, either. I don't want her scared, or giving me any sympathy bollocks. It happened, it could've been worse, it's over."

"How about at work?"

"Oh, carry on as if nothing happened. I don't run into Rick much as it is, and Gordon says he's going to be the point man on this big project, so hopefully he'll drop out of sight for a while. And I am going to stick like a plaster to Tai and Chi – no more cracks about men's buttocks from me. Oh God, cracks and buttocks... Ugh. Well, listen old man, don't tell a soul, and thanks for listening, it's really helped actually. Film night for you, isn't it? What have you got lined up?"

"*Solaris*."

"Which one? Not the Clooney's buttocks one? Oh hell, there I go again. I need another whisky. Enjoy. Talk tomorrow. 'Bye."

I said goodbye faintly and sat down, realizing that I'd been standing stiff as a surf board in the middle of the room all through the call.

* * *

"When are you going to tell him about me?"

Sra JJ stubbed out her cigarette in the thick white ashtray on the table, blew out smoke with a quick, decisive moue of contempt and said,

"Never."

The man smiled faintly.

Neither of them was known in Alicante, yet they both glanced this way and that from time to time, watchful.

The bright morning sunshine cut round a corner of the tall apartment blocks sitting elegantly back from the seafront, and across one side of the cheap metal table between them.

"'Never' lasts too long," said the man, offering her another cigarette.

Crossly, she took it. He lit it for her. He was a handsome man, strongly built, with the clearly defined features of the Basques.

"One day you'll have to tell him," he said, with his handsome head held back and his eyes closed as if inviting the air's caress. He ran a hand through his thick, silvered hair and Sra JJ watched, her expressive hands still for once, the smoke from her cigarette curling up into a suddenly anguished face.

He opened his eyes and caught her look. He smiled.

"Don't tell me 'never' Rosario," he said softly. "Never lasts too long."

* * *

This was the hero part, the adrenalin rush, the danger slot.

Right here, right now.

All the paperwork was easy – too easy for a man of his intelligence. True, only a handful of people could do what he could, but he couldn't venerate himself for what came so easily. What made him truly unique was his ability to play the numbers with such elegance – conjure up sparkling illusions to cast over drab corruption – and at the same time, be here, the means at his fingertips to lay waste the land before him and... the resolution to do just that.

Crouched in the arid beige landscape, dry grasses caressing his shoulders, he gazed out and across to the sea.

So much water, yet no salvation.

The fire trembled inside him.

Rosario... so contemptuous, so beautiful, so... *tied* to that tedious shrink.

"But I will set us both free," he crooned. "My beauty, my desire, delight of my eyes, companion of my endeavours – I am potent, I will set us both free... thus!"

His fingertips struck together on the thought, a small flame leapt into being at his bidding, the distant waters of the sea helpless witness.

Laughing softly, he drove away from the scene, unseen.

* * *

Sickened and sad, Carmen switched off the TV.

The fires, devouring land around Calpe. Small creatures running and burning, an ecosystem tortured.

Land of her childhood.

Land of sun and serenity, laughter and change.

To see it in flames hurt her physically.

Land of alegría.

Land of heat, a day of summer dust, a searing kiss...

A man who couldn't remember her name.

And she couldn't forget his kiss.

* * *

It had to be the hottest summer ever in New York. A heavy, damp blanket. Just sighing over it was too much effort.

Was I getting old? I missed the sea. Coney Island visits helped, but I kept thinking of that morning with Sra JJ at Manolo's all those years ago. The dusty dry heat. A red beast throbbing down through the hills, kicking up a dry dust, coming for... me.

Benido-m.

Benidoom?

"Here you go, son." My dad pressed a fresh, cold beer into my hand.

We were sitting on the deck above his garage, shaded by an old tarpaulin slung over metal poles. Mom was over at Hannah's. Dad looked older this year. I wondered if I did too. It had been a busy month at work. I'd helped Theo secure a contract for a new boutique hotel in Albany, upstate New York, and I'd enjoyed going up there to meet with the clients. It was an elegant town, a little old-fashioned, as Jules would say. That meant I could be out on my own without too much fear, and it was relaxing. Recently I'd felt obliged to go out with work colleagues in NYC to some hip bars and it just felt weird – I got tired of being always on the defensive.

"Next time you're in London, we're going to take you to the het cinema," Jules had promised me the night before, when he'd rung. "These places still exist, old man – they went through a really bad time; this one was closed down for a while after a het was nearly beaten to death there, but it's all okay now and nobody looks twice at you if you snog your girl – it is really out there. No police raids, no hassle. You know, old man, I really believe that the pendulum will swing in our lifetime and hets will be able to go everywhere and get on in life, get the great jobs, triumph in business and all that. I believe it. That cinema is always sold out, and you have to book now for that little het bistro I told you about where I take Chloe most Friday nights. Some of the punters now are gays coming to show how cool they are by 'accepting' us, it's actually getting a bit dangerous – wouldn't want any of my bank lot showing up there. But it's the trend. Hang on in there! Pecker up!"

I smiled just remembering the vitality in his voice.

"Something bothering you, son?"

I looked up quickly. My dad had taken me by surprise.

"No! Why do you ask?"

He flexed his fingers and forearms in a gesture I'd known since childhood, easing his muscles after a day spent in, under, around motors.

"Hm. Is Carmen coming over this year?"

I gave him look for look.

"Dad, it's July. I'm going over to Europe in September with Theo – remember? It wouldn't make sense. And she's busy."

I hate it when my dad looks at me with that certain look.

For a while, neither of us spoke. The tarpaulin, exhausted, it seemed, by the heavy heat, settled slightly and the metal poles groaned.

"I'm busy too," I said at length. "And I love my work, you know that."

He just looked.

"I don't think you know what it's like now, Dad." My throat felt heavy and closed, the words unnatural. "It's not like when you were young."

He just looked.

"I love my work and I need to be... I need... To stay, to get on, where I am, where I love... I need to, well, I need to play a certain game, Dad. I need to stay in with a certain set."

He half-nodded. Looked away from me. After another few minutes, he stood, his hand cleaving through the heavy air and coming to rest on my shoulder, strong. Strong, unbelievably heavy.

"Excuses, son," he said from above. "That's all excuses."

CHAPTER NINE
The right sort of beard

Dr JJ adjusted the dish of sweetmeats on the table in his consulting room and surveyed himself in the mirror, not without satisfaction.

"Bloody struggle," he muttered, thinking how long it had taken him to don the special garment tonight. But it was worth it. He always put it on the evening before his sessions with Mayor Ruiz, getting inside the skin of his patient, understanding more each time he took on the alien personality.

"You're beautiful," he crooned now to his reflection. "A handsome, handsome man. It's all going to be all right."

But tonight it had been a bloody struggle to don all this gear. Because it was hot. Hot, hot, hot.

"I desire you," he whispered. I don't know why, but you are irresistible to me." His gaze was fixed on the mirror.

He watched himself lower his hand.

"I wonder," he said aloud. "I wonder if he can open up to me yet."

* * *

"My, it certainly is hot this year," said Theo's voice above my head.

I almost jumped and lost the thread. I'd been deep in concentration, hearing again Carmen's voice last night on the 'phone while working on a trim for bespoke drapes.

Fires were ravaging Spain, including areas close to where she'd grown up, she'd said. Her friend Roberto over at Greenpeace had said they were sure to have been set deliberately.

She was upset. I could understand that, and said so.

It wasn't the first time she'd mentioned this guy Roberto. A couple of months back, he'd called her to say that there was some plan to build a huge casino somewhere in Europe – it was going to be called Eurovegas. He didn't like the environmental implications, was trying to find out more. Different countries were bidding for it – lots of jobs and money involved.

"Why did he call you to tell you?" I'd asked, but for some reasons didn't say I already knew about the project.

She'd giggled and said,

"What's it to you?"

I hadn't answered, I realized now. Why not? Carmen told me last night she was looking into it 'with Roberto'. Her fierce conviction that they could find and tackle bad things had struck me. She was so... straight.

"Nobody guides such a straight course as Jake," Theo said now, his hand light yet firm on my shoulder.

I turned to look up at him and saw he was with Mila.

"Mila!"

"Hi Jake," she smiled. "Don't let me interrupt."

Theo squeezed my shoulder slightly.

"Come into the office when you can. We've got some news. No rush. Raw silk has its own challenges," he told Mila. "But Jake has always had a sensitive touch – he understands just how much a fabric will withstand. As if by instinct." He gave me one of his quiet smiles. "As if by magic. It is a remarkable gift. He saves me a fortune in fabrics – I always used to have to buy much more extra to allow for spoilage. But not with Jake. Come when you can."

His hand was lifted, they drifted off. I was left to ponder how to achieve the perfect course at my fingertips, how not to ruin the fabric of my life.

"It's only a bit of bloody cloth!" Jules bellowed.

"Dude, it is $400-a-meter cloth, only available from one source."

"Oh right. Fair enough, then. Who's it for, Rockefeller?"

"Someone along those lines," I said. "You know I can't name names. Private client. Drapes for the master bedroom in the new mansion – he's getting married. We're embroidering in Swarovski crystal chips by hand – only Juanita or Rosa can do that really, but I'm getting the main stitching done and then I can watch them do the insets and practise on any remnants. It's kinda tricky because..."

"Yeah, yeah, I get the picture, old man! Listen, you can tell me all about it soon – I'm over for a two-day visit next week. You around?"

"Oh cool! You bet I am."

"Excellent! Right, gotta run."

"Wait! You haven't heard the news – Theo and Mila have signed contracts with Corey Rosenberg for this big new project in Europe. Eurovegas."

"They have? That's great! We'll be practically working together, old man! Gordon's got some strange PR role lined up for me on the same gig. Any clues where it is?"

"Not yet. Theo says Corey's playing his cards close to his chest as always."

"Ha! Same as Gordon. You know about the competition, don't you?"

"About France and Germany and the whole of Europe bidding for Eurovegas? Yeah, it's been in the news over here too."

"Well, time will tell. Right, I'd..."

"Hang on!"

"Now what?"

"Do you know a guy called Roberto? Works at Greenpeace in Spain. Madrid."

"Nope. Never heard of the guy. Not exactly our clients, Greenpeace. Why?"

"Oh, Carmen mentioned him."

"Really? Don't like the sound of that, old man. These Greenpeace blokes can pull – they're either buff young activists swarming all over oil rigs or legal eagles with conviction and piles of cash and the right kind of beard. Sooner you get your skinny surfer's ass over here the better."

"Thanks," I said a bit dully.

"Yeah, well, gotta go now. Really. Good luck with Flashboy's curtains. Ta-ra."

I sat and stared at the chair opposite for a while after hanging up.

Over in Madrid, Roberto and Carmen conferred over a coffee at a bar somewhere between their two offices, a map of Spain spread out awkwardly against the bar counter.

"Look!" Roberto exclaimed, jabbing at the map. "This is where the main fires have struck so far this summer. Here, here, here and over here. And this part to a lesser extent."

Carmen gazed at his profile admiringly. His conviction excited her. His clear signals of heterosexuality excited her. He had a beard, but it was the right sort – neat, not straggly with things nesting in it. She longed to touch it.

"I've ordered up independent reports into fire patterns and arson convictions for the past three years across the whole country," he was saying now. "I'm *sure* there's a connection between some of the fires and this damn' Eurovegas. I *bet* you this Rosenberg shit is going to locate it in Spain!"

Alight with fervour, his eyes turned to Carmen.

"We'll catch them out," he told her, covering her hand with his for one scorching moment. "If we can just get more evidence, so that when they announce the location of Eurovegas in August... We can do it! If only we had better information on Rosenberg. More inside stuff."

Gazing into his blazing eyes, Carmen heard herself say,

"I might be able to help with that."

Roberto's eyes widened in delighted surprise.

"You might? That would be terrific!" He glanced at his wristwatch and Carmen quivered – gay men used 'phones, not watches. "I have to get back."

"Yes, of course, me too." She stood up and slung her bag over her shoulder, glancing out at the stark sunny street.

Roberto put down some coins, called goodbye to the barman, and ushered her to the door, his arm almost around her.

"God, this has to be one of the hottest summers ever," he said, as they stepped outside. "It's been good, listen, call me if you get anything new."

"Yes, of course. You too."

"Yes, yes, oh! Are you free on Saturday night? My cousin's having a birthday party. Up in the mountains in Miraflores. I can drive us up if you're free – Mum can lend us her car."

"That sounds nice. Can I let you know later today?"

"Sure, sure." He leapt down the Metro steps and was gone.

Carmen stood gently quivering in the heat haze for a moment or two before heading back to her nearby office, fired by a new zeal.

* * *

"She rang me!" I told Jules excitedly. "This time, *she* rang *me*! I had no idea, we hadn't arranged to call. We normally speak at the weekends and it's Wednesday and *she* rang *me*!"

There was a slight pause and I was pleased – it wasn't easy to strike Jules dumb.

"What did she want?" he said, then.

"Nothing! What do you mean, what did she want? She wanted to talk to me!"

"That's all?"

"Of course!"

"And it's the first time she's called you at an unscheduled time?"

"Unscheduled! You're making it sound like the subway! But yes, unscheduled. First time."

"Hm. What did you talk about?"

"Work, mainly."

"Hm. What did she want?"

"Jules!"

"Think, old man. Carmen is Spanish, she is pragmatic. I'm serious. Think. What did she ask you about?"

"Work – I told you. She asked what I'm working on now."

"Flashboy's curtains?"

"Yes."

"And?"

"Nothing! Well, we talked about other stuff, like the Eurovegas project. She said Roberto – the dude from Greenpeace – has a theory that it's going to be located in Spain and he's trying to prove it by the pattern of rural fires across Spain because that's how unscrupulous developers clear land and..."

"And?" prompted Jules.

"And so she just asked if I knew anything about Corey Rosenberg."

Now we were both quiet.

Finally, Jules sighed and said,

"What did you tell her? No, don't bother. I already know. Everything. You told her everything you know and don't know or could come up with at that moment because you're besotted with a memory. You didn't tell her about the financial side, or that you know Corey personally, I hope?"

"Dude!" I reproached him, hot and confused. "No way! It's just for her work – I just talked about his place in Vegas that Millards worked on, nothing else. Nothing recent."

"You're going to lose her, Jake," Jules said.

"We talk every weekend."

"Yeah, yeah, and you Skype too. But a touch screen is not the same as touch without a screen, old man, and you are letting her go, you wet rag! What is this Roberto – buff activist type? Big shoulders, firm thighs, cock all primed and ready to fire?"

I took the 'phone away from my ear and stared at it with intense hatred but he was yelling now and I could still hear him.

"You should be pumping her for pleasure, old man, not having her pump you for information! What have you been playing at, messing around all these years? The girl needs cock!"

"Shut up! You're the one living a lie! You wouldn't know romance if it... *spat* at you!"

"Spat at me? Yeah, right. Listen, I may be living a lie, but I'm playing the game right and Chloe has her own business in London and we're both doing well and she gets cock every Friday night!"

"Oh, scheduled or unscheduled?" I sniped.

There was a slight pause before he said,

"Which night do you normally speak to Carmen – Saturday, isn't it?"

"Yeah."

"Bet you she's not available this Saturday."

Another huge pause – she'd already asked if we could speak on Sunday instead, without even explaining why, now I came to think of it.

He heard my silence.

"You're in trouble, old man," he said quietly. "You've got to grow a pair."

"Fuck off," I said sullenly. I don't know who put the 'phone down first.

Jules caught the Tube as little as he could. He could walk to work and the bank paid for cabs for pretty much everything else he needed to do.

Now, jammed onto the Underground on his way to see Chloe two days after talking to Jake, Jake's phrase 'living a lie' kept coming into his mind and he couldn't push it away.

Glancing round, he could see at least three other men shooting him meaningful glances. The train was busier than usual because of 'person under train' earlier, a nasal voice had announced. What kind of person? Jules wondered suddenly. Young or old, ambitious or plodding, ugly or good-looking, male or female? All we know is 'person'. Probably some poor desperate het who couldn't get a decent job or have a decent night out with his girl, Jules thought savagely.

"Yes, I'm living a lie," he said to himself, turning slightly as batches of passengers surged off and on the train, eliminating two lots of suggestive glances but gaining a new one. "But at least I'm getting on, I live in the right place, like what I do, play the game. Chloe's all right. We're together. We *are*."

And life in the 'hettos' – as the areas beyond Zone 2 had become known – had its appeal. The worst of the jam had thinned out by the time he emerged onto the platform at Turnham Green and breathed in deeply, glad to be able to move his limbs freely again.

"Living a lie," he muttered under his breath, bounding up the escalator and along to Chloe's house with almost angrily swift strides. "Living a bloody lie! At least I'm living, surf-boy! All fabric and no filling, his bloody life!"

By the time he got to Chloe's he'd muttered himself back to good humour and took her in his arms with more than usual enthusiasm.

"Wow!" she exclaimed. "Good to see you too!"

Jules flung down his briefcase and slipped off his blazer-style jacket – all the rage this season. Chloe hung it up while he kicked off his shoes and sniffed appreciatively.

"Smells good – I take it we're eating in this evening?"

"Yep. Got home a bit early and felt like cooking. But you get to take me out later for a celebratory drink."

He followed her into the kitchen, where the door was open to the garden and the table outside was simply set for two. He breathed a deep sigh of satisfaction and said,

"What's the occasion?"

With a huge smile, Chloe whipped a bottle of champagne out of the fridge and handed it to him to open while she turned to get glasses.

"You are not going to believe me, and I can hardly believe it myself, but T. Rantula came into the shop today!"

Jules stopped de-foiling the bottle and stared.

"You are joking! T. Rantula herself? I thought these designer divas always sent a flunky."

"So did I! But she came in and asked for me and she was really nice! Turns out she saw that magazine article in Phanie and her dad lives just behind Harrods, so she popped into my shop after going to see him for lunch and wanted to see everything I had and she stayed for nearly an hour asking tons of questions, and Jules – she wants me to do all the headgear for her winter collection in Paris next year!"

Jules popped the cork and grabbed her in a champagne-drizzled embrace, kissing her laughing face.

"It's true, it's true! I signed the contract later – I hope it's okay but honestly Jules, even if I lose money on the show, I couldn't *buy* the kind of advertising this will bring me. Can you *imagine*? T. Rantula's clientele! All the pop stars go to her shows, she does one-off creations for their videos and stuff, some of it gets auctioned off for charity later... It could be my big break!"

"Gimme the contract, I'll get our boys to take a look anyway. Living a lie, my arse!"

"What?"

"Nothing. Cheers, gorgeous, here's to Chloe's!"

* * *

Most Saturday nights I was either over with family or out with friends after a day spent swimming, surfing, hanging out at the gym. Because Carmen was five or six hours ahead, I'd call her when I got in from working out before heading off for beer and pizza with friends. I almost never went into Manhattan, but this weekend I decided to head down to the Village and see how things stood.

There's always a ton of stuff going on, so I booked a ticket to see some band at the Bowery and filled in the time till it started by taking a look in at a poetry reading on Bleecker St. It was a good vibe. Yeah, it was pretty aggressively gay, but I had a couple of beers and thought about the trip to Europe with Theo – only six weeks away now – and just loosened up. It was kinda nice just to listen to the poetry – some of it crap, some of it enjoyable – and feel the beer glass cool in my hand. Cool to the touch.

Touch.

Carmen's fingers, touching my face, when I kissed her that time in the car. Dr JJ's red beast.

"You look like a happy man," a voice interrupted my thoughts. I glanced round, prepared to act defensive, but somehow it didn't seem necessary. He was mid-forties, I'd say, with a deeply creased yet good-looking face, and thick careless hair going on above it.

"Hey. Yeah, it's all good," I responded. "Enjoying the poetry?"

It was a break, we weren't talking across anyone's poetic offering. He shrugged.

"Too gay for me," he said, and laughed at my consternation. "Oh don't worry, you won't get into trouble being seen with me. I'm Vincent, one of the Village's more flamboyant hets, and proud of it."

He held out his hand and I shook it.

"Jake."

"Are you enjoying it, Jake?"

"You know, I don't get out much, I don't have a lot to compare it against, but yes, I'm enjoying myself tonight."

"Got a girl? Got a guy?"

"Just enjoying myself, Vincent," I smiled, and he laughed.

"Cool, that's cool. Oh, they're starting up again. Get you a beer for part two?"

"Sure, thanks."

"It was interesting," I told Jules next time we spoke. He rang on Sunday to tell me Chloe had good news with her business. Neither of us referred to the last call.

"What, you get chatting to some washed-up old het at a poetry reading on a Saturday night in Manhattan? Christ!"

"He's not washed-up. He used to be in advertising, in with the top agencies, did really well for himself. Sounds like he had a blast, too. He said that when it all went a certain way, with the Change, and he was expected to play the game to keep his job, he jacked in his job and went solo."

"Yeah, yeah, what's he living off now? His old lady? His dad?"

His cynicism annoyed me.

"No, dude! He's got a thriving business, he does *only* het advertising and he's carved a great niche for himself. Says the lavender mafia – his words not mine – leave him in peace because he knows half of them anyway from before the Change, and it's good for them to be seen to accept a straight agency."

Jules was all attention now.

"Oh, I get it! Tokenism! Yes, that is really smart. Did you get his card?"

"Of course."

"And did you tell him you're in embroidery?"

I laughed.

"Oh, he's heard of Millards, believe me. He was impressed. It was fun."

"So Carmen had better watch out? You showed her what Saturday night's all about if she blows you off, didn't you? Listen, get off the line and give her a call. Bang on about your trip and tell her you can't wait to see her – not just *see* her. Lay it on thick, elbow this Roberto character out of the picture. Ta-ra!"

* * *

"At least it's a chance for a bit of a knees-up," commented UK.

Representatives from all the EU countries were rolling up at the Majestique in Brussels for the ceremony to announce which country was to become the home of Corey Rosenberg's billion-dollar project Eurovegas. Competition had been hot, with emerging economies particularly keen to get a slice of the juicy new pie.

"It's so vulgar," muttered France, sulky but elegant on the red carpet.

"Rosenberg's paying," Germany said calmly.

The much-publicised event was taking place at a hotel part-owned by Rosenberg, and he'd sent Earl's troupe over to lay on part of the show for the hundreds of delegates.

Croatia threw up from over-excitement. Germany tutted wearily but perked up when the excellent canapés started circulating.

And finally, the bright-lights moment arrived. A fanfare of music, a well of anticipatory silence, and then the proclamation.

"Eurovegas will be built in... Spain!"

The packed ballroom erupted into cheers – largely orchestrated, it has to be said, to drown out the boos and cries of disappointment from disgruntled rivals.

"Wow," said Jules later, catching a fragment on the news. "Must give Jake a bell and let him know."

"Torres popped up on videolink and congratulated his fellow architect 'bidders' – bet you half of them have been handed a nice little douceur to whack in a back-of-fag-packet design to up the prestige value of the competition – from other countries and banged on about how thrilled he is to be doing another major project for his motherland and all that. Usual guff. So, Spain! Looks like we'll all be working together soon."

"Where in Spain is it going to be?" I asked, pondering a dash of chilli for the cocktail I was struggling to invent. I could barely think for the heat.

"They haven't said yet. Give it a couple of weeks for Spain to get in a tizz and all the regions get hot under the collar saying they've got to have it because, because, because... Of course it's all been arranged, they're just spinning it out for the publicity value. So, how are things with you, old man? Have you got Carmen's interest back yet? Is she shagging Roberto?"

"That is so insensitive, dude," I murmured, not too put out. Despite myself, I was smiling, he must have heard.

"God, you are too laidback to get laid!" he said. "I'm beginning to think that boner in your shorts all those years ago was some kind of mechanical device. You do get some action, don't you? Not a 29-year-old virgin?"

"Hey, if Carmen would rather be with someone else, I have to accept it," I laughed.

"Don't you *care*?" he cried. "Seriously, don't you care? Can't you make some effort for what you want or are you too busy sewing on buttons for spoilt trust fund kids?"

Annoyed now, I said,

"Yes, I care, and yes I can make an effort, but I'll be in Europe in a few weeks anyway and there's no point hassling her."

"You've snipped off your manhood and stitched it into another bloke's bloody over-priced curtains!" he yelled.

"And I do not sew on buttons – we used crystal chips that..."

"That's right! They won't even let you sew on a button, will they? Christ Almighty!"

I'm pretty sure it was him who slammed the 'phone down first that time, but my hand was moving fast too. I knocked back the cocktail I'd been messing about with in one go. It tasted pretty good to me even without chilli.

* * *

"How bloody awful," said Dr JJ, padding across the tiled living-room at the Calpe villa to refill his wife's glass. He jerked his head towards the TV, which was full of Eurovegas and whereabouts in Spain it was most likely to be located. "All this endless debate about a bloody casino."

Sra JJ looked mildly surprised.

"What's so bad about it?" she said. "The Spaniards love to gamble, we've got tons of huge dusty open spaces doing nothing right across the country, I think it's great. Boost for the economy, all that construction. And we're great at tourism and catering."

Dr JJ relaxed his rangy body on one of their long sun loungers lined with bright cushions and gazed out across the terrace.

"Why are you so negative?" continued his wife. "It'll keep people away from the beaches on long weekends – I thought you'd like that."

He grinned at her suddenly.

"You're right, I hadn't thought of it like that."

"You Brits!" she sighed. "Always moaning about something."

He leaned over to slap her leg and she moved away, laughing.

"I spend all day listening to you Spaniards moaning, that's what does it!" he retorted.

"Well, it's your job and you wanted it," she said, picking up her ringing 'phone and going into the kitchen with it.

* * *

Corey Rosenberg cast a complacent glance over the financial screens, noting the uptick in Spain's stock since the Eurovegas news broke, particularly in the construction sector. His office had been inundated with bids from all manner of contractors, including interior design and furnishing companies. He'd told his people to ignore those.

"We've got the best, the contracts are signed, the companies involved are American and the Spaniards will just have to suck it up," he'd told the elite team. "We'll be bringing local Spanish companies in for all the sub-contracting work they can handle. But with Mila and Millards on board for the interiors, I'm not going to waste a nano-second considering two-bit mom'n'pop shops over there. And I don't want any of you doing it, either. Understood?"

Hecklow smiled when the email from Rosenberg pinged across his screen.

"Vamonos!" it said.

Gordon loosened his tie slightly and took a moment to glance out across the City through his huge windows.

Inside, it was deliciously cool, a suitable environment for making well-considered decisions, examining the risks and figures with a cool head, literally.

Outside, "it has to be the hottest summer ever," he murmured before turning back to his deceptively clear desk.

He was glad he wasn't an ordinary person.

Back in the den, Juan Antonio Ruiz bulged forward to top up Torres's glass. Both men were sweating. Torres wiped his brow with a large lemon handkerchief and wondered for the umpteenth time why Ruiz refused to get air-conditioning installed. Just too damn' old-fashioned. Smug in his own embodiment of avant-garde – his Manhattan skyscraper had changed the game with its energy-saving, architectural cooling method – Torres shrugged off the mayor's shortcomings and reached for his glass.

"Press?" he said curtly.

Ruiz waved a hand and opened his mouth to expound. Torres tried not to frown or glance at his watch. He wanted to get home. His wife would be there, but that was off-set by their state-of-the-art air-conditioning. And it was a big house – they didn't have to meet. He tuned back in and cut ruthlessly across Ruiz's babble.

"Sure, I can be there. Are you sure you have all the media onside?"

Ruiz looked offended.

"Who wouldn't come to a dinner of this type, with the unmatchable architect Torres, on the world-famous fashion designer Fornelli's yacht, with secrets to be shared only with them?"

"All of them? And what about Greenpeace?"

Now Ruiz laughed out loud. He really is unbelievably fat, Torres thought as the mayor's bulk wobbled before him.

"Greenpeace! Who listens to them? They have five members. No, no, my friend, no self-respecting journalist would be listening to Greenpeace when they could be dining with you! And then, when the crazy ecologists *do* get wind of the specifics of the Eurovegas project, all the contracts will be in place, the government committed... There is no going back. They may squawk here and there, but what of it? This is summer, this is Spain! The eco-mice may squeak, but nobody of influence will hear."

Torres nodded – he too knew how these things worked, and Ruiz was a wily old fox with plenty of experience.

"Fine," he said in the clipped voice that had found architectural expression in the sharp edges for which he was renowned and revered the world over. "I'll be there. But it has to be next week: I'm in Japan the week after. Make it Wednesday."

"Not Wednesday," countered Ruiz, and Torres glanced round at him, surprised at the hint of dissent.

Ruiz gestured broadly and beamed to rob his words of offence.

"Wednesday is impossible, my friend. Thursday. Hm? Good, excellent!" He offered no further explanation, just more broad beams as he ushered Torres towards the door.

How, after all, could he explain why Wednesday was impossible? He couldn't possibly reveal the delicious secret of his clandestine visits to Dr JJ. He'd taken to booking double sessions. The doctor had suggested it, and Mayor Ruiz found it all incredibly relaxing. Dr JJ had given him a kimono to wear, and although he'd thought it an odd notion, he'd tried it on and liked it. It was cool and comfortable and he could just lie back in its crisp embrace, reminiscing about his childhood or simply discussing the weather, until he drifted off into sleep on the waves of gently moving air and the doctor's understanding murmurs.

Ruiz sighed as he closed the door on Torres – he would miss the kimono sessions. They would end so soon, with the advent of the contracts and the diggers. Next Wednesday, in fact, would probably be the last. Dr JJ would have served his purpose in the grand scheme. But even so... picking up his glass, Ruiz reached for more tapas and suddenly realised he'd left the anchovies and crisps that Alfonso liked so much in the pantry.

CHAPTER TEN
The kimono sessions

"Why do you keep calling me?" hissed Sra JJ.

He just laughed and said,

"Usual place, Rosario. I'll be there at 5pm. Come, there's no harm."

He hung up, leaving her glaring at the empty 'phone until it suddenly rang again, making her jump.

It was her husband, to say he'd be late home this evening because he had his double session with Mayor Ruiz until 9pm.

"No worries, darling," she said at once. "I'll come up from Calpe and we can stay in Valencia tonight. I can nip over and see Papa first."

"Great, great," he said. That meant he didn't have to go and see 'Papa' too.

"I'll probably come via Alicante," his wife was saying. "There's a new furniture store I want to browse around."

Dr JJ smiled.

"Sounds good," he said. "Have fun."

"See you later." She hung up, staring a little doubtfully at the 'phone for a moment or two.

Then, with her characteristic surety, she shrugged and went to check the villa's kitchen and bedrooms to make sure she hadn't forgotten anything ahead of Jules' and Chloe's visit. Jake would be coming over too. She smiled as she went into the room he'd had almost a decade ago. Skinny guy, nice manners, that strange, intermittent memory loss... She plumped the cushions and wondered if he'd changed much. It would be fun to see him again and have a full house. She glanced at her watch. Time to set off.

* * *

Alicante flowed past them, apparently unheeding. Across the busy, tree-lined boulevard, beyond the lanes of traffic, yachts gleamed and swayed in the harbour. The entire sky was azure blue.

Rosario's brown eyes were fixed on his face, their expression troubled and pleading.

"I can't accept this," she said. "It's too much."

"Do you like it?"

The delicate necklace winked up at her, caressing her fingertips.

"It's beautiful," she said, and he knew she meant it. "But I can't accept it. You know I can't. What would my husband say?"

He reached across and took her hand, closing her fingers around the trinket.

"Your husband will fight to keep you, Rosario," he said. "Any man would."

Hands clasped, they looked deep into each other's eyes and a couple of teenagers from cooler climes turned their heads as they passed, struck by the intensity of that moment.

Dr JJ checked his outer office to make sure the receptionist had gone home. She had. All was quiet. He nodded in quick satisfaction and went to his main room to make all ready for Mayor Ruiz's double session.

"It's worth the struggle, it's all worth it," he assured himself, moving about the room. "Too much denial, too much fight. Tonight we must make progress. This man needs help. I must do this, only I can help him."

The doorbell rang and he caught his breath, nervous despite his conviction.

Coming up in the lift, Mayor Ruiz slicked back his hair and smirked at his dim reflection. Everything was on schedule, it was all coming together according to his plans and in his interests. He intended to enjoy this final relaxation session with the doctor he'd be throwing to the wolves within hours.

Dr JJ opened the door upstairs and Ruiz stepped out of the lift with his arms extended in bonhomie, a huge beam pinned to his satisfied face.

"Good evening!" both men cried, neither showing his sense that this session was crucial. Both canny, they each sensed a heightened awareness in the other, but any tension was glossed over as Dr JJ flung the door open wide and Ruiz boldly crossed the threshold.

Aware that she was responding to his intensity, Rosario tried to withdraw her hand from his, but he wouldn't let her.

"Rosario, when are you going to end this farce with the good doctor?" he said. "You know, when I arrived here at the bar today, the barman told me my wife had arrived and was in the Ladies."

"Oh God," murmured Rosario. "We shouldn't have come back to the same place."

"Do you know how that made me feel, Rosario? When he recognised you as my wife? Hm? Like a king! Like the king of the entire world!"

"Alfonso, you have to stop," she said gently. "These are pretty words, but I know about you and your women – everyone does."

"No!" he cried, startling her with his vehemence. "No. That is all done and gone. I used to think it was fun, but I want more than fun, Rosario. I want *you*."

His words clung to the hot, heavy air around them. Rosario felt paralysed.

"Let's end this farce now," he urged, leaning even closer, stroking back her hair with his other hand. "It's time. You need to be with me. We have to go away together. Calpe is over, it's done. Come away with me, Rosario. I have all the money we'll ever need."

His hand was oppressive on hers now, but still she couldn't pull free.

"What do you mean, go away? And what is this about Calpe? Why is it 'over'?"

He sighed and sat back slightly, but still held her hand with the necklace still in it. His gaze wandered out over the patterned paving of the boulevard, through its palm trees and traffic and across to the gleaming, swaying yachts in the harbour. Torres had one, he knew. There'd been a party on it one summer... A young woman – well, many young women, but one who'd gone down on her knees to service him in a glitzy bathroom. He remembered the gloss of the wooden trim over her head... He couldn't remember now what he'd done or was meant to do in return. But he remembered the beautiful wood trim inside that luxurious yacht.

Past. All past. His future would be better. Like that film, *Back To The Future*. He could make things right. He felt a pressure on his fingers and turned his burning gaze back to Rosario.

"Have you heard of Eurovegas?" he asked, finally.

"Of course." Unrecognised fear rose within her.

"They're building it here, in Calpe. Mega hotels, casino, the lot."

"What? Here? But where? And how do you know?"

There was a pause.

"I just do," he said.

Now she could withdraw her hand from his slackened grasp. He shifted under her disillusioned gaze.

"Alfonso, what have you done? You've known this for a long time, haven't you? Why now? Why tell me now?"

"The Salinas," he said quietly.

She stared.

"They're going to drain the Salinas. That part, I just found out."

The chatter and clatter and traffic noise receded as Rosario struggled to take it in. Alfonso watched, relieved in a way that someone else knew. And now, surely, she would see more clearly what was the past, what was the future. She was staring into the distance, across to the marina, eyes unseeing.

"But they can't," she whispered. "It's where we had our first kiss."

He was glad that she was looking into the distance because he certainly didn't remember that. But he wasn't the man to pass up an opportunity. He re-possessed her hand and said softly,

"Now do you understand? It won't be the same, ever again. We need to leave. Come away with me, my darling."

Her eyes turned back to him.

"Leave?" she said, her voice strong now. "What do you mean, leave? We have to *fight*. This can't happen. I need to think."

He stood as she did. Suddenly aware again of the necklace in her fingers, she said, "It is beautiful," and kissed him lightly, briefly, on his hungry lips. "Thank you."

Was that pity he'd tasted? he wondered as she walked quickly away, the necklace winking back at him from her slender brown fingers.

Dr JJ surveyed himself in the mirror of his tiny changing-room. It had taken 12 minutes of the mayor's snoring time to get the fat suit on, but the practice of the previous weeks had paid off. He was ready. And now, right on cue, a heavy thump and some snuffling from the main room indicated that Mayor Ruiz had fallen off the couch as usual.

Timing his entrance delicately, Dr JJ stepped back into the main room just as Ruiz had completed his struggle to stand up and was smoothing his kimono back into place.

He glanced up as the door opened, glimpsed the doctor, then did a double-take and gasped more loudly than the doctor had ever heard anyone gasp – it was almost a sob. Dr JJ was quite pleased. He advanced into the room and said,

"Hello. How are you feeling?"

As he'd advanced the few steps into the centre of the main room, the mayor had been slowly raising a disbelieving arm. The doctor stopped at the end of it, his chest almost touching Ruiz's outstretched fingers.

"How are you feeling?" he repeated, gazing sympathetically into the mayor's bulging eyes.

Ruiz gasped again, a strained, prolonged sound from deep in the lungs.

"What...?" he gurgled. "What the fuck... what the fuck are you *doing*?" His fingers wandered over the doctor's huge, unfamiliar form. "What is *that*?"

"This is the real me," answered Dr JJ, gently. "A fat person, like you. Obese, like you. We can do this together."

He grasped the mayor's arm as he spoke, swung him round to face the full-length mirror he'd occasionally used to great effect, though usually, he thought, for issues of anorexia or low self-esteem.

This time, the mirror could not contain the enormity of what it saw. Neither of them would have fitted, the doctor knew. Nonetheless, the effect was there. He could feel the mayor's laboured breathing, he could see the beads of sweat on his brow as the two kimono-clad creatures swelled before the mirror's gaze, bursting its boundaries, merging into one indeterminate balloon of fabric.

Ruiz was dumbstruck, sweating.

"It's time," Dr JJ said, in a firm yet gentle tone. "All these weeks, you've been so courageous, coming to see me about your obesity issue."

"What?" croaked Ruiz. "Obesity? What are you talking about? I'm a big man, an important man."

"Of course you are," crooned the doctor. "Of course you are. You are also fat. Obese. It's not a medical condition, it's something you have done to yourself and can therefore reverse yourself. You have the power! It's okay, I can help. Today we are taking a new step to help you come to terms with it, and start the healing process. Your courage has given me strength. First, we need to find the real you, uncover your real beauty."

He slipped the leash of his own kimono on the last words and it slid down over his shoulders and arms, away from his huge rubber torso.

"Aaaargghh!" shrieked the mayor, his eyes bulging into the mirror. "Aaaarggghhh! Aaaarrggghhh! What the fuck, what the fuck, oh my God!"

"It's okay, it's okay," soothed the doctor, who'd practised this so many times that his initial gut reaction – very similar to the mayor's, he noted with interest – had muted to calm. "Don't worry." He saw the mayor's gaze in the mirror slide to his nether regions and hastened to lift some of the rubber. "It's okay, I'm wearing boxer shorts – look."

"Aaaarrghhh!" shrilled Ruiz. "What the hell are you playing at, you pervert? What is *wrong* with you?!"

"You're having some denial," Dr JJ said. "It's natural. But I'm here for you, we can solve this together. If you could just open up and start to acknowledge why this began, why you lost control so completely, then we…"

He broke off, brought up short by the look in Ruiz's eyes, suddenly blazing and hard.

"Me, lose control?" hissed the mayor. "Let me tell you something, idiot, before I bring you down to where you belong. You don't even know what control means. You've never had any."

He glared menacingly into the mirror at the naked rubber healer. Dr JJ said nothing, just held that gaze.

The mayor stripped off his kimono and the doctor choked back an urge to scream himself. 'Get a grip,' he told himself. 'Study him, try to understand. Need to speed this up, though'.

"Perhaps your mother was fat?" he suggested. "Things unspoken in the family? Are you married? Perhaps your wife left when your penis was lost to sight? Look, whatever it is, we can tackle it together."

He was talking to the door of the changing-room. Within a very few minutes, the mayor emerged, fully dressed, a new menace in his bearing.

"I was looking forward to this session..." he snarled.

"Oh thanks!" said Dr JJ. "That's a really good sign."

"...because I knew it would be our last."

"Denial," said Dr JJ knowledgeably. "Hatred of the healer. That means you are so close to accepting the truth, the real beginning of ..."

"Shut up!" The mayor had picked up his briefcase and was by the main door now. "You, Dr JJ, you and your lovely wife, are finished. You hear me? Finished!"

For a moment, the two men stared at each other. Then Mayor Ruiz gave a small chuckle – not a pleasant sound.

"I'm going to bring you down," he said, putting his face very close to the doctor's. "You're finished."

Then he was gone.

Dr JJ closed the door and moved back a couple of steps, reaching with numb fingers for the zip at the back of the fat suit.

Inside it, he was sweating.

* * *

Jules' voice was crackling with excitement when he rang the Friday night before my flight to Europe.

"Thank God you're coming over, old man! There's all sorts going on. I thought we could have a couple of days in London but there's been a change of plan. I'll meet you at Heathrow first thing.

We need to get to Spain asap. Rosenberg's putting Eurovegas in Calpe! Hot off the press. More when I see you. 'Bye."

Earl managed a smile for Corey's senior executive assistant – she headed up a team of six personal assistants – as he passed her coming out of Corey's private rooms, but his heart wasn't really in it. She was a nice woman – all the EAs and PAs were – but Corey had been sexually demanding for the past few days, which was usually a sign he had big deals going on, and Earl was just tired and envious of the women because they didn't have to suck his cock or deal with his mood swings or stroke his ego.

Lucia's return smile was more genuine. Sure, the lavender mafia could be as misogynistic as the hets, but being able to work for a powerful man without him having any expectations on the side was a change for the better as far as she was concerned. All the women under her excellent supervision were ostensibly gay. In practice, Corey didn't care. The main thing was, they weren't regarded as part of the Rosenberg empire's attractions, so they were able to enjoy their jobs, status and substantial salaries without molestation.

Whereas Earl and his troupe... Lucia shook herself out of a moment's pity. They'd all had a choice and they'd made it. She smoothed her smart, understated dress, glanced at herself in a nearby mirror, and knocked on Rosenberg's door, stepping in a moment later to go through all the finalised travel plans and schedule for his imminent trip to Europe.

Eurovegas! She looked forward to the launch party. This job had great perks, too.

The news broke on the Friday after the plush yacht party for the media, making no great splash to start with, but creating ripples in some areas that fast gathered momentum over the ensuing hours.

"I *knew* it!" Roberto hissed between clenched teeth. "I was right about the fires. I knew it."

His colleagues came piling in through the door – Greenpeace's online platforms were on fire with the news.

"We need a plan," he said briskly, reaching for the 'phone with a muscular arm. "This can't happen. Get hold of Miguel, will you? And find out where Ester is. Media meeting at 11am. Carmen, hi! It's me, Roberto. Listen, we just heard Eurovegas is going to be in Calpe. Are you there? Great! I'll be coming down myself later today. See you soon!"

At the other end of the line, Carmen tingled with mingled excitement and horror. Roberto! Eurovegas! Calpe!

"Carmen, my love, there's some news on about Calpe and a big new building project by some American," called out her grandmother. Carmen was paying her usual late-summer visit to her grandparents at their flat up in Calpe's old town, perched high above the beaches.

"I know, I'll be right there!"

"Nice job, Lucia," Corey said approvingly. "All confirmed with Gordon Hecklow. Right, I'm heading off now, get in a bit of golf before the flight over to Europe."

Lucia nodded understandingly – golf was usually a euphemism for more business deals.

"I'll be on the move most of Wednesday so I've booked you and the other ladies of your team into the spa area of the Sans-Souci Palace Hotel for a full day. My treat."

Lucia exclaimed but Corey raised a silencing hand.

"I know you all worked hard. You've done a great liaison job on all the arrangements for Eurovegas and I appreciate your discretion as much as your efficiency. I'm looking forward to signing next week – something special about Europe, isn't there?"

He nodded dismissal and she left at once, with a smooth 'Thank you, sir', and the calm smile he had come to rely on.

Rosenberg glanced round the suite. He felt taut as a spring, clear-sighted, fired up. There *is* something about Europe, he thought. The US, Asia, sure, he had great projects and made a lot of money out of them, but this would be his first venture into the old continent.

"And the contract signing in London!" he said to his glowing, complacent reflection. "With Gordon Hecklow, no less."

He picked up the stingray travel folder Lucia had just been through with him and slipped it into his briefcase before closing the clasps with satisfying clicks.

Life is good, he thought smugly, and swung out of the door to the private elevator.

Theo had paid for my ticket over to London and I ran into my old friend Vincent, the Village's most flamboyant het, on the flight. We had a great time in the circular bar area in First Class, where he was sitting, while others slumbered their way across the Atlantic.

So I pretty much slept my way over to Alicante with Jules next morning, though I was conscious enough to get the inside skinny on the Eurovegas flap and have Jules shove a picture of Roberto in my face, which was just what I didn't need because I knew Carmen was staying with her grandparents in Calpe and I was really looking forward to seeing her. My dad's words about 'excuses' still stuck in my head; I knew he wasn't right, but...

"See all that brawn, old man?" Jules was saying shortly before I closed my eyes and ears. "Told you, ripped activist type. You'll have to do contrast. No offence, you look good, but it's a question of playing up the old skinny hips and beach-wide smile. And you can push your hair around, flick it and so on, which Roberto can't do. But don't flick it around too much or the girl might think you're being competitive and get cross."

He was still talking about it when he woke me just before landing.

To deflect his attention, I asked about Chloe and he said she'd left her kid brother in charge of the store and gone over to Calpe a couple of days earlier so as to get some sun while working on the T. Rantula collection.

"Don't know who hit the 'phone faster when the Eurovegas news broke," he said, "her or my mother. Quick draws, both of them. And you haven't heard the latest. I told you but I don't think you took it all in. No worries, Dad's taped it. Oh, there he is! Good. Hey Dad, did you bring the red beast to pick us up?"

Tall and rangy as I'd remembered him, Dr JJ said, "What else?" and gave us both a brief hug. It was good to see him. He smelt like a dad – wholesome and reliable, somehow. Whatever the 'latest' news was that had upset him, I was glad I was around to help out if I could.

They insisted I sit in the front so that I could remember the journey along the coast, threading a red track between the beige hills and the blue sea, every tranche of greenery speckled with ochre villas, and white boats glimpsed way down in the sparkling marinas tucked against the coastline.

It was a hot summer's evening, but different from the oppressive city heat of NYC, and I loved the wind whipping snatches of the Juliuses' talk – "fat bastard", "slimy old man", "corrupt bugger", "Manolo's", "protest", "do something", "need to be clever" – around my hair-whipped, jet-lagged head.

Huge hearty hugs and kisses from little Sra JJ, ciggie arcing round the back of my neck, as she exclaimed to see me again. A more restrained, sisterly embrace from Chloe, whose spray of freckles looked cute in the sun.

"You've got a while before dinner," said Dr JJ. "Maybe you want to go for a walk or a drink or something?"

"No way," said Jules at once. "We need to bring Jake up to speed on all this shit. He kept nodding off on the 'plane while I was trying to tell him."

I nodded.

"Carmen's coming round for dinner," he told me, "but this Roberto prick's coming too because he's Greenpeace."

"Hold on!" cut in Dr JJ. "You don't even know the man – you can't call him a prick!"

"I don't want to know him," said Jules. "The old hippie here has been dragging his feet with Carmen, and now she's getting cosy with this activist beefcake."

"Oh dear," said Sra JJ to me. "Why haven't you got things clear between you and Carmen yet? You don't want to lose her."

Her straightforward look dismantled me.

"Oh, it's just work and the situation – you know, I really like my work but you're kind of expected to..."

"...be gay," put in Chloe. "That's how it is in London and New York. Both their bosses think they're a couple."

Dr and Sra JJ stared at us for what felt like 10 minutes.

For once, Jules was quiet, and I couldn't locate any kind of defense or explanation.

"Well, for God's sake let's take one thing at a time and sort out the immediate business first," said Dr JJ. "Back here in 20 minutes after you've had a wash and brush-up?"

"Yes, sir," I said, and raced Jules up the wood and tiled staircase to the sublime upstairs views.

"I'm not sure how much longer I can take this, bro," Earl was saying to his best friend Caleb, who ran a health store in Bel Air. They were sitting at a local bar out back, having a beer. "I mean, the boss was *rough* this week. I can suck his cock and manage his neediness 'n' all that shite, but I swear, it felt like he was tryin' to tear me up. I can't send him the young ones – he had one crying this week and the boy just up and left. One week before the next Eurovegas gig, over in Spain! It's fucking with my choreography. And my own ass, literally."

"But he uses a condom, right?"

"Hell yeah! Of course he does! Caleb, do you think I'm crazy? Anyway, he can't afford no diseases – he could afford the treatment but any time spent not making him money is losing him money, know what I mean?"

Caleb shook his head.

"You gonna quit?"

"Not yet. Just saying, it's affecting my performance. It's getting so I have to adjust the choreography 'cos it hurts too much to do what I wanna do, or I have to give those moves to another dancer. I can't be doing that. No, I'm planning to see the Eurovegas one through and network like crazy every trip to Europe."

They were both silent for a while, sucking at their beers, nodding to old friends.

"You know what, bro?" said Earl suddenly. "I envy the ladies. 'Cos that's what they're called. Me? I'm Corey's No 1 Cocksucker. The ladies, they had all this shit for, what, centuries? And now they're mincing around taking the perks with no ass involved. And the high-rolling gay ladies who swing as much punch as the guys, well, I tell you, they're nicer. Don't want to rip up a girl's snatch just to show their firepower. I know some gals who got real sweet deals with gay-lays they met in business circles."

Caleb looked sympathetic, but said,

"At least you only got one ole queen to keep happy, man. At least he don't let his friends loose on you when there's a big deal going down. And he lets you do your dance work. You hang on in there, keep the ole man sweet and like you said, network like crazy and get yourself known over there in gay Paree."

"Paris is not in Spain, you dumb-ass."

"Yeah, I'm the dumb-ass, but you the one getting a loose ass. Hey, here's my delivery – you can help me stack 'em."

Dr JJ flicked off the switch and said,
"There!"

They all seemed to be looking at me as the newcomer for a reaction. We'd all been watching footage of the mayor of Valencia's response to the news that Eurovegas was to be located in his region, in Calpe, and it had all been very cleverly woven in with shots of him embracing Dr JJ at the smoking ban protest, looking all buddy-buddy.

"Man, the mayor has really done a number on you," I said, and they all burst out talking.

"He has, hasn't he?"

"I knew it!"

"It's not about Eurovegas, the man's got issues that..."

"Can't believe how he gets away with it time after..."

"Jake, do you really get the issue here?" Chloe asked suddenly, cutting across the general off-loading.

Again, they all looked at me.

"Sure I do. Mayor Ruiz has got his way with Eurovegas and he's using Dr JJ as a pretend ally to cloud the fact that he's onside with the central government on the nationwide smoking ban. He puts out footage to make it look as though he's in with the locals, can't do anything about the ban, that kind of thing. Result: he'll stay popular, collect plenty kickbacks, enjoy the political leverage, and Eurovegas and the smoking ban both go through. Government gets to play both the public health concern and job creation cards."

They were all quiet. Jules nodded and said,

"That's about it. We don't want Eurovegas here, but the way Mayor Ruiz is spinning it on TV, it looks as though Dad and most of the locals are really behind him."

"But there's more to it than that," I said, feeling that old familiar rush of confidence as my board leapt along the front curve of a wave. "You do realize, don't you, that Corey Rosenberg won't build unless smoking is allowed in the casino?"

Massive silence.

"Are you sure?" said Chloe.

"Sure I'm sure. Remember the Las Vegas launch, Jules? How pleased you were to be able to smoke indoors with your Vegas Virgin?"

"That's a cocktail!" he put in fast. "Yes, I remember. It was great! Great idea, great business."

Now they were all staring at him. Chloe was the first to respond.

"Jules, are you thick?" she said. "Eurovegas will have to be exempt from Spanish national law if what Jake says is right."

"I'm right, it's all documented, you can find it on the internet. Some states in the US have pushed back, but mainly, Corey just does what he wants 'cos he brings in the big bucks."

"So?" Jules still looked puzzled.

"So, Ruiz must have negotiated with the central government for smoking to be allowed in Eurovegas, so as to secure the deal. It's illegal! Rosenberg's from the US, he's not even Spanish!"

"So?" said Jules again. "I think it's great – at least there'll be somewhere we can all still smoke indoors!"

"But I don't want to go to bloody Eurovegas to be able to smoke!" cried Sra JJ. "I want to go to Manolo's! If it's a nationwide ban, okay, it was going to happen. We'll smoke outside. But for a foreign company to come in and just set up under its own laws – no!"

"Dude, you have to get clear on this," I told Jules. "Your mother's quite right."

"But it could work really well for Manolo and people like him – he could get a concession inside the casino and..." His voice trailed off. "Okay, that's not going to happen."

"For heaven's sake, Jules!" exclaimed Chloe. "A ban is a ban is a ban."

"Yes, have a little conviction," I added, and that really set him off.

"Conviction?" he hissed, rounding on me. "*You* talk about conviction? The hippy-dippy who hasn't got enough conviction to get the girl he fancies and has been messing around for a whole bloody decade?"

"It's not a decade," I muttered, but he had the room, I could tell.

At that moment, there was some noise in the hallway and a voice called out "Hola, hola!" and Carmen herself entered.

And something in me just snapped.

I strode right over to that blaze of beauty, grabbed her and kissed her with all the pent-up passion of real, crystallized feeling after years of pathetic uncertainty. I don't know what made me so sure so suddenly. I just was. Whatever it takes, I thought, as her eyes smiled up at me and I went down under the waves again. She was in my arms and we hadn't spoken a word. I could see Chloe grinning from ear to ear over Carmen's shoulder.

"You must be Roberto," I heard Jules say to a shape in the background. "I'm Jules, what can I get you to drink? You do realize Mayor Ruiz must have negotiated a deal with the central government to allow smoking in the Eurovegas complex, don't you?"

"I don't care about that," snapped Roberto. "Of course he has. What Greenpeace opposes is Eurovegas, full stop. It's an environmental disaster backed by political and corporate greed."

"You don't know the worst," Sra JJ said.

"I thought Ruiz setting me up over the smoking ban was the worst," said Dr JJ.

His wife shook her head, exhaling smoke.

"No, darling, there's more."

We all stood quiet and waited, Carmen's body fitted against mine.

"They're going to drain the Salinas to make room for Eurovegas."

Carmen pulled away from me with a gasp of shock.

"But they can't do that!" cried Dr JJ. "It's where we had our first kiss."

Sra JJ nodded sadly.

"I know. We have to stop it. Enough building! The Salinas is beautiful, we need it. Roberto, we'll do whatever we can."

"Hold on, how do you know?" said Dr JJ.

"I just do." She stubbed out her cigarette almost defiantly. "I heard. Reliable source."

"I'll check it out," Roberto said. "It's a peg for protest, it'll mobilize everyone – not just the smokers. And it'll get media attention. The media's been bought, but enough may respond if we put up a good campaign."

"Ruiz is a nasty, greedy old man who's done too much damage in the region already," said Sra JJ. "They will drain the Salinas over my dead body."

"We'll stop them," I said, fired by her passion.

"Oh, what are you going to do?" said Jules. "Chain yourself to a flamingo?"

"That sounds kinda beautiful but I can see you're being sarcastic," I said.

"We could dress him as a flamingo and get him to stand on that little island in the Salinas," said Roberto.

I opened my mouth to say, "Sure," because Carmen's face had lit up at the idea, but Jules scowled at Roberto and said,

"Don't be ridiculous."

Roberto looked offended and said,

"We've had a lot of success with our polar bear campaign – dressing activists in polar bear suits and placing them on ice or boats where there's oil drilling in the Arctic. It really grabs people's attention."

"It's true," put in Carmen. "The first one went viral on social media and we've had four activists arrested while doing a polar bear stunt. Roberto did one, didn't you?"

He looked modest. Jules scowled and waved his arms.

"Oh yeah? Well, good for you. Did you get arrested?"

It was extraordinary how fast Roberto deflated. I don't think anyone else – except possibly Dr JJ – had even noticed there was an ego to be pricked there, but Jules had got right in amongst him with that one question. As always, I felt protected by Jules.

"No," muttered Roberto, "but..."

"Well, there you go!" Jules steam-rollered over him. "I'll tell you what will get you arrested, though, and that's if you dress Jake up in a stinky hot flamingo suit and stick him on an island with no shade in 40-degree heat for six hours and he flops over and dies! *Then* you'll see a headline and some handcuffs!"

There was a silence. Jules stopped waving his arms and strode over to pour himself some water from the jug on the sideboard. Roberto looked defiant but slightly discomfited and I just watched Carmen, who'd stopped looking at him and turned to me.

"Yes, it would be cruel," she said.

"Well, I did it," Roberto put in. Unwise.

"That was in the fucking Arctic!" Jules fired at him. "This is Spain in the summer, you codpiece!"

The native English speakers all laughed, but Carmen, Roberto and Sra JJ didn't get it, so I stopped pretty fast.

"I'll do whatever I can," I said, my eyes locked with Carmen's.

"We'll think of something," she said. "I think Jake would be brilliant at peaceful protest."

Jules snorted and said,

"Well, he'd be half brilliant. Fine with the peaceful bit."

"Can't you get Rosenberg on the smoking ban exemption?" queried Dr JJ. "Like an Al Pacino thing?"

"No." Roberto was firm. "We've had a look at the contracts through an insider. Everything to be signed just before the national total ban comes into effect. Twenty-year period before reassessment. Watertight, he's a clever operator."

"Legal eagle *and* beefcake activist," I murmured to Jules.

"You're a jammy bastard," he muttered back. "Don't know how you do it. But it takes more than a kiss, you know. She's a prick-tease like the rest of them. She'll want the date set and the house bought and the kids' names agreed before you see any pussy."

My eyes followed Carmen, who was conferring with the others.

"That's okay. Whatever it takes. We'll make it work just fine. Theo's looking at setting up in Europe."

"He is? That's great news, old man, but if you lose the Eurovegas gig, that'll throw a spanner in the works, won't it? It's a big contract."

"There's plenty of space in Spain, isn't there?" I said, a bit puzzled by his talk of losing the contract. "We'd do the work wherever Rosenberg builds, but Spain's got the contract and surely it could go somewhere else here without doing too much environmental damage?"

"Tell that to your rival."

We both watched Roberto juggling 'phones, TV remote controls and various electronic devices.

"Just spinning his wheels," I observed, and Jules turned to me with a surprised chuckle.

"Jake, under that hippy-dippy exterior you are a laser beam of precision and I never realized it! Outcomes *and* analysis – who'd have thought it?"

I remember giving him a shove, Carmen's smile across the room, a powerful sense of purpose, a lot of noise, and then Jules saying, "Who's that?" and a stranger in the doorway.

CHAPTER ELEVEN
Red-hot revelations

"Who's that?" said Jules.

The chatter around us died away, all eyes turned to the stranger in the doorway. I glanced around to see if anyone showed any sign of recognition – after all, this dude was standing right there, inside the house.

Dr JJ stood looking over Carmen's head at the newcomer, his nostrils slightly flared as if assessing the first winds of a hurricane. Jules looked so like him in profile, but with more charge, less coil. Characteristically, Jules was the first to move and speak.

"Hello, Mr...?" he said, taking a step forward and speaking in both English and Spanish.

The stranger didn't move or look at Jules. His eyes were fixed on Sra JJ, who held that gaze, her head tilted back in an odd gesture of what looked like resignation. And, recognition?

I took the stranger in. Forties, early fifties, maybe, good-looking in a classic way – thick dark hair dusted with grey, olive skin, strong features, dark eyes. He wasn't tall, but he had presence. A strong presence.

It was as though there was an invisible connection between him and Sra JJ. The girls seemed strangely apprehensive – they weren't scared, but their eyes were anxious in a way I trusted.

Jules stepped closer, trying to break the link between the stranger and his mother.

"Can we help? Are you looking for someone?"

There was a fraught, frozen moment, then the dude suddenly smiled – and after years of operating in a work environment where I had to gauge men fast and accurately, I can honestly say his presence just tripled... but the girls still held anxiety in their eyes, their tensed shoulders – and said, without moving or detaching his gaze from Sra JJ,

"I'm just looking for my wife."

Relieved, Jules said,

"Oh okay, well, no wife except the one accounted for, so perhaps we can help you find the right house?"

The stranger turned his head slightly to look at Jules and the girls both intensified, Chloe's eyes huge in her pale, freckled face, and Carmen's turning blacker with that undefined suspicion.

The stranger spoke again.

"Perhaps I haven't been clear," he said. His eyes went back to Sra JJ.

"I'm looking *at* my wife," he said, then.

It was like a key moment in a movie – the girls gasped, Roberto stopped fussing with his 'phone, Jules made an odd snorting noise and waved his arms in a futile way.

"Yeah, right, that's my mother, maybe you're pissed."

"Maybe you're illegitimate," the stranger shot back, and this time, Jules, his dad and I all gasped, our heads swivelling round toward Sra JJ.

"Alfonso, don't be ridiculous," she said, from behind a small cloud of smoke. "You really are the limit."

She ground out her smoke in a nearby ashtray and gave a more ladylike version of Jules' snort.

"Illegitimate!" she scoffed, lighting another cigarette.

"Does your son know?" he retorted. "Does any of them know?"

He took a step toward her but Dr JJ blocked his way.

"Who the hell are you?" he growled.

"I'm Rosario's husband," said the stranger, with another dazzling smile. "Her *real* husband."

We all stood with our heads turning this way and that between him, Dr JJ and Sra JJ. Jules, for once, was speechless.

Dr JJ didn't seem as freaked-out as I would've been, or Jules clearly was, but then, I'd always thought he was a seriously cool dude. He didn't waste time asking his wife if she knew the stranger Alfonso – she obviously did. Instead, he said,

"Rosario, is this true, what he's saying?"

She shrugged her shoulders – more in irritation than helplessness, I thought – and said,

"I don't think so."

"You don't think so?! Oh great!" The outburst was from Jules. "You're not sure, maybe, who you're married to? So I may actually be illegitimate, like 'Alfonso' says?"

"Oh shut up, Jules," said Chloe. "This is *so* not about you. Honestly, who cares whether or not you're legitimate?"

"I care!" he cried.

"Yes, well, that's a slur on your mother and you should be ashamed of yourself," she said. "And a slur on your dad too, since we're not sexist. And nobody cares anyway. Just *sshshh!*"

During this interchange, the three main players had stayed where they stood, the two men with their eyes fixed on Sra JJ. Now Dr JJ spoke again.

"Rosario. You don't think so? Really? You're not sure whether this man is your husband?"

She took three quick, angry puffs at her smoke, as if Dr JJ's gentleness unnerved her more than the stranger's brashness.

"No! I'm not! I don't *think* so – I was 17, under age. I was staying with a cousin in Pamplona. I met Alfonso there. He told me he was involved with ETA – sort of, not really. He probably made it up. I was so young, I thought he was brave and exciting..."

"I was!" cried Alfonso. "With you, for you!"

Sra JJ shook her head.

"ETA wasn't exciting, Alfonso. People died in their attacks, whether you call it terrorism or separatism. Anyway, it was a mad, hot summer. We went to some man who said he was a priest but it can't possibly have been legal – there's no paperwork or anything."

"Christ!" cried Jules. "There was no bloody paperwork for anything back in those days! I *am* illegitimate!"

"Jules, shut *up!*" said Chloe. "Did you go to church for the, um, wedding?" She shot an apologetic look at Dr JJ but he was still staring at his wife – if that's how I thought of her, goodness knows what he was going through.

"No, no," said Sra JJ. "No church, just this 'priest' guy. I told you, it was a mad thing."

"It was a *real* thing," put in Alfonso, heatedly, and I could feel the words 'like Coke' trembling on my lips, which were stretched in a weird rictus of disbelief.

Sra JJ shrugged again.

"Well, whatever. But not for long. I came home here and..."

"And I came to, to be near you," cried Alfonso. "Until you were of age and we could tell the world our beautiful secret and be together openly, proud man and wife!"

Dr JJ's eyebrows flickered up and down and I thought it was a mercy he had all that psychiatric training at his back. He was better prepared than most. Even so...

Still looking at Sra JJ, he said,

"Then what happened?"

Alfonso's turn to shrug, emanating a gust of disgust.

Sra JJ blew the smoke slowly out through her nostrils, her eyes on Dr JJ's face.

"Then I met you," she said, simply.

Well, it was romantic, but in a really tense way, you know?

The silence held for about 20 seconds, then Dr JJ looked down and started patting the front of his shirt. Jules whipped out a packet of cigarettes and gave him one and lit it for him.

"Thanks, son." The doctor blew out the first cloud like a visible release of tension and said,

"Christ, Rosario, I thought you were a virgin. All that bloody creeping around being scared shitless of your dad, getting you home by 10-o-bloody-clock, months of dry humping..."

Her slender brown wrist flicked, she took a quick drag and said,

"Yes, I'm sorry. My father couldn't know, he'd have killed us all. Me first."

Dr JJ nodded slightly.

"What about since then? Have you been seeing each other?"

"No! Of course not!" she exclaimed. "He's just surfaced in the past few weeks – we've had coffee a couple of times, that's all."

"Yes, that is *all*, that is everything! It is all-important!" cried Alfonso, who seemed to be quite the drama queen.

"Why did you meet him?" asked Dr JJ.

His wife shrugged.

"I don't really know. Old times' sake? Curiosity?"

The doc didn't pursue it. Nana would've called him wise. He was probably Aquarius – they intellectualize emotions a lot, she says.

"And what did you, er, talk about?" was his next question as, without really looking at Alfonso, he took a glass over to where the stranger stood and poured him some wine.

Alfonso accepted the wine and said a bit sulkily,

"I wanted her to go away with me. She was my wife first."

Sra JJ tutted impatiently.

"He's got this crazy idea after decades of being Mayor Ruiz's right-hand man and shagging anything that moved."

"I told you, none of that meant anything."

"It doesn't matter. I'm not going anywhere. I like it here. But the point is, Alfonso's the one who told me about the plan to drain the Salinas. I bet he's been in on all the other backhander deals but he's got cold feet on this one and wants me to go off with him while they turn Calpe into a theme park! I told him no, I have to stay and fight."

The rest of us were all still pretty stunned and silent. After a moment, Alfonso drained his glass and said,

"It's true." He stood up. "And that's why I came today, Rosario. You are right. We must fight. Ruiz and Torres have gone too far. Rosario's right, that's why I love her, she reminds me of what I should be. It's time to fight. But I can't just hand over the paperwork."

Sra JJ snorted.

"You mean you're scared of being clapped up in prison because you're up to your neck in the paperwork."

"No," he said. "No paper trails, nothing connects me to all their shady dealings. The point is, I know this project inside out now, and the truth is that it would be fine for Spain if it were located properly. It's an economic coup. Germany's let it come to Spain because a lot of the construction work is going to German companies who've already built up most of the coast and are starting to move inland now."

"What's Germany got to do with it?" I asked.

"Germany runs Europe," Jules replied shortly. "He's got a point. They'd grab it for themselves if the Spanish bid folds, or hand it to somewhere like Croatia, where they'd be able to control the build and grab all the infrastructure construction work and loans too."

He rounded on Alfonso.

"But that doesn't explain your change of tune. You must have millions in the bank if you've been creaming off from Ruiz's projects."

"Yeah," I added.

"You don't give a toss about the environment!" pursued Jules.

"That's not the point," snapped Sra JJ. "We need to stop Ruiz in his tracks. We can't let him ruin Calpe. And apart from anything else, he's made David look stupid with that TV report using footage from the smoking ban protest – he's made it look as though David's on his side and people are going to think we're behind the draining of the Salinas too! We've got to stop it. David, he's misrepresented you, he's made you look ridiculous. David!"

Dr JJ turned slowly away from the window he'd been gazing out of and said,

"Not as ridiculous as I can make him look."

There was a pause – quite a long one – then Jules said,

"Where are you going with that, Dad? Some kind of David and Goliath mission you're on? Just because your name's David?"

"Not at all." Dr JJ moved around refilling glasses. He hadn't touched his wife since the revelations began, but the romantic tension had pretty much left the air, and once again I was thankful he was a highly trained psychiatrist. I also marveled at Sra JJ's composure. There was a lot to be learned from these two, I thought, as Carmen squeezed my hand and smiled at me.

"Ruiz has been one of my patients for quite a while now," Dr JJ was saying. "He's been doing double sessions recently. I've learned quite a lot of things he'd probably prefer not to have made public."

"Christ!" exclaimed Jules.

I think we were all pretty shocked.

"What kind of things?" asked Chloe, which shocked me even more, even though it's what we all wanted to know.

"David!" said Sra JJ. "You can't reveal that kind of thing! Remember your psychiatrist/patient confidentiality!"

"Ah, but I'm not technically a psychiatrist," said Dr JJ, putting down the bottle and standing tall, sweeping the room with an unexpectedly hard smile. "I never completed my studies. I never took the Hippocratic oath. That fat manipulative bastard will get no mercy from me. I can reveal all I want."

Well, he'd revealed quite enough to stun us all back into silence. Another momentous moment etched onto my memory – at this rate, it would be sheer filigree by the end of the day. The sun sat around the house, a scorching setting for these red-hot revelations.

Then the sharp intakes of breath, murmuring, some of us stirring, some still motionless. Now, Sra JJ did move over to her husband.

"What?" she hissed at him from close range. I can understand her being mad, can't you? "What do you mean, you're not qualified? My father only let me go out with you because of your qualifications, your prospects! For heaven's sake, David, he lent you the money to set up your plaque!"

"Well, that's the thing," he admitted. "I had to impress him somehow, and the medical profession always goes down well, but obviously I wasn't going to start operating on people. So shrinkage seemed the safest bet. On my plaque, it only says 'psychological treatment', and that's fair enough – I did study for six years, just never completed."

"But you lied! And you've never told me the truth!"

"You never told me you were married!"

Alfonso sat up, sensing a second chance.

"It's not the same! You've been lying to your patients all these years!" cried Sra JJ.

Dr JJ shook his head firmly.

"No I haven't. There is a document on my consulting-room wall that clearly says I am not qualified as a psychiatrist. It's just a matter of which words you put in big font, and the fact that nobody ever looks at these things closely – they just want to get some help. And I have helped."

"But you've been practising for what, 20 years?" said Chloe. "Surely somebody must have noticed?"

"Only one. A Swedish journalist who went behind the desk to look properly. She said, 'Well, at least you're honest' and carried on seeing me for three more months. She'd been on the edge of the Gulf War as a journalist and came down here to get over it. She realized she wasn't cut out for war reporting and retrained as an aromatherapist."

"Aromatherapist!" echoed Chloe.

"Yes. Went to work in Paris, set up her own business there. We were both ahead of our time. It was thin pickings for me at first, you know – everybody in Spain was happy, no problems to talk about really, and if they did, it was to their friends and family – but aromatherapy and shrinkage both boomed eventually. It worked out."

He looked down at his still seething wife and stooped to kiss her but she turned her head away.

"Come on Rosario," he begged. "I've done no harm, I've done quite a lot of good, kept on top of latest developments in the profession. And I did it for us – I knew I could make it work for us if I just had a little bit of capital, but my dad had cut me off without a penny..."

"Well, you shouldn't have shagged his wife," Sra JJ shot at him.

Silence and gasps, if you know what I mean.

"Dude, they're coming over the plate way too fast for me," I said to Jules out of the corner of my mouth.

"For you and me both, old man," he whispered back. "But that wasn't, you know, my grandmother, obviously. Second wife scenario."

"She wasn't his wife then!" Dr JJ was saying heatedly. "They met through me and she and I stopped, you know, seeing each other after that! We'd only had a few dates, older woman thing, it was fun but it wasn't going anywhere. But he was a stubborn old man who wanted to hold onto his money."

"Well, it was his money," put in Chloe, and Dr JJ wiped his forehead and said that was absolutely true, but things had gotten very unpleasant so he'd left and never gone back.

"If they met through you, you should have claimed an introduction fee," said Jules.

"I expect he was glad you left, in a way," said Chloe, whose insights were beginning to scare me. "He was probably afraid you two might, you know, strike up again if they had a rough patch."

"Yes," nodded Carmen. "And if you had not left England, you would not have met your wife."

"*My* wife," said Alfonso, but his heart didn't seem to be in it any more.

"So what have you got on Mayor Ruiz, Dr JJ?" persisted Chloe. "Sordid sex secrets, or is it all political?"

"Nothing much political," admitted the doctor – I still thought of him that way. "He was discreet about his political intrigues, but he did have a lot to say about hiring fat girls and having cream bun fights."

"Christ!" yelled Jules. "Disgusting old man!"

"You wouldn't want to get the girls in trouble," said Chloe.

"How much worse trouble could they be in than having to chuck sticky buns at fatso Ruiz and pretending to like it?" said Jules.

"Well, at least he paid them – I expect he paid them, didn't he?" She looked at Alfonso and he nodded.

"Yes, yes, I know he paid the girls, but I know nothing about what he got up to with them," he said.

Sra JJ snorted and stubbed out her smoke.

"Well, it's all perpetuating the trade, but the cream buns things has to be better than, you know... having sex with him," said Chloe. "I mean, that is one huge advantage of the Change over in London – city hookers at least have a lot less rough sex and so on to deal with. I should think it's the same in New York?"

I nodded.

"Sure, in general. Vince the ads man told me there are studies showing the impact on society as a whole – women have more choices and actually earn the same as men now, which is a huge shift, and it's having a trickledown effect from the big cities."

Carmen and Chloe were gazing at me but I sensed I'd lost the rest of the room. Dr JJ had walked out altogether.

"Exactly," said Chloe, briskly. "So, Dr JJ, what have you got?"

He strode back in and across to a laptop at the end of the sideboard.

"You mean, cream bun fights with paid company isn't enough?" he said, opening up the laptop.

"Oh yes," said Carmen, "we can get a lot out of that."

"You're absolutely right, unfortunately," chipped in Roberto. "The public doesn't give a shit about Greenpeace's work or preserving our planet, but they'll love bits of filth like this. I know just who to leak it to – no names, don't worry, just 'a source close to the mayor's office' and then a series of sensationalist details dripped out over a week."

"Pity there aren't any visuals for social media," said Carmen, "but even so, I can certainly get it moving among the anti-prostitution campaigners, just to start with."

Dr JJ finished fiddling with the laptop and waved us all over.

"Gather round, come on."

The screen came to life. At first, there was nothing much, just a big, pleasant-looking room decorated in shades of yellow, terracotta and amber, then we all gasped as a door opened and Mayor Ruiz, clad in a blue and white kimono, lumbered into the foreground and lay down on a couch.

For a few minutes, he and the doctor's voice off camera discussed the weather. The gaps grew longer, and then Ruiz nodded off. Dr JJ put the footage into fast forward, which was pretty funny because the mayor shifted about in a bizarrely lumpy way and Jules kept saying, "Ugh, he's revolting," but then the doc brought it back to normal speed and we all leaned right forward like a football front line with a touchdown in sight while Mayor Ruiz shifted too close to the edge of the couch and gradually, inevitably, fell right off it in his sleep, dragged over by his enormous belly. He landed with a crash, snuffling and snorting like crazy, and Chloe and Carmen both started laughing like crazy, about four seconds before the rest of us reacted.

Not everyone laughed: Roberto was too intense for this kind of banana-skin farce, but he did look pleased; Jules was whooping and jumping around; Alfonso looked horrified; Sra JJ chuckled softly and Dr JJ stood back blowing smoke rings.

"Well?" he challenged, after Carmen had played it through three times, once in gut-bustingly hilarious slo-mo and finally in x16 fast forward and Chloe was clutching her stomach saying it hurt. "Can you do something with *that* on social media?"

* * *

Back in London next evening, Jules flung himself onto Chloe's bouncy, welcoming bed and buried his face in the puffy pillows, breathing in her fragrance. Their fragrance. It must have something of him, he reasoned, but hers'd be the sweet part.

He'd left her in Calpe, explaining to his parents why he and Jake pretended to be a couple, while Carmen and Roberto busied themselves with laying out a media strategy to put Mayor Ruiz in the laughing-stocks, and Jake... What *was* Jake doing? Walking on the beach, communing with the sea, probably, thought Jules. But he'd secured Carmen, just with one embrace. How *had* that happened? He would make it work, he would somehow stop living according to the terms and conditions of the Change.

"But what about us, what about me and Chloe?" Jules agonised.

He took another deep, un/satisfying breath and then sat upright abruptly with what sounded to his own suspicious ears almost like a sob.

"Get a grip," he told himself aloud, and went along to the het cinema to take his mind off things.

The cinema wasn't that full. The film had already begun. He found himself a seat tucked away to one side at the back, and was grateful for the darkness.

"Don't hesitate so much," his mother had told him, just before he'd left for the airport. "English women need romance too."

"You don't understand," he'd said, and left it to Chloe to try and explain how her business, his job, their social life and entire future depended on compliance with the Change's changes.

Staring at the screen but unaware of the film, he replayed the recent revelations, Jake entwined with Carmen, his parents' hugging each other and kissing briefly as everyone (except Alfonso, of course) cheered, himself saying, "great, so I am the illegitimate son of a congenital liar," and Chloe's burst of the derisive laughter that somehow always reassured him. He needed her here, now, to remind him tartly that it wasn't all about him, put her hand on his thigh during the film, hell, to tell him what to *do*! But of course, that wasn't romantic. He had to work something out on his own. Was he capable? Was it expecting too much? His not-too-positive mental meandering came to an abrupt halt as a couple several rows in front kissed, and as the man's head turned towards the woman, Jules realised with blinding clarity that it was his boss, 'Gay Gordons' Hecklow.

* * *

Theo moved through the lobby of the London Ritz like a king. He liked it here. Though he was in the business of luxury, he ran on tight margins and it was a treat for him to stay at the early 20th-century hotel. Thanks to Jake, his entire stay in a suite overlooking Green Park came courtesy of the Ritz itself: the banquettes in the ballroom were in need of re-upholstering, and Theo was in town to finalise the details. The contract would give Millards a small foothold in Europe, where the craftsmanship he steered was recognised and valued.

"Europe appreciates, the US pays," he'd told Jake.

The Heritage Director greeted him with smiling suavity and led him into her office. Theo spotted a tiny piece of fluff on the chair next to the one where he sat down, and the director, catching that fastidious glance, picked the fluff quickly away before taking her own seat.

"Jake!" cried Theo next morning, entering the breakfast room at the opulent Wolseley restaurant, just across a side street from the Ritz, and seeing his protégé at one of the coveted corner tables.

Jake leapt up and embraced him.

"Good news," Theo said, sitting down and letting the waiter dexterously flick a pristine napkin onto his lap. "There's a new dimension to our meeting with the Heritage Director this afternoon. We met briefly yesterday, and she wants us to prepare a bid for replacing the Jacquard and damask silk drapes in all the guest rooms and suites."

Jake's mouth fell open.

"Wow, Theo, that is a *really* big deal!"

"I know, I know, we have to get busy, fast. She'll show us some rooms later on, but we'll need all our time after breakfast to prepare. Now, where is Jules? It was so kind of him to send a car to the airport for me."

"I haven't seen him today," said Jake. "I stayed at his place last night, but I had an early night and he wasn't ready when I left to come here. He just yelled at me through the bathroom door to order coffee and juice and he'd be right... Oh, there he is!"

A gleam of burnished gold, and a discreet but warm welcome from the maitre d' signalled Jules' arrival, then suddenly, like a blast of warm air, he was with and around them, hugging Theo and slapping Jake on the arm.

"Have you told him?" he said, downing a juice. "Mm, that's great, can we have some more of this?" The waiter flicked the napkin and nodded. "Well, Theo, what do you think?"

"Oh, it's marvellous," said Theo at once. "I've never been here in my life, and it's absolutely lovely."

"Yes, yes, the Wolseley's fine, but I meant the situation," said Jules impatiently.

"What situation?" inquired Theo calmly.

"For God's sake, you haven't told him yet?!" Jules turned accusingly on Jake, who smiled and said,

"Jules, cool down. Theo arrived about one minute before you did. Let's order so that we can enjoy this awesome breakfast you've told me about. The situation won't go away in the next half hour."

Jules fumed for a moment and then said,

"You're right. Sorry, Theo. Now, recommendations..."

Forty minutes later, fed and informed, Theo took a sip of coffee and said,

"Well, it's obvious. You'll have to switch the contracts on Corey Rosenberg."

The two younger men stared, stunned.

Theo carried on calmly.

"So that Corey, without realising, signs a watertight contract which places Eurovegas in a different location. Everyone happy. Well, except Roberto perhaps, but I dare say he can find an acceptable location. Greenpeace happy enough, Spanish government happy, Corey keeps his precious Eurovegas, your boss Gordon keeps the financial plum, and Millards keeps the interiors work."

Immaculate in a grey-green suit with a deep amber shirt and fresh floral tie, Jules continued to stare, his hands clenching and unclenching, his face working. Alongside him, Jake, skinny-chic in his now trademark tight jeans, crisp white shirt and Texan tie, was motionless.

"Are you insane?" cried Jules suddenly.

Theo carried on sipping his coffee with impregnable poise. Jake said nothing.

"Oh all right!" Jules exclaimed 20 seconds later. "All right! I can probably arrange it. You!" He glared at Jake. "Always a bloody drama! Always having to fish you out of something! Theo, great to see you. Go and sew up that Ritz deal. Oh sorry, bad pun. Breakfast's all taken care of – unlimited coffee. Damn, damn, damn! All right, I'm on it. *Fuck!*"

Like a gust of wind, he was gone.

"That's *Jake*?" asked Sra JJ, disbelievingly, peering at the photos Chloe was showing them from the big party at Jules' London flat.

"Yes!"

"What, in all those sequins?"

"Yes, yes, yes!"

"The one draped all over Jules?" Dr JJ was calm but clearly interested.

Carmen leaned in to look too. The air was thick with smoke.

"Yes, that was the plan, to convince Jules' boss Gordon Hecklow that Jules is definitely gay."

"Even though he's not?"

Chloe nodded.

"That's right. Jake agreed to pretend to be his couple, because that's how it is in London and New York and other big cities. You're just not 'in' unless you're gay. Men or women. Look, there's me with Kate, my friend who really is gay; she's just adopted another child with her partner. Being seen with Kate at a party like that makes me look good, makes me accepted, you know? It's okay for me to be one of Jules' gay circle, but if Gordon knew Jules and Jake were both straight, he'd cut Jules loose in a heartbeat and it'd be impossible for Jules to get a decent job anywhere in the City. We could move to the provinces, but he loves the City, and I want to make my business work too, and it all depends on being 'in'."

Sra JJ was flicking through the photos, her husband leaning over her shoulder to see.

"Looks like a good party," observed the doc.

"Oh, it was amazing! The waiting staff were all like supermodels on roller skates, and of course the views are fantastic and yes, it was fun."

"But don't you girls mind?" inquired Sra JJ.

Carmen blew smoke and said firmly,

"Jake can come to live and work here. We'll visit London, New York, but it's best if he is here."

Sra JJ smiled approvingly.

"Jules and I do have a plan," said Chloe, a little defensively. "This is only for a couple more years, till my business is really, really established. Then maybe we can move somewhere else without too much damage. Or things may change... back, you know, so that nobody cares if you're straight and you can just be yourself – like things used to be." Her tone at the end was almost wistful, her thought almost a plea.

Carmen patted her arm consolingly.

"Sure, things may change. And it's good that you have a plan. And you're not poor."

Dr JJ said,

"Well, I mind. These boys are too bloody convincing. Look at this photo! Christ Almighty! Jake on sparkling form! Who the hell is this?"

"Tai and Chi," giggled Chloe. "Apparently they're really good at all the cut and thrust finance work, but they double up as Gordon's goons, and Jules says they always dress in dental floss outfits for parties."

Dr JJ filled glasses, but kept coming back to one photo in particular.

"Don't like the look of this bloke," he said.

Chloe leaned over to see.

"Oh, that's Rick," she said, her laughter dying out. "No, I can't stand him, but Jules says I'm silly about it."

"Looks like nasty piece of work," Dr JJ said. "Right. Let's go and have dinner. That was interesting but I need to get back to the straight and narrow now."

Rick snarled as he swept into the waiting area outside Gordon Hecklow's office and spotted Jules sitting on one of the low leather chairs.

Glancing up, Jules felt the usual fleeting tingle of fear, a quick reminder of his terror the night they'd been entertaining Corey Rosenberg at Duro and Rick had assaulted him in the men's loo.

"'Morning, Rick," he said casually, glad Gordon's executive assistant Margaret was close by, and hoping he'd be in to see the big man before Rick.

"Hello, Jules. "

Rick took a chair situated just too close for comfort and eased it so close that his ankles brushed against Jules'. Jules shifted position but Rick still subtly crowded him. Jules tutted quietly and carried on perusing the FT.

Rick picked up a magazine from the neat low table in front of them and waited till Margaret was on the 'phone before saying,

"So! The big signing with Corey Rosenberg approaches!"

"Soul of discretion as always," said Jules, with a contemptuous glance.

Rick laughed harshly, setting Jules' teeth on edge.

"Oh, Mr Discreet needn't worry – he doesn't know anything important enough to give away!"

Jules had a momentary flashback to Mayor Ruiz, engineer of lucrative land grabs and entire forests of shady deals, falling off the couch in his father's consulting room, and smothered a grin.

"I'm looking forward to the celebration at your place," Rick continued, leaning over and placing a hand on Jules' thigh. "I mean, really looking forward to it. Nice of you to send me an invitation."

"Somebody else takes care of all that," Jules said evenly, turning a page and hoping Rick couldn't sense the revulsion throbbing through his nerve endings. Was his thigh damp?

Rick laughed again and stroked Jules' thigh. Hard. A threat, not a caress.

Jules looked at him over the FT.

"Rick, get your hand off my leg."

"Ooh, what? Doncha like it?"

"No, and I know Jake wouldn't like it either," said Jules.

Rick pulled his hand away in an exaggerated way and said,

"Ooooh! Jake! That's right – mustn't upset the little lady, must we? You know, I am really looking forward to seeing Jake at the party. I've always thought he and I could understand each other so well if we just got a bit closer."

He sat back, teeth slightly bared in a non-smile, a threat in his steel-blue eyes.

Jules lowered the FT, images coursing through his brain: Jake waving him off as he called out 'See you at the poof pad for the party!'; his parents' puzzled looks; Chloe saying, 'Don't worry, I'll tell them how it works' as the taxi pulled away. Jake in a potato field a decade ago, lighting a smoke, always on the listen for what the bloody waves were telling him, even in a potato field in the middle of Spain. A slow, sure anger fizzed up inside Jules.

"Rick, you don't need to get anywhere near Jake, let alone close. Do you hear me? Nowhere near him."

Rick held his gaze, maintained that arrogant smirk.

"*So* protective, Jules! I'm impressed."

Margaret had finished a call, the 'phones were silent for the moment. Jules stood up and folded the FT carefully.

"Rick, are you sure this aggression of yours isn't just a front?" he said loudly. "I really get the feeling that maybe it's a little pussy-plunging you're yearning for, but none of the ladies would have you, so you're picking on the guys now. Hm? You're just so unconvincing, which probably means you're unconvinced. Think about it."

Rick's eyes gleamed hard; he was rising to his feet with aggression in his balled fists when Gordon's door was flung open and Gordon himself came striding out, his formidable presence washing through the room in an instant.

"Rick!" he cried. "I'm going to need another half hour, see you then. Jules." A lifted finger, a small gesture, and before he knew it, Jules was in the lift with Gordon, heading back down to earth. They were both silent till they reached a small local park and sat with their sodas, weak sun patting their cheeks.

"Nice one, Jules," commented Gordon then, his tone admiring. "Below the belt, you naughty boy! But quite right, he shouldn't needle you about Jake."

"You heard?! But that means the waiting-room must be..."

"Bugged? Yes. Very useful."

"Christ!" said Jules, staring at Gordon and the leaves that stirred behind him.

"Oh, don't worry about that. What did you want to see me about?"

Jules glanced round briefly and sat back on the wrought-iron bench, suddenly relaxed. His dark-gold hair gleamed as he turned his head towards the man with the multi-billion-pound portfolio and said simply,

"Gordon, I know your secret."

The silence between them accentuated the tweeting of nearby birds, distant traffic noise.

"My dear boy, which one?" cried Gordon lightly, but his eyes were wary.

"I was at the het cinema in Turnham Green last night," said Jules quietly. "I saw you there, snogging a woman."

CHAPTER TWELVE
Grab it with both hands

Finally Gordon spoke.

"It was an experiment," he said. "Just thought I'd see what it felt like."

"Bollocks," said Jules, lobbing his can with satisfying accuracy into a bin. "You were kissing a woman and it was not an experiment, Gordon. I'm not stupid. That's someone I reckon you've known for a while and kiss a fair amount. And when I followed you..."

"You followed us?!"

"Yes, well, not for long, that was a bit weird, sorry about that, but the point is that the two of you were holding hands, close, just... I dunno, familiar somehow."

Gordon stared hard at him.

"My parents are straight," said Jules. "They get on pretty well. So I can see when people are, you know, used to each other."

The sun was dipping in and out of sporadic white clouds. It was good that the clouds were white, not any shade of dirty grey, Jules thought inconsequentially. He shifted his weight on the bench and looked back at Gordon.

"Well, and what do you plan to do now?" said Gordon in a hard voice. "Use your knowledge?"

"Christ no!" Jules exclaimed. "Well, only a bit. And I don't want to. What I want is for you to be in agreement with something I need to do, that's all. No harm done. Business as usual."

Gordon laughed suddenly and leaned forward to massage Jules' shoulder, running his hand lightly up and down Jules' shirt front.

"I like you, Jules. I always did. And you're shrewd, that's why I wanted you to come and work with me all those years ago. Straight to the point, working out what you want. No time wasted asking me why."

"I know why," said Jules. "Your career was taking off just as the Change hit. You'd have been toast if you'd come out as straight. No multi-billion-pound portfolio, no glittering lifestyle, no elegant retirement."

Gordon nodded slightly, sombre again.

"I didn't realise the Change was going to endure so long," he admitted quietly. "It was all just a bit of a giggle to start with. I enjoyed being in with the lavender mafia but suddenly there was nothing else – you were either with them or out. When I roped you in, I was in way too deep myself to change lanes. And I've had a lot of fun, make no mistake. But we've really felt it the past five years, she and I. Living a lie, Jules. Always looking over your shoulder."

"Why the hell did you have to rope me in at all?" cried Jules. "All I did was shout 'Poof!' in a pizzeria and next thing I knew you had me in golden gay handcuffs and I had people like Rick treating me like a piece of meat he was hungry for!"

"Don't try and pass the buck, darling," Gordon said in his familiar drawl. "Rick's an exception and you've done very nicely out of the job. You wouldn't be able to maintain Jake and that fancy pad of yours without a good solid background. Oh, of course! You could have made it on your own, you and Jake, in the lavender mafia. But would you, Jules? Would you have got so far so fast without my helping hands?"

Acutely aware of his screaming heterosexuality, Jules scowled and said,

"Why do you keep stroking my chest?"

"Making sure you're not wired," said Gordon. "And keeping up appearances. Rick'll be watching somewhere, somehow, and he needs managing."

"He's a shit – he tried to rape me!"

"He is a shit," agreed Gordon. "I realise that now. I was hoping he'd get it on with Corey Rosenberg and leave the country, but I suppose they're too similar. Anyway, let's get on. It's a busy day. What do you want me to be 'in agreement with', dear boy?"

His manner and tone were restored to their usual rather flamboyant suavity. Reassured, Jules swiftly outlined the need to switch the Eurovegas contracts on Rosenberg.

"You won't notice a thing," he assured Gordon. "It's only the location that'll be changed. But we need to work out how to, well, make the switch."

"Ah! A bit more than just being in agreement, then?" Gordon quizzed him.

Jules ran an impatient hand through his unruly hair and tutted.

"Look, this Greenpeace bloke Roberto is realistic – he's recommended a location that will cause minimal environmental damage and another, er, associate can get the government to re-sign, but..."

"Yes," said Gordon thoughtfully. "But. Well, I won't kick up a fuss – I won't query a thing when we sign the contracts. But to make the switch, you'll need to distract Rosenberg – he's the sort who'd refuse to sign just out of spite. I sometimes think I'd rather be dealing with Trump, but the bastard's running for the US presidency so he's scaled back on business commitments."

"Trump for president?" said Jules. "You have to be kidding."

"I'm afraid not, dear boy. You'll see it in the papers in a day or two. Anyway, the way it works is that Rosenberg and I walk into the signing room and the contracts are already on the table. If you plan to switch them, you'll need to do it between the moment when the lawyers place them and Rosenberg and I step in. So you're fine with me going in – I can be distracted by looking out of the window for a moment, but you'll need to delay Rosenberg for at least 90 seconds."

Jules stared.

"Okay. Right. You're right, we need a distraction but not such a big one that it'll stop Corey going on in and signing."

"Well, you have the perfect tool," said Gordon, at his most urbane.

Jules looked an inquiry.

"Jake!" pronounced Gordon. "Rosenberg has the hots for him. Use Jake!"

He stood and strode away, leaving Jules with his mouth open and a fast-beating heart.

Carmen's dark eyes snapped with satisfaction as she ran the final version of the video of Mayor Ruiz falling off the couch in Dr JJ's consulting room.

"It still lacks something, but it could go viral in certain circles," she told Roberto as she pinged it over to him in Madrid.

Pushing back her dark hair, she stood and stretched, satisfied with her part in the strategy they'd sketched out together.

"Idiot!" she snapped at Ruiz's image. "Stupid, greedy, nasty man. We will make you look so, so *stupid*. You will lose your position and have to run. Well, waddle."

The sound of Dr JJ's Testarossa growling into the driveway reminded her of the day she and Jules had found Jake in the bar down the hill and picked him up in it. Spaced-out, confused. He couldn't even remember her name, but as her grandmother used to say, you'll see the truth in his eyes. And then they'd kissed. All those years apart... Never mind. He was still best for her, she just knew it.

Sra JJ called out to her to come down for a drink on the terrace and she snapped off the computer, smiling as easily as she'd scowled before.

In Madrid, Roberto pursed his shapely lips, pondering the video Carmen had sent him, and her comments on it. She was right, it was still just a funny film of a fat bloke falling off a couch. He rang his younger sister, a journalist who was finding it hard to keep a job at any of the main news outlets because of her strong left-leaning convictions.

"Maite, I'm sending you a video," he said briskly. "In confidence. I think it lacks impact. It's urgent."

Maite was back on the line three minutes later.

"I've got great ideas for this – it's going to be a terrific satire once we've got some statistics on it."

Roberto smiled – she was absolutely right.

"I've got some good stuff, but what we really need is an inside source who could give us some figures only Ruiz would know, or secret deals or something – you know, really give it substance."

"Hold on."

Roberto turned to Alfonso and explained. Two minutes later, he told Maite he was passing her on to a reliable anonymous source he could vouch for, who would be able to supply some bombshell facts and figures about Ruiz's financial shenanigans to add to the footage.

And *that* was the video that went viral.

It was also the video that, when previewed to the EU regional director Mariano Gonzalez early next morning, impelled him to pick up his pen and sign the amended contracts without demur.

Before him, he saw the past and the future: Alfonso, who'd undoubtedly assisted Mayor Ruiz in all his wrongdoings, now presenting himself as a picture of virtue, almost a hero, the government's only hope for eluding an international mess; and Roberto, rock-solid in his campaigning convictions. He reminded Gonzalez of his own son, who was training to be a lawyer and had that same attitude of 'step aside so that we can put things right'.

Gonzalez sighed inwardly. Well, at least Roberto was reasonable. Badajoz was an inspired alternative, and the government would be able to claim environmental kudos as well as point to thousands of jobs created in one of Spain's poorest regions, which had little to offer touristically. At least Spain hadn't lost the entire deal.

As his signature scratched across the pages, he felt like one of those high-up people forced into an uncomfortable decision on that US Law & Order series his son watched non-stop. "Interesting ethical dilemmas, real legal conflicts," he'd intone. What a drag the boy was getting to be…

At 49, Gonzalez was marooned on the lower slopes of the mountains already scaled by the likes of Mayor Ruiz and even this Alfonso weasel now watching him sign. They'd made their stash and would hang onto most of it, despite slaps on the wrist, whereas he, Gonzalez, was in for nothing but contempt from the hordes of determined young campaigners he could see approaching across the plains beneath him, intent on recapturing their country.

He threw down the pen and, still intensely irritated, took a 'plane down to Valencia while Roberto flew the fresh papers over to London, and Alfonso bathed in whisky and his newfound sense of virtue.

Jules came to meet us for a drink after work at the Promenade Bar inside the Dorchester Hotel. When he said Promenade, I'd been expecting an outdoor venue, but in fact, it's a long, ornately decorated area leading back from the main lobby, with an oval bar at the end. Lots of gilding and palm plants, it was generally very lush. Jules had said it was a must-see and that Theo would love it, and as usual, he was right on the money – Theo expanded like a flower in water as he relaxed into one of the stud-finished velvet and leather chairs close to the exquisitely lit bar.

"This place is loaded with history," Jules enthused when he whirled in a few minutes later. "I thought you'd like it. Still draws the latest celebs. Must be the most-mentioned hotel in literature. Except Raffles, maybe. Have you ordered? No? Great! I recommend the Smokey Cup – fantastic spin on the whisky experience. How did the meeting go?"

Theo filled him in succinctly but without rushing – the man's pace is just perfect, always – and then said exactly what I'd been thinking.

"But you look a little on edge, Jules. How did your Eurovegas efforts go?"

"Pretty good, pretty good," said Jules, but I didn't like the way he was looking at me.

"What's up?" I asked, straight out.

"Well, it's all good really. Really good – Gordon's agreed to sign with no comment on the location, so if Alfonso's done his bit and got the new location onto the contracts signed by the Madrid government..."

"He's done it," I said. "I spoke to him this afternoon."

"He has? Blimey! What a weasel – how can he possibly get national documents altered and signed within 48 hours?"

"He knows the system," I said mildly, but Jules still scowled and muttered 'weasel' a few more times before Theo said,

"And so?"

"Oh, sorry! Yes. Right. Well, the thing is, we need a diversion of maybe two minutes when Corey Rosenberg's about to go into the boardroom to sign the contract. The portfolios containing the new contracts will be placed on the table by the legal team at 13:55, just before the two big boys arrive from separate entrances. So, we need to focus everyone's attention elsewhere while we do the switcheroo. Gordon won't fuss if he sees me apparently straightening folders on the table, but we have to keep Corey out of the way, and rattle him enough to take the edge off his concentration during the signing, but not so much that he jibs and refuses to sign or something daft."

I thought it sounded silly, and said so.

"It's not as though he cares where it's located, does he? He just wants to make money."

"But he is a control freak," Theo said unexpectedly. "He also has a mean character – if he feels he's been manipulated or swindled in any way, he will turn nasty and could be unpredictable. I assume plenty of other countries would love to have the Eurovegas investment?"

"Of course they would!" said Jules. "And now you mention it, that's probably how Alfonso got the contracts altered – he knows who to leak what to. It'd be massive egg on face for the Spanish government if they were seen to let this kind of investment slip through their fingers, and they can't let that happen, especially with elections coming up. Keep the dosh, change the location, hey presto! There'll be some protest over the smoking ban being waived, but something's got to give.

"Anyway, the point is, we need a distraction in the hallway Corey will be coming along, and Gordon said we should use you for that, Jake, because Corey fancies you."

Jules sat back and took a slug of his cocktail. I wanted to reach for mine, but felt paralyzed.

"Jake. Jake!" Theo's voice was quiet but urgent. His concerned face stood out against a pale background as I fought to keep visual hold of the bright warm colors I knew were there.

"No!" I whispered. "No!"

"Oh come on, old man," Jules urged. "We've all been running around like blue-arsed flies to get this sorted so you can keep your interiors contract, apart from anything else, and you've just been sucking up cocktails and hanging about on the edges doing bugger all. Now's your chance! Grab it with both hands!"

"I'm not going to grab anything with any hands," I said, as the nausea rose.

Theo reached out a hand and pushed Jules gently back into his chair.

"Let's reflect," he said. "It does sound like a feasible proposition..."

"No," I cried, sitting forward. "Listen, Theo! I'm straight! I love a girl called Carmen. She's in Spain. But I love my work with you. I don't want to lose either of you. I can't snog Corey – Jules, you know what'll happen!"

Theo raised an inquiring eyebrow at Jules, who sighed and ran a hand through his dark-gold hair.

"Theo, I'm sorry we've been deceiving you," he said after a few moments. "You know how it is. Professionally. But Jake's got a point. He'll pass out if Corey so much as touches him. Years ago, I kissed Jake – just once, no tongue – and he's been having blackouts ever since if a man comes on to him."

Theo looked at me and I nodded.

"What I was going to say," he resumed, "is that I don't like the idea of Corey being encouraged in any way to make a move on Jake. Corey is not a buffoon. He's a very dangerous man, especially when thwarted."

We both stared.

"Why do you say that?" I asked. "I thought you hardly knew him."

Theo took a composed sip of his Smokey Cup and said,

"No, in fact I know him better than most people do: I lived with him for 17 years."

I guess we were in a state of shock, because the barman asked us about three times if we'd like another cocktail, and then it was Theo who answered him.

"Crikey!" Jules managed finally. "Why'd you, why did you, you know, stop living with him?"

"There were various reasons, but essentially, Corey is too fond of coercion, sometimes, quite violent coercion. We had a lot of fun until he began to make it big and his personal urges became... distasteful. I changed coast and set up business in New York."

Nobody spoke until he said,

"If you need a distraction for the signing, you might want to contact Corey's Cocksuckers. They'll probably be in town with him."

"Corey's Cocksuckers?" cried Jules, recovering. "Who or what are they?"

"Well, as well as the obvious, they're the dance troupe. He always has a favourite – I'll ask Mila who it is. You could visit him and make him an offer he can't refuse in exchange for setting up a diversion." Theo was texting as he spoke.

Over in San Francisco, Mila was dropping the kids off at school when the message came in. She reached over to straighten Kylie's braids, watched both little bodies safely into the building and frowned over the question Theo had put to her.

"Yes, yes, I know the troupe, I know the guy... but his name? I know, I'll ask Corey's EA, Lucia. She'll know. She knows everything."

It was a superb day off, all the girls were enjoying it. They'd swapped business and beauty tips, marvelled over the luxurious surroundings as they strolled from one pamper session to another, clad in plump white robes, and were now about to head off for the famous oval-shaped pool, which Rosenberg had reserved for their exclusive use.

"I'll be right there," Lucia called after her colleagues, turning into the changing-room – which would house her entire apartment, she thought – to check her emails and messages. Only a handful required attention, including a text from Mila, the interior designer Corey had such a love/hate relationship with. Lucia pinged back the information and turned her back on business again, taking a satisfied peek at the woman smiling back at her from the sparkling mirrors before pushing open the door to the next chunk of paradise.

Jake and Jules were just finishing dinner at a tiny restaurant nestled under bridgework at the South Bank when Theo's message came through. He'd gone back to the Ritz to enjoy room service and an early night.

"His name's Earl, he's been Corey's favourite for three years, and the dancers are staying at the Comfort Inn near Waterloo," Jules read out. "Christ, what a cheapskate Rosenberg is! I would've thought he'd want Earl closer at hand, in his hotel. Apparently he's at the Savoy. That's not too far, in fact. I suppose he just calls for Earl if he needs that kind of room service. Right, let's get along to the Comfort Inn."

After they'd waited just over an hour in the lobby, Earl swung in through the door, his easy gait and something in his presence denoting the dancer beneath his loose, understated clothing.

"Sure, I'd like out," he agreed half an hour later, sitting with a beer in his hand. "I need to progress my career. And that is strictly between you and me, amigos. But Corey pays me well, I'd need something to go to, to make it happen. And people I'd like to work with think I'm earning so much they can't afford to make me an offer. Y'know, London is *cool*! Me and the guys were just at a performance in some place I'd never heard of, it was so great, but me, I'd need money to set up here. Money and contacts. Oh well, I got a few days. Thanks for the beer, guys, good to see y'again, Jake. I need to get over to the Savoy, welcome Corey – he just got in today."

"We're going that way," Jules said at once. "We'll drop you off. I've got a business idea that might interest you."

Twenty minutes later, Earl leaned back into the taxi to shake Jules' hand as he got out of the cab at the Savoy.

"Man, you get me work with T. Rantula and I'll create any kind of diversion you want tomorrow."

"Great, here's where to meet me for breakfast, 8am. We'll go through the plan then. Oh, and here's £20 for cab fare to get there." Jules thrust a card and the cash at Earl and rolled his eyes at Jake as the taxi moved on.

"Dude, why'd you promise him work with T. Rantula?" said Jake. "You can't guarantee that!"

"Only thing I could think of. Shut up, I need to call Chloe."

In Calpe, Chloe threw her 'phone down and turned to the others.

"Jules has gone nuts! He's promised some dancer bloke a contract with T. Rantula and says I've got to get it! In time for the Eurovegas signing! That's in... 13 hours!"

Carmen looked shocked but Roberto merely threw her an impassive glance, and Alfonso, the man who'd got contracts swapped and signed by the Madrid government within 48 hours, actually said, "Pah!"

Sra JJ asked where T. Rantula was, and Dr JJ beckoned the waiter over to their table at the lively harbourside bar, saying,

"Sounds as though we'll be here for a while, let's get more drinks."

"But I'm only the milliner!" wailed Chloe. "I can't wake T. Rantula up over some dancer I've never heard of!"

Dr JJ glanced at his watch and said,

"Wake her up? It's only 1am – that's midnight in the UK. She shouldn't be in bed by midnight at her age."

"You have his number?" asked Carmen.

"Her number. Yes. But..."

"Call." Carmen pushed Chloe's 'phone back across the table and gave her a vigorous nod. "Call now."

Earl smiled and stroked and sucked with hope that night.

Corey luxuriated in the surroundings of the Savoy and the careful attentions of Earl – really, the boy was better than usual today – his mind meandering pleasurably between the signing of a money-spinning new contract with the incomparable Gordon Hecklow tomorrow, and vague visions of Jake. Elusive, elusive – that was the word. Corey glanced down at Earl's bobbing head and sighed with deep satisfaction, biding his time, choosing his moment... elusive... effusive. His excitement grew, he felt his control slipping away for that delirious, dangerous moment... Earl's inviting back gleamed beneath him. Suddenly, he pushed Earl's head aside and released his load over that beautiful back, his own body shuddering and his mind playing over Jake's smiling face.

"He's in!" Jules texted to Jake at 08:20 on the morning of the contract signing.

"Oh cool, Jules has got Earl lined up to provide a diversion today," Jake told Theo over breakfast. "Thanks for that tip about Corey's dance troupe, Theo – it really saved my skin."

"You're welcome," returned Theo. "What time are we due at Jules' office? I can't wait to hear about the possible investor interest he mentioned."

"Yeah, exciting. It'd be a great boost for Millards' European expansion. You've got a terrific business, Theo. Jules'll come through – he doesn't make empty promises."

Theo smiled at Jake's easy confidence.

"He said we should have lunch first, after our meeting at the 5-Z hotel, and be at his office just before 2pm. That way we can meet while the signing is going on upstairs, and say hi to Corey afterwards."

Theo raised his eyebrows.

"No need for you to see him, Theo, if you don't want to, but Jules said it's good for me to show up, just to remind everyone at his place that he and I are a committed couple, and so that I can represent Millards the firm, just nudge our interests along kind of thing."

"Yes, of course. That is sound thinking."

"And the signing will be up on the top floor. Jules' office is on a lower floor, he said. Then there's the entertainment Corey's hosting this evening in the vaults of what used to be the Bank of England or something. I'll need to turn up for that. We're all invited – by Gordon."

"What are you going to wear?" inquired Theo. "Perhaps we should take a stroll down Jermyn Street."

CHAPTER THIRTEEN
Set a thief to catch a thief

Pablo Torres's wife Elisa watched the television news next day with gathering disbelief. Eurovegas was being relocated! Her husband had told her nothing of this.

Suddenly decisive, she hurried into the bedroom Pablo rarely shared, picked up a soft, bright pashmina to fling around her slender shoulders, and drove herself down from the heights where their opulent villa sat, to her favourite café in Alicante centre.

"Hola Elisa!" the chatty young waiter hailed her. "The usual?"

She nodded with a smile as he prepared a bombón – espresso with a shot of sweet condensed milk – moving over to her corner table while she rang her lover for their usual morning chat.

It was good to feel anonymous but known. She smiled up at Pepe, who only knew her as Elisa, when he put the neat cup and biscuit in front of her. The sun warmed her shoulders. She took her first sip and smiled even more broadly when Lucia answered at the second ring.

Ten minutes later, she rang her husband to say she wanted a divorce.

"Don't tell him you're gay," Lucia – her lawyer as well as her lover – had advised. "He'll accuse you of having withheld his marital rights or something and cut your settlement."

Elisa laughed.

"I just want to get out of that cold house," she said. "It wasn't deceit when I married him, you know."

"I know," said Lucia. "It's just the way things were. Men marrying women, nuclear families. I get it. But frankly, Elisa, I don't care about how things were back then. This is now. I just want your permission to get busy on the settlement and give him a jolt up his complacent, uncaring backside."

Torres himself felt aggrieved rather than shocked. He'd always assumed Elisa would hang around and just enjoy the money his success had brought. Who was going to run the household while he was away on his business trips now? he wondered suddenly.

* * *

The heart of the City. London's financial center. I like it. Buzzy but classy. I wouldn't want to take it every day, though. Like Manhattan – not my scene.

An amazing old guy with what sounded to me like a Cockney accent waved us over to a seating area furnished with large, plush white chairs and a profusion of papers and magazines on the huge low table in front of it. Financial information oozed across the screens above us.

"Is he what you call a geezer?" I asked Jules when he appeared minutes later to fetch us.

"George? Oh yes, he's a diamond geezer, aren't you, George?!" He winked at the receptionist as he swept us into an elevator lined with what looked like beaten copper.

Theo gave it an interested glance and said,

"I hope we're not too early?"

"No, no, perfect, gives me time to show you round a bit and get you a cuppa for when I'm upstairs. Phew! My God, can't believe it's actually happening!"

He swirled us up into his office, pausing to joke with his PA about keeping an eye on us and make sure we didn't nick anything while he was with Gordon "for the signing".

We all shivered in anticipation. His office was small, but had a window and felt small in a discreet way rather than a mean one.

"Welcome!" cried Jules and for a moment we all just grinned. It was all working out.

"So Chloe got a contract for Earl out of T. Rantula, then?" I said.

"What? Oh. No."

"But you promised Earl work on her videos if he did a diversion today!"

"Yes, well, I know. Chloe's still trying. I couldn't let that stop us. Calculated risk, old man." He looked at his watch.

"Dude, you are lying again!"

"Jake, shut up. This is not today's problem."

He was edgy and I guess he was right. I shrugged.

"Right," said Jules. "Emily will bring you some tea and stuff in a mo. Right. Eight minutes to go. How can you two look so relaxed? Bloody Americans! Oh thanks, Emily."

Theo moved in toward the teapot with visible pleasure at the ceremony.

"Leave it!" cried Jules, his cell 'phone going off. "Needs four more minutes. Sorry, hold on."

Well, we weren't expecting trouble, but it was trouble callin'. I hadn't thought Jules could get any tenser, but the skin on his face became stretched taut as a drum while he listened to the caller.

"What!" he yelled, suddenly, thumping the desk. "What?! You've what? Wait! Wait!"

For a flabbergasted moment he stared at the unresponsive 'phone with horror taking hold of his face, then he turned to us and looked at his watch again and gulped,

"That was Earl. He's stubbed his toe."

Theo raised an eyebrow and I think my mouth opened.

"He's stubbed his fucking toe on a bit of uneven sodding 'sidewalk' and he's on his way to Emergency, he says. He's not coming here! Emergency!"

"Well, he is a dancer," said Theo, "and he is performing tonight."

"Yes, yes, yes – all right, ALL RIGHT! But he was going to distract Corey bloody Rosenberg's attention in..." an anguished look at his watch, "...exactly four minutes."

Total, eternal nano-silence. Then Jules began to moan and suddenly my world became very calm, the answer coming in on an unseen tide, the waves telling me what to do.

"Let's go," I said, grabbing Jules and moving toward the elevators. "Bring the contracts portfolio."

The gilded doors were opening at the Directors Only floor. Jules stopped moaning and said,

"What? What?"

"Get in there and do the switch. Now!" I said calmly.

His insane stare turned on me and I smiled.

"I've got this, Jules. I've got this. Just GO!"

"That way!" gasped Jules, pointing down the hallway. "Corey's coming in from that way!" He was gone.

Stern faces stared down from portraits lining the walls. I felt the floor moving but was reassured. This was a wave I understand, I could read its movement under my feet.

The moments ticked by. I kept my eyes and all my senses fixed on the elevator doors Jules had pointed out. I heard its approach, quiet though it was out there on the gold carpet waves.

I took a deep breath, adjusted my balance, spread my hands at each side and watched the doors open to reveal Corey, slightly rippled at the edges by the haze of my intense focus.

Alone, he strode the waves toward me. I could smell his astonishment as he came to a halt and said,

"Jake?"

My hand touched his arm, my voice low and urgent.

"Corey, I don't mean to hold you up, but something's... happened. May I just have a moment?"

Something in my eyes or my touch must have convinced him. Although no-one was around, we stepped into a curved alcove displaying some kind of Chinese vase on a pedestal.

"Jake, you look so troubled. What is it?"

His hand was on my arm, creeping up it.

"Jake, you're shivering! Are you ill? What's happened? Let me call help."

"No! No, Corey, thank you. I... I just need a moment. I'm so sorry. I know you're signing the Eurovegas contracts now – Jules told me."

"Oh, Jules. Yes, of course he would be here."

"I don't want to hold you up, but I didn't know who else to turn to..."

I let myself sag a little and both his arms came up to steady me.

"Jake! My dear, dear Jake, don't you pay that a moment's mind! Gordon Hecklow can wait a few minutes. My concern is you. Tell me what's happened!"

I calculated Jules needed another minute so I breathed hard for a few more seconds and then said,

"Last night, Jules and I went out and we ran into one of your dancers. Guy called Earl."

Corey's eyes narrowed.

"Earl?"

"Yes, he'd been to see a dance performance and I recognized him from the show at your casino in Vegas, so I said hi."

"Yes?" Corey's voice was hard. I let myself shiver, thinking of the surf's first cold touch.

"Well, we had a beer or two all together and then he said he had something to ask me."

"Yes?"

"Well, I said sure, and we stepped outside. It was quiet, round the corner where he led me. And then he... Corey, I hate to tell you, but I just need you to know because we're gonna be working together again – he made a move on me."

Corey's eyes narrowed to slits and I caught a glimpse of the danger Theo had spoken of.

"Look. It's not a big deal and I really don't want to get him into trouble, but..."

"Trouble!" Those eyes were blazing with menace now. "He can say goodbye to his dancing career!"

"Corey! You must not hurt him!"

There was a pause then the grip went out of his hands and he nodded reluctantly.

"Very well, Jake. As you wish. But he leaves my employment tomorrow. He didn't, hurt you, did he?"

"No, no, it was just a misunderstanding. That's why I don't want him punished, Corey."

"He leaves my troupe tomorrow," repeated Corey. Then his expression softened, which was scarier than his anger. "But that's all, Jake, I swear. I won't harm him. He's been useful to me, but things change. Satisfied?"

He gave me a little shake and I glanced up shyly like I'd seen Princess Di do, and said, "Thanks, Corey," and he pulled me close and his lips were on mine.

I remember the sound of an opening door, a rush of sound and draft, the gleam of Jules' gold hair, then the riptide took me down and the world gasped black.

* * *

When Torres's soon-to-be-ex-wife Elisa saw the video, sent to her by Lucia, she laughed so hard that Pepe came over from behind the bar to ask what she was watching. Eyes streaming with tears of laughter, she pushed her laptop round and said,

"It's Mayor Ruiz, Valencia."

Pepe watched the video in delight and indignation.

"This is what we've got to stop!" he cried. "This corruption! I am forming a new political party to do just this!"

"You are?" Elisa was surprised – she'd thought he was just a barman, hadn't looked beyond. Suddenly, she was ashamed. "Tell me about it."

He told her about his degree, his ambitions; showed her the foundations of his political party. An hour later, she joined it, encouraged by his dynamism and optimism.

"I have time," she said, as though realising it for the first time. "I'm 52, the kids are grown up. I'd like to help. Are you sure you can make a difference?"

"We," he corrected. "Can *we* make a difference? Yes, of course we can! Claro que sí!"

"Claro," she repeated slowly. "It's a good name for a political party – it means 'clear' and 'of course'."

* * *

A handsome, concerned face hovered above me and I smiled.

"There! He's coming round!"

A familiar voice. Separate from the handsome face. I turned my head and saw it belonged to another handsome guy, younger, with dark-gold hair that waved naturally.

"Did he sign?" I asked.

The younger guy gave a yelp and said,

"There you are! Lucid as a bell! Told you I caught him before his head hit the pedestal! Sodding Chinese ornaments all over the place."

"Did who sign?" the older man asked me, gently. "Do you remember his name?"

I screwed up my eyes but nothing came to me.

"Are you my friends?" I asked.

"Oh bloody hell," said the younger one. "Yes, old man, we are your friends. Don't worry about a thing."

"Good," I murmured. The ocean beckoned. "You're nice. I have to go before the surf fades. I hope his toe gets better."

When I next opened my eyes, the most beautiful woman in the world was standing by my bed.

"Hello Carmen," I said, and one of the other people with her yipped excitedly.

"He's back! He's remembering names! It used to be mine first – now it's you, Carmen – quite right too!"

"Who are you?" I asked, though I knew perfectly well it was Jules. The world was clear again.

For a split second, he looked crestfallen, then he said to Carmen,

"Okay, he's not round yet – excellent moment to tell him you're engaged and you'd already picked out the ring together so you need to nip along to fetch it. I'll tell you the best places to go and you can get something you really like before he knows what's what."

She laughed and said,

"He knows who you are."

"Yeah, I'll handle the details, Jules," I said, and he made a lunge at me but I was saved by my 'phone ringing. Dr JJ's voice booming calmly down the line.

"Jake – you should know it's all over the news here that the Eurovegas location has been changed. It's created quite a stir. The EU regional director was on to confirm that the government had relocated it to an area where it would most benefit jobs and general development, and Roberto got his face on too, saying, 'Greenpeace just wasn't going to let the draining of a national treasure like the Salinas at Calpe go ahead', and taking most of the credit, but they're clearly in it together and perfectly happy about it. Nice work! Carmen will tell you about the video of Mayor Ruiz – Alfonso says he'll never live it down and his political career is over, and that he – Alfonso – is going straight and starting a new job up in Madrid with the central government! He really is a piece of work. Still, set a thief to catch a thief. I just thought you should know urgently about the news on the telly because of Corey Rosenberg – he may not have heard yet but he damn' soon will and you need to be prepared. Jules talks too much on the 'phone, so I'm leaving this with you. Good luck! 'Bye!"

He rang off without me having said more than 'yes' and 'got it'. I filled the gang in and Jules said, "Oh my God!" and clutched his face; Chloe clutched his arm; Theo raised an eyebrow; and Carmen got her ciggies out and said,

"That's excellent. We can clear it all up fast. Jake, you need to call Corey and tell him you've just heard he's had the location changed for environmental reasons and you really admire that decision. At Millards you wouldn't have understood the negative implications of the Calpe site, and this is so much better for business all round. Show no sign of remembering what happened earlier today when he kissed you. Jules, you need to call the architect Torres and thank him for steering Mayor Ruiz away from Calpe. That should checkmate them – they'll both want the credit. I'm going for a smoke, then to change. See you!"

She kissed me and was gone.

"Christ!" exclaimed Jules, dialing. "What a brain! Mind you, old man, you won't be able to get away with anything. Hello, is that Pablo Torres? Pablo, hi, this is Jules Julius, we met in the loo at Corey's Las Vegas... Oh, you remember? Great! Listen, I won't keep you, just wanted to say I've just heard that Eurovegas has been relocated and I suppose you influenced Ruiz on that one, thank God! I mean, Christ! – draining the Salinas! What a madman to come up with that idea! You saved my skin, too – Gordon Hecklow would *not* have been amused to be in on the financing of such an environmental disaster and he'd have blamed me for not giving him advance warning. I owe you big time! See you at the party tonight!"

He clapped his 'phone down and said with satisfaction,

"He didn't have a clue – could tell by his silence. Well, now he's got his script. Thanks to Carmen. Right, gotta go change – come on Jake, call Corey, we need to get moving."

So I did and we did.

"I don't know what's happened!" Torres hissed when an irate Ruiz rang him.

"But you must!" shrieked the mayor. "It's all over the news here! They've changed the location! They're sending Eurovegas to the city of Badajoz, right over in Extremadura!"

"Are you implying I was somehow in on this change of location?" Torres snarled.

Ruiz moderated his tone.

"No, no, not that. but I know what I set up on the contracts and it was coming to Calpe! I've had the German engineering company due to drain the Salinas on my back all morning and I don't know what to tell them!"

Suddenly Torres felt grateful for the swap, whoever had engineered it. Rosenberg was the man to keep in with, not Ruiz. He'd done well out of the mayor's intrigues but it was time to go completely international, leave Spain's petty local kabals behind. They would not last forever – there was a new trend afoot, he sensed it in a way that stodgy old Ruiz, mired in his old ways, never would.

"I know as little as you do," he snapped. "But it's happened, it's real. I've had Rosenberg on the line and..."

"What! What did you tell him?"

"What do you expect? I told him Badajoz will give us more scope for architectural innovation..."

"You what?!"

"...and that in my opinion, it was a smart move by the Spanish government that would in no way affect the value of his investment – on the contrary. You can't expect me to go up against the government, Juan Antonio. We'll have other projects for Valencia further down the line. Goodbye."

The mayor stared down at the receiver in his hand, reality sinking bitterly in, succulent kickbacks oozing out of sight.

Alfonso. Where was Alfonso? If anyone knew what had gone wrong, it was that weasel. He punched in the number but it just rang and rang.

The street outside was unexpectedly quiet. The mayor stood surrounded by unaccustomed silence. His mind a blank, he glanced up at the clock, subconsciously aware of something amiss.

The reliable antique clock – a gift from a construction company president – had stopped.

Mayor Ruiz felt cold even as sweat broke out down the back of his neck.

"Mariano!" exclaimed Juan Antonio Ruiz, opening his front door later that day. He'd stayed away from the office after his press officer had tipped him off about the video that had just surfaced on social media, until they had a response planned. Now he stepped back at the look on Mariano Gonzalez's face.

"You stupid, greedy, fat *idiot!*" hissed Spain's regional director to the EU, coming in and slamming the door behind him. "Drain the Salinas! Create an environmental catastrophe! Implicate the national government! You stupid, stupid, *stupid* man!"

Juan Antonio spread his arms deprecatingly, but Gonzalez was in full flow.

"Have *you* seen that video?"

Juan Antonio nodded; he began to say,

"It's only a vid…"

"No, it is NOT only a video!" snapped Gonzalez. "It is an indictment of political corruption in Spain, and you are going to have to serve time for it, Ruiz."

There was a slight pause. Both men stood in the dim hallway, away from the scorch of the sun, while Gonzalez breathed heavily in his anger and Ruiz's crafty brain reassembled reality.

"How long for?" he asked.

"How do I know? I'm not a fucking judge. Ten, 12 years maybe."

That means out in four, reckoned Ruiz, running through the photo opps in his head. The government couldn't treat him too shabbily – they'd let him get away with it all for too long. They wouldn't want him to talk – he had too much to tell. His money would still be waiting when he got out. There was a very well-known actress who would come and visit him, cry for the cameras, and in general lend some romantic colour to his image, if he paid her an adequate fee. He'd have time to write a book.

"That video," Gonzalez was saying, "is the perfect illustration of what's wrong with Spanish politics."

"Well, you should know what's wrong with politics, since you are at the centre of government," Ruiz shot back, and Gonzalez ignited.

"Shut up!" he snarled. "Don't threaten me! That video shows greed embodied. You know what it's called – The Fall of Corruption! You, falling off a bloody couch, interspersed with all those financial figures about your scams and kickbacks and footage of you at construction sites and God knows what! You have been indiscreet and greedy, greedy, GREEDY! And now it shows up on a bloody video which people will watch and understand because it all shows up because you are so FAT! You hear me? Fat, fat, FAT!" He ended on a kind of scream and poked Ruiz sharply in the belly.

"Hey!" protested Juan Antonio, and Gonzalez stepped back, disgusted at everything.

"I have to go," he said, turning.

"Wait! Will I be allowed, you know... female company, in prison?"

"Prostitutes? No, you bloody well won't! You'll have to wank."

Ruiz was disappointed, but resilient. He'd find a way – he always did.

"I will need to see a shrink," he called after Gonzalez's disappearing back. "You cannot deny me that! I will need it. I have a good man in mind!"

"I told you it was all about the fat!" Dr JJ told his wife triumphantly. "Ruiz rang today – he wants to continue treatment with me!"

"I hope you told him to get lost," said Sra JJ.

"No! Why should I? It's an interesting case. He didn't even ask about the video."

"Well, prison experience will be good for your CV," she said. "Just make sure you're always close to the door."

Dr JJ stared.

"Prison?"

"You bet! That greedy old shit's going down. Alfonso says so."

"Oh, Alfonso, Alfonso," grumbled the doc.

"Come on, let's go and get a drink down at the harbour."

Their mutual exasperation subsided with the sun and the wine in the bottle, each happily secure that they were right.

* * *

Theo had thought it would rattle Corey, and it did.

The event at the old vaults was a select affair but Gordon Hecklow had been happy to include Theo and his two companions – Chloe and Carmen – on his own guest list.

By 7pm, guests were flowing into the main underground space via an immense silver safe door.

"I feel like James Bond," Jules muttered to Jake as they entered together.

"You look like him," replied Jake, sotto voce.

As a couple, they had opted for the professional, ostensibly conservative approach – Jules in classic black DJ, Jake in narrow black trousers with a fitted white shirt, shoestring tie and dull silver blazer – and they moved about together, though there was little to suggest intimacy in their body language.

As co-hosts, Corey and Gordon were initially stationed together for the meet and greet over circulating champagne cocktails. They were now standing with Rick, Jules and Jake, set to move into the more informal mingling phase before the entertainment, when Theo and the girls arrived.

Theo's exploration of the sartorial extravagances on display along Jermyn Street hadn't tempted him to alter his own wardrobe. He was wearing a gorgeously embroidered cream frock coat from the Millards atelier over exquisitely cut peach shirt and trousers, and his entrance – accompanied as he was by exotic Carmen on one arm and a fiery Chloe on the other – made quite a stir.

"God Almighty, who is that?" exclaimed Rick, displaying his fundamental coarseness as the group watched Theo stroll towards them, his handsome head held straight between the ornate, high-standing collar points of that coat.

Cheerfully aware of some kind of intrigue, Gordon shot Rick a quelling look and said,

"That's Theo Danes, owner of Millards, the firm that handles Corey's wonderful casino interiors. Jake's boss."

Rick snorted.

Theo was before them. Gordon grasped his hand warmly and turned to Corey.

"Corey, Theo – I take it you two have met?"

Pole-axed, Corey silently extended his hand. He flinched oh so slightly as Theo took it and held it, saying urbanely,

"Yes indeed! Though it's been a while, hasn't it, Corey? It's Jake who brings the personal touch to our more far-flung clients these days."

His hand felt so smooth to Corey. Theo was as magnetic, as handsome, as disapproving as ever. Completely unaware that he was silent and still hand-fast, Corey stood remembering. Images of flamboyant orgies, sex in theatrical surroundings, wild wild parties, flashed through his memory, interlaced with the smooth colours of the utter calm that Theo had brought him. Then he had left, leaving Corey's world colder, harder. 'This man tortured me,' he thought. Seventeen years together. Seventeen.

"But enough of the reminiscing!" Theo joked, releasing Corey's hand. "We must mingle! We are, after all, in a unique setting!"

"Yes, yes, you must come and look at this door, the engineering here is just incredible..." Gordon drew Theo away.

Corey's eyes followed them. Into the awkward silence, Jake finally said,

"We're looking forward to working on the Spanish casino very much, Corey."

Corey glanced at him. Jake, the continuation of Theo's pull. Until now, he'd held up his resentment at Jules' blazing look of reproach earlier that day as a shield against his own feelings. He'd yielded Jake to Jules with a sharp, "He fainted. I'm late for the signing", and hurried on to join Gordon in the Directors' room.

But now, Corey felt suddenly stripped raw, disarmed and naked by Jake's purity and Theo's living memory. The two of them lived on the right, the bright side of a line he couldn't even discern, thought Corey bitterly. But it was bitterness against himself, his choices. All at once, he felt his own brashness, the cutting emptiness of his existence.

Jake's eyes were understanding now.

"It was genius to have Eurovegas relocated," he said quietly, but it was Jules' forthright,

"Yeah, too right – you'll make a killing at the Extremadura site and improve your image no end on the environmental side of things" that brought a wry smile to Corey's thinned lips.

"Am I beyond redemption?" he asked, to their consternation.

Seeing that Jake might be taking the question seriously, Jules leapt in again.

"Christ, no! Well, maybe. Actually. But there's only one way to find out, Corey, and that's to do things differently."

All three held silence for a few moments. Rick had wandered off.

"Corey," Jules said tentatively. "What do you think about Rick?"

Corey and Jake both turned to stare.

"Well, I just thought you two might, you know, hit it off."

"Rick?" repeated Corey. "Rick?" he gave a burst of harsh laughter. "That's my answer. I must be truly beyond redemption if you think I could hit it off with an... oaf like Rick."

"Oh, well, sorry."

"It's okay, Jules, it's okay. You're right. Do things differently."

"But not the money-making! You're great at that – no changes needed, eh Jake?"

He'd lost Corey's attention – Theo was walking back towards them.

The two older men stood facing each other. Jules and Jake held their breath and the noise around the former lovers receded from their bubble of silent, shared emotions.

"Well, Corey?" challenged Theo, in total command.

Corey half-smiled.

"Well, Theo. I've decided to do certain things differently, thanks in part to our two young friends here. Too late for you and me, of course."

"Of course. I admire your intention."

"But you don't think I can do it."

"I know you *can* do it," said Theo calmly. "I don't believe you will."

Corey winced.

"Always cruel," he said.

Theo flipped his fingers elegantly along his embroidered sleeve and said,

"Well, Corey, it's a crewel world I live in."

Jake, the only one to get his pun, chuckled softly.

EPILOGUE

Six months later, I moved to London to set up the European side of Millards. Carmen and I are buying a home in Alicante, but I use Jules' 'poof pad' in London as the main office. It's a lot of travelling, but I enjoy that, and it means Carmen can carry on with her work in Spain.

Jules and I give the occasional party to help maintain the couple image until he and Chloe are ready to cut loose from their financial shackles and do what Carmen and I are going to do, which is to get married.

Eurovegas is taking shape, with good old Roberto hopping about to make sure all the environmental clauses in the swapped contract are fulfilled. Ruiz tried to smear him and Greenpeace back after the video fiasco brought him down, but Carmen headed him off at the digital pass and it didn't go anywhere.

Earl's moved to Europe too – courtesy of Rick, who hooked up with him after hearing about Corey's 'oaf' comment, which Jules leaked to him.

Dr JJ's studying to sit his finals and has carried on working in the meantime. He came clean to his patients and most of them were pretty unfazed by his lack of credentials. Like he said, that was his problem and they were really more concerned with their own.

At Millards, we're underway already with Mila on some of the interiors for Corey Rosenberg's casino in Spain. Corey says he wants to make our leather trapunto a feature of his casinos worldwide, so unless he loses his Midas touch, Millards has a bit of financial security for some time to come.

It was hard for me to leave Theo's NYC atelier, but Jules told me not to be daft – Theo needs me to run the European expansion, and we'd never have got the trapunto contract if Corey hadn't stuck his tongue down my throat and felt bad about it afterwards, so I helped business there too.

I shivered at the memory.

"It's all worked out absolutely fine," Jules said. "You and Theo have got it all nicely stitched up – well done to the two old biddies! You've got work lined up for years, you're getting good new contracts in Europe, and Theo will love coming over to visit. It's all great, old man!"

He clapped me on the shoulder, his hazel eyes gleaming.

"And none of it would ever have happened if I hadn't shouted "Poof!" in a pizzeria 10 years ago!"

Printed in Great Britain
by Amazon